HARLEM CONFIDENTIAL

HARLEM CONFIDENTIAL

COLE RILEY

www.urbanbooks.net

Urban Books
74 Andrews Avenue
Wheatley Heights, NY 11798

©copyright 2006 Cole Riley

ISBN 1-893196-41-0

First Printing February 2006
Printed in the United States of America

10 9 8 7 6 5 4 3 2 1

*This is a work of fiction. Any references or similarities to
actual events, real people, living, or dead, or to real locals
are intended to give the novel a sense of reality. Any
similarity in other names, characters, places, and incidents
is entirely coincidental.*

Submit Wholesale Orders to:
Kensington Publishing Corp.
C/O Penguin Group (USA) Inc.
Attention: Order Processing
405 Murray Hill Parkway
East Rutherford, NJ 07073-2316
Phone: 1-800-526-0275
Fax: 1-800-227-960

Acknowledgements

For Cheryl D. Woodruff, a true friend and editor extraordinaire, who literally saved my life and without whom, this book would not exist.

For Carl Weber, a damn good word wizard who earned my honor and respect for as long as I shall live, and without whom the wolf would have been in my living room.

"Harlem is sex, sin, vice, any number of evils all rolled up in one. It is concentrated corruption, pure temptation, undiluted larceny. Go behind any door, and you will see what I mean. Harlem represents the unwritten law of the jungle with the cats not playing by any rules whatsoever."

—Chester Himes
1964

ONE

Harry "Cootie" Chambers was lucky to be alive. The streets in Harlem were not plowed yet as the big snowstorm blanketed its main and side streets with thick powder and treacherous black ice underneath. Once loaded into the ambulance, Cootie was on the gurney bleeding, losing life, while the vehicle was slipping and sliding on the ice, and almost didn't make it to the hospital. Two civilians pushed the ambulance out of a deep snow bank. The bullets did their damage to Cootie but he would survive, the sum of him being slightly less than whole. When Red shot him, that maniacal gleam in his yellow eyes transfixed him just seconds before the slugs penetrated his flesh. He could not forget those eyes. Nothing about the first few days in the hospital after the shooting was within his recall. Everything went black. Red stomped him after he shot him, busted some ribs and a cheekbone on the right side of his face. Several visitors, after he returned to consciousness, commented on how he almost died.

His older sister, Barbara, a heavyset woman who always smelled of lemons, got a few digs in. "I thought Red was your friend," she said, sucking her teeth. "You always brought him around to the house. He even ate Thanksgiving dinner with us that time after he got out of jail. You treated him like a brother. He's a snake, if I saw one."

"That's okay," Cootie said calmly.

Barbara's husband, the subway conductor, stood with his hands in the pockets of his uniform. He was small, almost a midget. Balding, always with a smile on his little kid face. They were a Mutt-and-Jeff of a couple, love at first sight. Cootie overheard her telling his father that he might have been small but he was well-equipped, built like a horse. His old man had to laugh after that.

"What God is trying to tell you is that you have to give up the way you're living," his sister said, pointing at him. "You know that, right?"

"Yeah, you almost died." Her husband had to bring up that crucial point. One of the bullets burned right through an area of his body inches from his heart, inches from putting him into his grave.

"What kind of a con man are you?" she asked. "What happened to you?"

"What do you mean?" He was suddenly tired, worn out from this questioning.

"You used to be a decent man," she continued. "A hardworking man."

Cootie tried to roll over, helpless to adjust himself in the bed. "Barb, will you pull my pillows up so I can prop myself up?" Truth was his sister knew nothing about him.

His sister helped him lean forward as her man tugged the pillows underneath Cootie's head, and then she let him gently fall into their softness. She knew not to press him for an answer. He could be stubborn and downright ornery when he wanted. He was not out of the woods yet, for his whole body showed his lack of strength and will. Or maybe he was just acting. He was a great one for putting on a show.

"I'm pretty damn tired," Cootie whispered, waving her to him for a kiss.

Grover, her husband, was curious about the care the hospital was giving him. They lived on the outskirts of Mount Vernon, in a black middle enclave, away from the crime, the projects, and the slums. "They haven't even plowed the streets around here in Harlem. Is Harlem Hospital treating you right? You know these nigger hospitals . . ."

"Hey, they kept me alive so I can't kick. I'm really bushed."

"You want us to go?" she asked, upset that she couldn't score all of the points she wanted. "When do you want us to come again?"

"Thursday." Cootie winked at her.

As they were going out, the cute little nurse who took care of him throughout the day was coming in. She was Asian, maybe Filipino or Thai. She was very attentive but demanding. Other than the doctors, she was extremely watchful of his company during visiting hours—no long stays, no aggravation. Her name was Lucy, pretty yellow woman. Sometimes she sat with him and chatted, but never about herself, only about him and his life of crime.

"How are you feeling today?" she asked, carrying a tray with some soup and a carton of lukewarm apple juice.

"I'm good to go." He smiled, a weak one.

But they both knew that it would be a while before he would be at full strength. Still, his power was coming back slowly. He could feel it surging into his arms and legs. The taste of solid food no longer made him sick. However, the doctors didn't give him too much of it. He spent less and less time sleeping.

"How did the visit go with your sister today?" the nurse asked.

"Okay. She asks too many damn questions."

The nurse laughed, hiding her mouth with her hand. "She's just concerned about you. After all, she's your sister. Do you have any other family?"

He didn't want to talk about it. "Can I get a pain shot for my chest wound?"

4

"I'll ask the doctor." She was quick to pick up hints. Only on two occasions did she mention the shooting, the funny-money scam, and the double-cross that landed him in the hospital fighting for his life. Lucy refused to let him feel sorry for himself. It was the thing he enjoyed most about her, her innate wisdom, the nurse's sense of clarity about the significance of life's lessons.

The visit he dreaded most finally came during that next day. Philbrick, the detective, had been kind enough to not kick him while he was really down. Flat on his ass. He waited until Cootie was getting to his knees before he let him have it.

Philbrick had one of his guys stand outside of the door, like the criminal was going to flee. The cop was tall, pockmarked in the face, oily black hair, and smelled like cigar smoke. The white man wore a really cheap corduroy suit. His stubby fingers yearned for a stogy, its absence made them edgy.

"Well, Cootie, I understand you're not going to leave us after all," the cop said in that radio announcer's voice of his, milking each word for its irony. "You're going to live."

"Yeah, I guess I am." Cootie played it safe. No excess dialogue.

"What are we going to do with you?" the cop asked. "You've got some real bad boys mad at you. You know that. And fucking around with Red's wife, that wasn't cool. I'm surprised that they haven't made a play on you in the hospital. Red never forgets nor does he forgive."

He was silent.

"We're trying to find Red before he makes good his promise to kill you. We're rounding up his boys. We're watching his places, even his casinos and restaurants. Nobody's talking. Everything on the streets is mum. Nobody knows nothing."

5

He remained mute.

"What do you know?" the cop asked. "All we want to do is help you. We don't want you. You're a little fish. We want Red. Can you help us?"

"I don't think so." He was not a snitch, a stoolie.

"We let you do your business without bothering you," the cop said, getting more pissed. "We knew about your funny-money schemes, but we knew you weren't moving any volume. We had records on you this thick." He gestured with his fingers spread wide. "We had surveillance and video on every one of your operations. Let me tell you something. We could have taken you down at any time we wanted."

Cootie propped his head up with his arm. "So why didn't you?"

"We were biding our time," the cop answered snidely. "We wanted to get you where there was nothing to prevent you from doing long time. We wanted you cold."

"That's bullshit," he said. "You never could catch me."

"Almost . . ." The cop grinned. "We almost had you before Red did a number on you. You compromised the department with your crap. I'll be honest. There are many people down there calling for me to bring back your head."

Cootie understood the error of his ways. He had violated his cardinal rule: never let chasing tail get in the way of doing a successful caper. He lusted after Red's wife, mad lust, and wanted to bounce between her thighs even if it was just a quickie, but he knew he lost out. The bitch blabbed to Red, and that was that.

"Will you help us . . . to land Red?" the cop was almost pleading.

But Cootie's mind was elsewhere—the shooting, the betrayal, and his ending up in the hospital. "I fucked up big time. I know that."

The laugh from Philbrick's mouth was cold and sardonic. "You're damn right you did. I don't know what the hell you could have been thinking of. How could you do some stupid shit like that?"

He frowned at the cop. "I don't know. I really don't."

"Cootie, I'll do what I can for you, but I can't make any promises," the cop said matter-of-factly. "You're in some deep shit. I know it's hard for a man not to think with his prick sometimes, but you have to weigh the consequences. Is the pleasure worth the consequences? You see, that's a lesson every man has to learn at some point in his life."

"Fuck you, Philbrick," Cootie shot back. "I'm not some damn kid. Kill the lectures. I knew what I was getting into and the consequences."

"We can get your stupid, black ass anytime we want."

"Oh yeah, anytime you want. You have nothing on me. You found nothing that would incriminate me in my apartment, in my office, or in my car. You didn't even find a gun. What do you have me on? Some parking tickets, huh?"

Philbrick stood near the bed and squeezed the black man's shoulder. "You wouldn't last any time in prison. Remember your last stretch?"

"Is it still snowing out there?" Cootie grinned up at the craggy-faced white man.

The cop touched him on the arm lightly, said take care, and walked briskly from the room. He took his sidekick with him.

Cootie tried to lie on his side, but the wounds throbbed, still he remained quiet almost for an hour after the cops left. He thought about what this shooting and the vendetta cost everyone around him, especially his two young daughters and his family. Day after day, he had been screwing around, living a secret life that he thought he had hidden so well from the outside world. Red's wife betrayed him. He couldn't even speak her name. The bitch.

His phone rang, snapping him out of his self-examination and self-flogging. It was his old partner, Gillette, an ex-con he met during the last stint in stir. Gillette loved Cootie like a brother, although he would be quick to recognize, the con man was a cockhound and would do anything for pussy. This dog loved women. This dog loved sex. He was always making choices that almost cost him his life.

"Man, you lucky fucker," Gillette said, remembering the miles of bandage and gauze encasing Cootie's long, lean body. He snuck into Cootie's hospital room earlier when one of his crew distracted the cop outside. Chuckling, he recalled Cootie resembled Boris Karloff in the old film classic, *The Mummy,* all wrapped up and no place to go.

"Philbrick visited me and wanted me to rat out Red," Cootie said. "I'm not a rat. I don't snitch. I told him that. Fuck Philbrick."

"You know you are one lucky fucker," Gillette repeated.

"I don't know how lucky I am yet," Cootie said mournfully. "I was telling you Philbrick was up here a minute ago, and things don't look good. He's just waiting for me to make one false step. Gillette, how can one person make so many dumb-ass mistakes? I should have seen this coming."

"I hope the pussy was worth it," Gillette teased. "A couple of inches higher, and the folks at the morgue would have been giving the deluxe Y cut. A couple of inches lower and you'd be wearing a dress. Either way you'd been fucked."

Cootie's eyes moistened. "I knew what I was doing, and I did it anyway. But I will never let any women lead me around by my dick after this. I swear to God. Men are idiots."

"My mother has been saying that for years," his friend joked.

"You know what hurts most about all of this, Gillette?"

"What?"

"It's what all of this has done to the kids," Cootie said sadly. "This must be hellish for them. I can't imagine the kind of stupid, thoughtless things people are saying to the girls. How are they holding up?"

"Have they visited you?"

"No. They haven't even called me. Barb visited me but they haven't."

Gillette laughed ironically. "Alicia called me. She's doing okay. She's one strong girl, reminds me of Faith. I don't think you realize what a jewel you have there."

"What about Audrey?" Cootie was afraid to ask. She was the younger girl, nineteen, and Alicia was two years older. Audrey was the more volatile, excitable, and a live wire like he was. And no, Alicia couldn't have reminded him of Faith.

"Alicia says she hasn't seen her for days, since this whole thing began," his friend replied. "She's worried, but then she's disappeared for days before. Maybe Audrey is with some of her wild pals."

Cootie thought of their mother, Faith, who died at thirty-eight from a drug overdose. He found her naked on the floor of the bathroom. The needle was still in her arm. Some bad shit. He had run his old man to the clinic to get his new Medicaid card so he could restock his high blood pressure meds at the pharmacy. When he returned home, he opened the bathroom door and found the water overflowing from the tub and her curled up in a corner. Cold and dead. That was five years ago.

"I've got to go," he said, moaning into the phone. "My pain is rearing up. It hurts like hell. I'll call you back later. Okay?"

"Yeah, cool," Gillette said. "You need anything?"

"No. Just let me know if you hear from Audrey. And tell Alicia to call me, please. Tell her that she shouldn't be afraid to call me. I'm not mad at her. I'm mad at myself for getting into this scrape. Tell her that."

A grinding surge of pain shot through Cootie's chest to his stomach down to his legs. He placed the phone down on the table. For a moment, he couldn't catch his breath. Lucy the nurse returned right on time, saw the pained expression on his face and ordered him to hang up the phone. "Rest, please." She gave him something for the agony, fluffed the pillows one more time behind his head, rearranged his legs under the sheet, and exited.

"Oh yes, one more thing, a bath in an hour," she told him.

Once the nurse was gone, Cootie pulled himself from the bed, a mass of burning muscles, aching bones, and shooting pains. He hated the bed. He hated being waited on hand and foot. With great effort, he dragged himself to the window where he could see another part of the hospital, snow on the roof, and a parking lot in the distance where cars were spinning their wheels on the ice. Try as he might, he couldn't get the window open.

He wanted some fresh air, not recycled hospital air. The thought of smashing the window open with a chair crossed his mind, but he lacked the will or the strength. All of this was going through his brain's circuits when he suddenly felt hot, feverish, and weak, and then the power left his limbs, and he felt his head bounce hard against the hard tiled hospital floor.

When he was revived, the doctors and nurses were working on him, checking his blood pressure, checking for a concussion, checking for broken bones, checking for anything out of the ordinary. He heard Lucy the nurse saying through the fog that she left the room just for a minute and when she returned, he was on the floor. They talked of urine and blood samples, and an MRI in the morning. There would be another battery of tests before they considered his release in another week.

"I think we should keep a close eye on him tonight for any unexpected complications," one doctor said. "This fainting could be nothing or it could be an indication of something we haven't picked up."

In his grogginess, Cootie saw the nurse pluck a thermometer from nowhere, shake it, and felt it slide into his mouth. The thermometer tasted of alcohol but he tolerated it. She flashed a kind smile at him, removed it from his lips, and recorded the temperature on the chart. He couldn't hear what she said to one of the doctors since it was out of the range of his hearing. Finally, the repair work was done, and the crowd of medical crew departed.

On her way out, Lucy the nurse leaned over and whispered, "Don't worry. It's nothing serious. You just had a little too much excitement today."

Alone again, Cootie refused to stay still. That damn bed. It was killing him. Getting up this time took more effort for some reason. His legs did not want to obey. He used the bed to brace himself as he worked his way to the window again. The glass felt cold to the touch. There was a nasty lump on the side of his head from his fall. The knot of angry flesh was tender. He moved back from the window and plopped into the armless chair, the one reserved for visitors, staring at the cars driving in and out of the parking lot.

He had asked the nurse about what happened to the patient who occupied the empty bed next to him. She said he had a massive stroke and died during the night. Another patient was going to be in the bed in a few hours.

Soon he'd be free of this place. Soon he'd be able to start putting his life together again, free to repair some of the wounds he'd inflicted on his loved ones and friends. He eased the dresser open and searched under the hospital-issued magazines for his buried treasure. As he found it, a smile came to his lips. It was a black-and-white photograph of Faith and the girls taken in Central Park a few summers ago. The gang picnicking in happier times—before the shit hit the fan, before Red's bitch, before the shooting.

"Damn, damn, damn." He picked up the photo, examined it with narrowed eyes in the fading afternoon light. A sob caught in his throat. He eased the snapshot back into the hiding place under the magazines and closed the dresser.

Sighing heavily, Cootie hobbled to the bed, groaned as the pain overcame the drugs for a second, slid back under the sheet, and closed his eyes. There was no relief for him. No solace. For a second, he glanced at the window again and noticed the start of more wind-whipped snow gusts. It only served to make him sadder. He cursed himself to sleep.

T W O

Perhaps the old Delta bluesmen Son House and Howling Wolf would call it the blues. Cootie felt it. Overpowering, continual, and painful. One of his old cellmates, a reader of books, said the French called it *delection morose*. A mental S&M thing. Black folks, he thought, called it feeling sorry for yourself, wallowing in the muck. But he wanted to suffer, wanted to pay for what he had done to the girls and his family. Something was eating away at him. Yes, he had the blues—or the blues had him—and the suffering made it all real for him.

"How are you feeling today?" Lucy the nurse asked.

"Shitty," Cootie growled.

The doctors were worried about him. The cops were pressing him. Cootie dummied up, keeping silent. Everything was bad. His body was healing but his soul was broken. He felt pent up, trapped, and tainted in so many ways. He transferred his disgust and anger, and turned it inward on himself. Night after night was spent brooding, replaying the scenes on the final day at Red's penthouse, the big man and his gun, him getting plugged and the gunshots. One, then the other.

Everybody said don't worry about this stuff you can't change, just move on with your life. None of this kind of talk made him any less anxious. He felt like shit, helpless, hopeless, and not worthy of a second chance.

"I think you're suffering from clinical depression," Lucy said one afternoon. "The doctors are trying to decide if you should be prescribed Prozac, something to level you out until you can get a grip on your life. We're worried because you're not sleeping or eating properly."

"I'm not depressed, just wore out," Cootie defended himself." There's nothing wrong with me that a stiff drink couldn't cure."

"Not true," the nurse said. "You've got to stop beating yourself up. What's done is done."

"If one more person tells me that, I'll. . . ."

"Mr. Chambers, it's the truth," she replied curtly. "Your attitude is jeopardizing your health and recovery. You have some serious injuries, and the self-abuse is not helping you get well any faster."

"I don't need to hear this bull again," he snapped.

"You don't need to snap my head off," the nurse said. "I'm just trying to be helpful. I want to see you get back on your feet."

She walked out of the room without looking at him. He could tell he had hurt her. Everything she said was right on the money. He was venting his anger at someone who really cared for him. The woman did her job well. A good nurse. Maybe something Philbrick said a few days before was true: go through it, absorb the lessons, see what it was in you that made you make those stupid choices and what that says about who you are. Then turn your back on it all and grow from it. Nothing happens to us without a reason.

Or he could dwell on another thing Philbrick said, about how he couldn't do another stretch in prison. He was right. Prison life was hellish these days. It was nothing to sneeze at when he was in the joint either. He almost died there.

He had a visitor the next day. One of Gillette's girlfriends, Marita, came out to the hospital to see him. The guys had a joke about her, about her being somewhat tiny with large—very large—breasts and a big

14

ass. Gillette teased her about getting a boob job. Cootie had known her since he was a bouncer at a strip club near Wall Street. She brought a fruit basket, some *Sports Illustrated* magazines, and a giant bag of Fritos, which she knew he couldn't eat without doing internal damage.

"So, are they letting you out pretty soon?" she asked, after cutting off the football game on the TV. Favre and the Green Bay Packers were making mincemeat of the Philadelphia Eagles, racking up score after score.

"The doctors keep postponing it, finding new things for me to worry about," Cootie answered. "Hell, I may never leave this damn place."

"You look pretty good for someone who's been shot a coupla times," she joked.

"Looks are deceiving," he said. He hated small talk. "Have you seen my girls?"

"I ran into Alicia the other day downtown at Macy's and we talked," she said. "She didn't mention you. I asked her about her sister. She shrugged."

"They haven't been to see me at all." Sadly, he looked out the window.

"We're getting old, aren't we?"

"I guess," he replied. "But that doesn't explain why they haven't come." They had been friends for years since he saved her from being knifed by a pimp. Marita and him. In fact, they knew each other before Gillette.

She started munching the Fritos, laughing. "Why is it you chase these stupid bird-brain impossible situations, then get bent all out of shape when they bite you in the ass?"

"I don't know what you mean."

"Yes, you knew the game from the beginning. Quit playing the victim. It doesn't do you any good."

"Where do you get that from?"

She crunched the chips extra loudly. "Look, boo, when a person tells you in the beginning that she's still dealing with this psycho, that's a wake-up call right there. You knew Red. You knew he was a wack case. You're the one who convinced yourself to move forward with pursuing his wife. Stop playing the vic."

"There is no vic here," he snapped. "The victim part was that I believed the bitch. Tell me that you haven't been lied to in your life."

"But now she's the bitch." She grinned. "You rolled the dice and took your chances. Hey, I'm doing the same thing with me and the married guy. I know up front what the deal is. I can't get mad at him if I get burned."

He was ticked off. "That's the past. I'm not messing with any woman."

"You sound bitter and pissed off."

"No, I'm not." She was going to town on those Fritos, smacking away.

"You can be nice, just make sure it's with the right person," she said.

"Tell me about the married cat," he said. "What's up with that?"

She crossed her legs and pursed her lips. "I was getting bored with myself so I decided flying solo wasn't so much fun, so I hooked up with this guy. Turns out he's hitched. Society bitch, snooty. He says she doesn't understand him or his needs."

He laughed. "Men always say that."

"Won't even give him head," she said. "He and I talk. I see him on weekends mostly. But my head isn't there like it was last year. I've put some distance there since nothing is going anywhere. I think it's more of what we had, which was at one time really good, but that's gone, and there's not a desire to re-create it now if ever."

"What did he say? Is he going to split with his wife?"

She shook her head, her eyes weary and dim. "Now he's singing the song of staying until his son is out of high school. I appreciate he's a family guy, but I think that's also his excuse to stay where he is. Not that I would want him to walk away from his family since that wouldn't be cool at all, but I let him know I can't spend the next couple of years hanging out for possibly nothing."

"Do you love him?"

"So that leaves him and me nowhere. . . ."

"Do you love him?"

There was a faraway look on her face, dreaming and wishing for things that could be, but were impossible. "Yes, I do. Very much so. Always did. We broke up once before. I didn't leave him because I didn't love him. At the time, I just didn't think I would have been happy with the life he wanted to give me."

"How so?"

"I didn't know who I was or who I could become."

"How long have you been together?"

She folded the cellophane chip bag and put it into her purse. "I would have always been looking across the road wondering what could have been there for me. That would have made me dissatisfied with him in the long run and I probably would have left him or been where he is with his wife now, stuck and unhappy, doing it for the kids. So I chose to leave him."

"But you went back?"

"Yes, I went back," she said. "The love trap is stronger than ever. Old loves."

He slid forward in the bed. "Why would you risk unhappiness to be with a married man? I knew we— Red's wife and I—weren't in love with each other. I just loved the sex."

17

"See, that's the difference," she said. "I really like him. We clicked mentally. We always had lots to talk about, just fit very smoothly. No drama. Also he's a Cancer, so we have much of the same things in common."

"Hmmm. And the sex?"

"He's a damn good lover," she said. "But it was more than that. There was the pull there of what we had, the possibility of having that again, knowing that I haven't had it like that with anyone since then in that way. Old loves are dangerous. Love is always a risk, so I have my eyes open. I know it's not the best situation or one I should be in, which is why I started distancing myself."

"If you met him now, would you go after him?"

"I'll put it this way, if he were someone I was just meeting, I wouldn't be in it at all," she said, frowning. "He's a real heartbreaker. He's spoiled me for every man after him."

"Yes, you're right about old loves."

"Hey, maybe I'll meet somebody new and settle down," she said, smiling. "Are you back in circulation?" She was just messing with his head.

"Kinda."

"Why not?"

"I have some unfinished business," he said. "After that, I'll—"

"How did you get involved with Red's wife?" she asked.

"I had some business with Red," he replied. "She was always around and flirting with me. One day, I took her up on it, and we started screwing around. Everything was all right until she blabbed to Red about cheating on him."

"Oh, shit," she said. "Didn't anyone ever tell you not to shit where you sleep?"

"Yeah, right."

"So after you take care of business, are you going to be on the market again?"

He smiled like a fox eyeing a fat hen. "Oh sure."

"See, for you guys, it's about the booty, then you wonder how you end up knee deep in some crap. Then you beat up on women who want stability and a stiff dick." She laughed, and he joined in.

"Ever see Pam around?"

Marita's eyes lit up. "Oh, she's fine. She used to be great pals with your wife. Remember? Pam had a rough time of it for a while there, but she's back in the saddle. I saw her two weeks ago. She's taking really good care of herself. Looks ten years younger."

"Is she still stripping?"

"Yep. Over at Eve's in the Bronx. They got busted a month ago."

"Drugs and sex on the premises," she said. "Vice caught Pam and this other girl doing a private show. Pam had the guy's dick in her mouth when they nabbed her. Couldn't do shit but go quietly."

"Why hasn't she called me?" He looked at her closely. She had a cute face, those balloon tits, and a rail-thin body. She was forever dieting and working out at the gym.

"Pam will call you when she feels its right for her. I think you understand why that might be difficult for her. She's trying to set her priorities now, and you aren't really one of them."

"Why not?" He narrowed his eyes.

"You know she had you under her skin for some time now. And this thing with Red's wife and the ruckus it raised didn't sit well with her. She really loved you. She would have done anything for you, but you had to go and fuck that up. When you get your head on straight, then she may call you."

"So that's why she hasn't visited me?"

Marita opened the cellophane on the fruit basket, reached inside to retrieve a pear. She rubbed it for a moment on the sleeve of her red silk blouse, then bit into it. "You don't get it, do you? Pam loved you but she never really liked you as a human being. She kept giving you chances, and you kept hurting her."

He watched her run her fragile hand over her close-cut, curly head. "Marita, we both did things—bad things. We both hurt each other."

"She never hurt you like this. You disgraced her in front of everybody, dissed her like a common whore. No woman likes to be shit on in public. If I were her, I would never talk to your tired ass again."

"Then why are you here?" Cootie looked at her angrily. He knew. Marita was fucking Pam. He had known she was attracted to her, and she had used this shooting to move in on her. Women in the stripping biz went both ways, men and women, so he wasn't surprised. Especially the females that were bi. What did Gillette call them, carpet-munchers. Sick bastard.

Marita stood, hands on her narrow hips. "I was hoping to find you half-dead, but no such luck. It's a pity the bitch was such a bad shot." She laughed evilly, kept on laughing, laughing as she tossed the magazines in his face and walked quickly past the nurse on her way out.

"What was that about?" the nurse asked.

He grabbed the fruit basket and emptied its contents into the waste bin. "Hell if I know. She knows my girlfriend."

"You're not too popular, are you?" she asked.

He was watching her flat ass and her swaying of it. "I guess not."

T H R E E

Good news greeted Cootie three days later. The doctors decided to parole him, and he made the necessary calls to ensure he had somewhere to go. He called everybody but his family and friends, except Gillette, whom he knew was down in Atlantic City, gambling and losing money he didn't have. He left a number of messages on answering machines both in Harlem and the Bronx. He didn't get to Brooklyn yet. Cootie didn't care what the deal was as long as he had a roof over his head. Somewhere to sleep. He was just glad to be out of the hospital.

He called Momo, a boxer friend of his at a midtown gym. Some pug said he wasn't there, but he would be around warming up about five. He stopped at a diner for a bowl of greasy chicken noodle soup, lukewarm tea, and half a doughnut, then he flagged down a gypsy cab for the ride to the gym. The traffic was light. The snowplows were out on the side streets on the West Side and down through what used to be San Juan Hill in the Lincoln Center neighborhood, doing a thorough cleaning of the steep mounds of the white stuff and slush.

Walking around the corner, he trotted up the stairs to the second-floor gym. He could smell the pungent odor of male sweat as the groups of fighters sparred with each other in the three rings set up. The managers, coaches, and handlers were monitoring their boys, tallying their assets and defects. There were about fifteen people standing around, no more than that.

He peeked into the weight room off to the left at a few muscle-bound guys taking turns on the leg press. Some

21

of them were admiring their bodies, checking the veins on their huge arms and the marbled bulges of their shoulders and chests. Preening peacocks.

"This is a closed gym, no visitors," a broken-down pug whispered.

Matt, the manager of Momo, walked up dressed like a butler, as he always was, carrying his derby and mahogany walking stick. The man liked to think he was a fashion plate. He was a humpback.

"Cootie, I heard you were shot," Matt said, the question transformed into a reply.

"Yeah," Cootie answered, flinching at the memory of the bullets. As he turned from the manager, he suddenly saw a pair of tree-trunk legs fill the space of his vision as Momo climbed into the ring. Matt wisecracked that the boxer was doing his workout and that he would be able to come out to play later.

"Hey, Coot," the boxer yelled, finally seeing him. "Heard you was shot."

"You can talk to Momo when we finish up here," Matt said firmly.

"Shut up, white man. I need to see my man now." The boxer climbed back out of the ring, grabbed Cootie by the arm, and yanked him toward the door. Matt stood there with a corner man, towel over his shoulder, red in the face, and mumbling he wouldn't stand for the black man's insolence.

"When you finish with him, can we get back to the matter at hand?" his manager growled.

"Yes dear," the boxer wisecracked and bowed. "I've got to talk to you. It's kinda important. It concerns your kid."

"Which kid?" Cootie already knew he meant Audrey.

"Audrey. This spic bastard has turned her out," the boxer said. "She's been sleeping around, doing hotel trade, turning tricks and shit. She even tried to crack on me for some bread. The spic was there, overseeing the action. Audrey was just a sweet girl. I hate that asshole."

"How long has she been doing this?"

"Probably not long. Probably since you was in the hospital."

Cootie was stunned. Maybe this was what Marita tried to tell him. And Gillette. And they were afraid to do it. His baby girl turning tricks, damnit, no way.

He noticed Momo was all business when he went over to the makeshift ring, a medium-sized circle of sweat-drenched canvas. The boxer sat on a stool, clad in trunks and pro-fighting shoes, as his trainer began wrapping his outstretched hands with tape. Another guy slipped the headgear over his bald dome. The boxer kept a murderous expression on his face, completely deadpan, possibly to frighten any spies from the opposing camp. He wanted to look mean.

"Matt says youse a guest of his and anything youse wants, ahm suppose to git for youse," one of the gofers said to Cootie, handing him a cold bottle of ginger ale.

He smiled at the broken-nosed guy and returned his gaze to the boxer being readied for mock battle. The tape was being applied over his thumb, over the top of his left hand, and finally between his fingers. The trainer did it so fast, so efficiently, that it was apparent that this was a ritual he could perform in his sleep. He stepped back and watched the boxer flex both hands, turn them over, and examine both sides. The boxer smiled for the first time, saying they felt good, strong, tight. He was ready to go and get some.

The gofer came back and whispered hoarsely into Cootie's ear. "Saw youse at da gym before you was shot with a nice little piece of white ass. Young thing. Something lak da champ here would cripple her in bed.

23

Wear dat pussy out. He's lak Tyson lak dat, loves da honeys. At least da ole Tyson before he went to da joint on da rape charge and cleaned up his act. Youse git any of dat white trim?"

Cootie ignored him.

"Was dat the broad who got into the trouble?" The gofer was relentless.

"No, it was a Negress," Cootie said, laughing. "Not an ofay."

He walked closer to the ring. Standing in the middle of it, the boxer pushed his hands into a pair of heavy gloves and put his rubber mouthpiece into his mouth. He bounced up and down, getting the blood going in his legs.

"Momo's lak Dempsey, Tunney, Louis, Ali, and Robinson all in one," the gofer muttered, his eyes gleaming when the boxer did a rotation number with his neck. "There's some Duran, Armstrong, and Tyson in there too. He one powerful man."

Cootie could feel the man's awesome power, his menace, his need to hit something, to hit someone. He was anxious, constantly moving, mumbling to himself. He was a killer in the ring. Finally, his trainer yelled for the boxer to spar with a Spanish guy, who was all flash but a good jab. The guy, Hernandez, possessed quick hands and feet. The trainer walked over and stood next to Cootie, barking instructions to the fighter.

"No head hunting, work on the body," the trainer shouted, and his boxer responded, cutting off the ring to trap his foe against the ropes. "Go to the body. Get off first. Nine-three-one-four. Forget the uppercut."

The boxer ripped a series of bone-numbing punches to Hernandez's body, methodically working him over, aimed at the kidneys, heart, and liver. Hernandez tried to spin out of the corner, tried to counter with a couple of shots to the side of the fighter's head, but the boxer, Momo, seemed oblivious to them. The onlookers were entranced by the brutal nature of the assault. The boxer grunted with each blow, some of which lifted the Spanish guy's body off the canvas.

"Let Hernandez out of there," the trainer shouted. "Momo, don't bust 'im up."

The boxer stalked Hernandez around the ring, feinting and slipping punches, constantly moving forward. Hernandez was on his bicycle, dancing laterally away from the occasional roundhouse blows from the boxer. Some in the crowd applauded his wily legwork. The boxer scowled, cursed under his breath, and moved effectively to the man's right. Hernandez was trapped again. Then it happened. The boxer launched a terrifying array of punches at his prey, ending the combination with a wicked left hook, a sizzling right cross, and a swift Tysonlike uppercut. Hernandez went down hard on the canvas and did not move. Silence.

"Damn," Cootie mumbled.

"He's a bad man, a very bad man," his trainer said of his fighter.

The trainer and two handlers leaped into the ring, pushing the boxer away from the fallen fighter. One checked Hernandez's cloudy eyes and neck before they helped him up on a stool. Cootie watched the scene with a knot in his stomach. The man appeared really shaken by the latest series of blows. However, Hernandez shook his head, and coughed up a little blood when the trainer administered a couple of whiffs of smelling salts.

"Don't worry, everybody," the gofer yelled happily. "He's jes a little groggy. He's all right. Momo jes rocked his world a little bit."

The boxer lifted his headgear, saw Cootie watching, and nodded. He faced his trainer and asked who else was back there for him to spar with, to get in some rounds. The trainer mentioned a few names and added that the boxer needed the veteran fighters to sharpen his skills. Pushovers were useless. You needed guys who knew tricks, knew how to mimic other guys' fighting styles, knew how to make him think in the ring.

"Yeah, I know that, so where are they?" the boxer asked.

Cootie watched the boxer take off his gloves and wave to the crowd, who were delighted with the impressive show of power they had just witnessed. Momo was the product of a rigid Spartan training routine: diet, exercise, and combat. He was a marvelous example of black manhood—sculpted body, smooth skin, fairly handsome except for the busted nose.

"How did you like that?" Momo asked.

"Damn, you sat him down on his ass," Cootie replied. "What a punch."

"Want to go a few more rounds?" Matt asked, indicating another boxer.

The boxer motioned to Cootie that he would talk to him more as he made quick work of the latest bum brought forward for the slaughter. Cootie waved back, okay. The trainer smiled; there was a surprise waiting for the cocky youngster.

Max Burns, the seasoned Irish vet who had been in retirement for some time, climbed into the ring, and the crowd clapped and whistled their approval of the old champ coming out to show the kid a thing or two. He was the Irish Archie Moore, an old pro. Everyone knew what Burns was capable of doing. He was still one of the strongest heavyweights ever, with a big advantage in reach, and deceptive speed. During his reign, he had faced several rugged fighters and had demolished most of them with little problem. Larry Holmes, the successor to Ali, had cut his career short by giving him eye damage.

Burns walked to the younger man, tapped gloves with him, and whispered something to him. He was tall, strong, muscled, and very pale. Freckled. Red hair. The young boxer yelled toward the crowd that he was going to whup the old man's ass.

"You in trouble now, old geezer," the boxer taunted the veteran. "I'm going to send you back to your rockin' chair, pops." He did his version of the Ali shuffle and raised his arms in a gesture of easy victory.

Burns smiled knowingly, adjusted his headgear, and began circling the boxer, moving beautifully. His left arm was extended and his right was held close to his body, protecting his chest and chin. The boxer pounced on him, swinging wildly, but he couldn't land anything solid. He was frustrated with the clever old-timer, who was jabbing him to death with his left—*pop-pop-pop-pop*. The boxer leaned away from the punches, giving his opponent an angle, hoping to make himself a harder target to hit. But Burns moved with him, smashed with a chopping right to the boxer's headgear, rattling him momentarily.

The trainer laughed. "Take the boy to school, Burns. Take him to school." Burns missed with a jab, and the boxer dug one shot, deep into the veteran's body. Discomfort could be seen on Burns's face for a second, but he tied the younger man up with his hands, and spun him away from him before he could throw another punch. The boxer, sensing the damage, rushed in, missing with a flurry of hooks and jabs. He wanted to fight the old man on the inside, where his superior youth and speed could take a toll.

"Take it to him, Momo," his trainer yelled. "Show him what you got."

Angered, the boxer, throwing caution to the wind, charged once more, throwing a torrent of punches. All of them went wide of their mark. Conserving his energy, Burns went into a deep crouch, bobbing and weaving expertly. He avoided much of the attack. Finally, one of the boxer's roundhouse rights caught Burns backpedaling, staggering him and sending him back against the ropes. The crowd was stomping, screaming, and yelling for the boy to finish off the older warrior.

"Patience, Momo, patience," his trainer cautioned wisely. He had seen Burns fight before and knew that the cagey fighter was most dangerous when he was hurt.

The boxer stopped thinking, pressed forward in his attack, digging more shots to the body. Burns winced twice and covered up. The younger fighter moved to the left, his right hand cocked. Instinctively, Burns dipped and hit the boxer with a crunching blow to the kidney, and his younger foe wobbled. A look of surprise crossed the youth's face as he tried to retreat, but the old man was on him. Burns crossed the kid's feeble left jab with his own hamlike right fist. It landed right on the chin, and it was followed by two more lightning rights. The boxer would have fallen to the canvas but the ropes were close, and he sagged into them. He grabbed the top strand of the ropes while Burns belabored him with a barrage of punches.

The trainer was going to halt the sparring, but held back to see what the kid had. If he was going to go for the gold, he had to learn to take punishment as well as to dish it out. That was the lesson Ali taught Foreman in their fight in Zaire, the Rumble in the Jungle. Anyone can throw punches, but you got to learn how to take them too. That was how it was in life as well.

"Get off the ropes, kid," the trainer shouted at his young charge. "Fight back. Don't wimp out on me. You ain't on queer street yet."

The boxer wobbled once more. He tried to hold on to Burns, tying up one of his thick arms, but the old man managed to pound him savagely to the body with the other one. He wanted the boy to give him some respect. He was mad. The boy had no idea who he was fucking with.

There was a steady stream of blood coming from one of the younger boxer's nostrils. Nobody had ever made him bleed before. No doubt he had fought some stiffs, handpicked opponents, but there were a lot of serious contenders on his record. Nobody had cut him before. He was trying to go light on the old geezer, but now Burns was shaming him in front of his people.

It was a mighty uppercut that turned things around for the boxer. He loaded up the punch while bent over, absorbing a furious series of hooks to the head. He planted his feet, shifted his weight, and put all of his power into an uppercut that launched Burns from the floor. The crowd went silent. He dazed Burns with the shot and moved in for the kill. Two lefts to the head, three rights to the head, one kidney punch, another uppercut, and a power shot, a right to Burns's jawline. The old man draped over the ropes.

"Momo, back off," the trainer shouted, realizing that the youth could hurt the veteran permanently. "No more, no more punches."

The boxer was satisfied with neutralizing the old man. He popped him twice more on the side of the headgear, and Burns pitched forward, his eyes rolling back in his head. He was unconscious before he hit the canvas. He landed hard on his face and sprawled there, outstretched. Out cold. The young boxer stepped over him, showing his disrespect, a move that triggered boos and moans from the crowd. This was sparring, after all.

His trainer tried to stop the boxer to chew him out, but he pushed past him roughly and grabbed Cootie by the elbow.

"Fuck them," Momo said.

"That was unnecessary back there," Cootie said. "You proved your point. You didn't have to pound on him like that."

Arrogance was one of the things about the boxer that always found itself in articles written about him. And Cootie could see why. He strutted like a proud bantam rooster, full of himself, gloating over his devastating punishment of the man who bloodied him.

"Anytime you get into the ring, it's a war," he told Cootie, winking. "Burns knew that. He was landing some good shots so I knew I'd make him pay—and pay big-time."

"Shit, it was only a warm-up, sparring," Cootie shot back.

"Fuck you and him," the boxer replied sullenly. "You got a place to stay?"

"Hell no. I can't go back to my place. I need a place to crash until I get squared away. Don't you have that room up on Lexington?"

"Yes. You can use it. I need to talk to you. Let's talk about my problem. I've got other things on my mind other than some washed-up has-been pug. Some serious shit's going down."

Cootie looked over his shoulder. "Burns must be all right, on his feet again. So, what's the problem, champ?" he asked.

"I'm not the champ, and I may never be," the boxer said flatly. "You saw the champ's last fight, didn't you?"

"Yes. What about it? It was over in a minute and a half. KO."

"Right, but it was a charade. Everybody knows that. He fights nothing but bums. The division ain't shit. One guy went down before the punch hit him, and another one was bleeding so bad that my trainer wondered what was on the champ's gloves. These guys are bums, and the people feel ripped off."

"He's the Great White Hype," Cootie said. "Ain't he from Russia or Croatia or some damn place?"

"I don't care where he's from," Momo said. "I can whup him."

"Do you really believe that?"

"Shit yeah," the boxer replied. "Everybody said Jordan, his last opponent, had a glass jaw before he took this fight. He went down from a light left hook that my kid would have shaken off, and then he hops up to beat the count, not really hurt, but he collapses on the ropes just before the ref gets ready to send him out to face the champ again. It was bullshit. I can whup his ass. I know I can."

"So why don't you?"

"The Vegas mob says I got to lose," the boxer said angrily. "Don King don't even fuck with these guys out there. I'm to carry him for twelve rounds, land a few good shots, but the champ's supposed to deck me one minute into the last round. The mob says he'll give me a rematch and a bigger purse the second time around."

"What does your trainer, Aliano, say?" Cootie asked, watching his face.

"He doesn't like it, says if I lose this one, they'll never give me another shot at him," the boxer answered. "The mob, he says, wants me to fight the champ because I'm good for the fight game because I'm a warrior, and I give it my all. It's to clean up his image. He's a fuckin' bum."

31

Cootie laughed. "Yeah, you got heart. I have to give you that much."

"I've been in a few wars, but I'm still in my prime," the boxer said. "If I fought the champ in an honest match, I'd expose his weaknesses and set him on his ass. Everybody knows that. Even he knows that."

"What does the mob say will happen if you don't take a dive?" Cootie asked.

"I'll have an accident," the boxer said sadly. "That's crazy mad. They said they'd fuck everybody up, everybody that's close to me or has ever been close to me."

"What are you going to do?"

"I'm going to whup the champ's ass," he said. "And then I'll deal with the consequences."

Cootie let no emotion show in his face. He felt the boxer watching him for a response. He knew boxing was a dirty game. Very few got out what they put into it, especially the boxers and the trainers.

"Mr. Chambers, what do you think I should do?" He was like a little boy asking for approval from his father.

Cootie looked at the burly black man's glove-covered hands, then at his impressive Adonis body, shook his head, and shrugged. "Kick the champ's ass and deal with the consequences." Then they laughed.

"Oh yeah, you got to get Audrey away from that spic," the boxer said, digging into his tote bag for the room key. "They've got her on crack. She looks like shit."

He stared at the boxer in alarm, shaking his head. "Oh damn." This crack news coming from Momo only confirmed everything he'd been hearing from people around the hood. His baby girl was going down fast—real fast.

F O U R

It was two days before Cootie finally caught up with his older daughter, Alicia, a tall, big-boned beauty who looked like his late wife, and she was not pleased with meeting him. Only when he told her through Marita, Gillette's friend that the safety of her children was involved if she didn't agree to see him. It was a big lie. Alicia insisted the meeting place be public. He was irked with her, but he was forced to go along with her bullshit. She held the trump card, the clues to his baby girl, so there was very little he could do to force his will upon the situation.

They met in a small but comfortable Ethiopian-Eritrean restaurant in Harlem, off 128th Street and Lenox, which specialized in vegetarian dishes. There were only ten tables in the eatery. Native art from the Northern African countries decorated the walls, giving the surroundings an authentic feel. Music from the region played softly in the background. Only three of the tables were occupied, which made Cootie feel much easier in case there were verbal fireworks between them. Alicia was known to get loud. Nothing like an audience to inspire a domestic argument.

A beautiful young Ethiopian woman came to their table, asking what they wanted to order—lunch or an early dinner. Cootie always loved the color of their skin, the Ethiopians, the flesh of a smooth nut brown. He glanced at Alicia, who wondered what appetizers were available. The African woman laid two menus on the table.

"We have two very popular appetizers, *fitfit* salad and *azifa*," the woman said in a delicately accented English. "*Azifa* is very good. Its whole cooked lentils with a mustard sauce. Delicious."

"Do you have anything in a soup?" Cootie asked.

The woman smiled, with her oval black eyes flashing in warmth. "We have a traditional chicken soup with egg noodles or a *kebasa* soup with rice, red lentils, green and yellow split peas. Either one is good."

"Are the doctors letting you have solid food yet?" Alicia asked.

"Yes, but it takes a little time to get used to it," her father replied.

"Does it hurt?" Alicia referred to his wound.

"Not as bad as it did. The pain was really terrible before. Hurt like hell."

The woman was still standing beside the table. Cootie smiled up at her and chose the chicken soup. He asked for a cup of strong coffee to go with it. Alicia, who looked incredible in her yellow sweater and tight-fitting jeans, went with the *fitfit* salad and decaffeinated tea. She told him she was taking aerobic and weight-lifting classes at a neighborhood gym. Her body—slimmer hips and waist, and less around the middle—reflected the new interest. Even her face was thinner, her cheekbones more pronounced. All of that was accented by her new haircut, closely cropped with a streak of henna across the front. She looked younger, stylish, hipper.

"You're looking well," Cootie said, not knowing where to start.

"I didn't want to visit you at the hospital because I didn't want to lose another parent," Alicia said somberly. "I've lost too many people in hospitals. I kept in touch with Marita and Gillette as to how you were doing, but I didn't want to go there."

"Your mother didn't die in a hospital," he said, suppressing his temper.

She sat with the fork poised above her salad. "I know all that. Did you want to be a parent? Did you want to be a father with kids? Because sometimes it seemed that you wanted to be out in the streets rather than with us. Especially after Faith died, you just had that itch to be out there."

He stared at the patrons nervously. "I'll be honest. I didn't feel like a father, like a dad. Just because I had two babies didn't mean I wanted to settle down. Being a father meant being responsible, providing a roof over your heads and food to eat. Like a lot of cats, I thought fathering a kid just meant you screwed a broad and she got pregnant."

"Did Faith feel the same way?" She watched his restless hands.

"I don't know how she felt," he replied. "She had some serious issues she was trying to wrestle with: drugs, booze, and depression. Both of us weren't ready to be parents. Both of us came from households where our parents were from the street life. I can't speak for her, but I knew it was impossible to have me playing a role that I never saw in my own childhood."

"What do you mean?"

"My mother died in childbirth having my younger sister, and my father hustled numbers and women," he said. "When I turned twelve, he started dealing drugs. He got a short stint in the big house, and we were turned over to his sister. It's almost as if life is repeating itself. He was very cold and distant. I hardly knew my father."

Alicia thought back on the old neighborhood. "Yeah, there were a lot of fatherless families around there. I was always proud that we had a father, although you loved to run the streets. Before Faith died, she'd have boyfriends or guys who gave us gifts and candy, hoping to get the pussy. We knew what they were trying to do.—Get the coochie."

"I knew she had guys, marks, and lovers," he said. "But then I wasn't exactly faithful either. I always had chicks on the side. We accepted that outside thing as a part of our marriage. I never asked her any questions, and neither did she."

"Did you love her?"

"Hell yeah," he answered. "I loved her so much. She was special."

If she had been Audrey, she would be bitching about men, their cheating, their lack of ambition, the inequality of the sexes in society, her usual gripes, but that was not the case. That was not what she did. Alicia talked about her new man—her new fella as she called him—her stable UPS friend, Harold. She drawled on and on about how he was a hardworking guy, always seeming carefree, never worrying about anything.

"Where did you find him?" Cootie wanted a drink.

"At a Christmas party given by my job." She smiled. She talked about how she went through a brief period of auditioning men, about how there were so many lost brothers out there, but quite a few good ones as well. She was totally different from her mother, who always thought black men weren't shit.

"How does he take to your boys?" he asked, recalling her little ones were three and five. Her old man, the boys' real father, was doing a bit, a nickel, at Sing Sing for armed robbery.

"He's okay with it, but it's sometimes hard for him because they remember their father," she said. "He spent time with them before he was locked up. So Harry has some mighty big boots to fill. And he tries. I guess it wasn't very difficult to raise us, being girls and all."

He grinned. "Sure. You girls had two different personalities. You were so confident, laid-back, and independent, whereas Audrey was a live wire and volatile. Boy, she had a hot temper, would stay mad for hours. I had a woman come in to help out because I couldn't have done it if I wanted to conduct my street business. But a lot of times I was by myself, juggling school, naps, television, and lunches. I recall Audrey didn't like milk and salt, and you didn't eat meat."

"I never liked meat," she said. "But I remember you would always read to us those spooky stories. We'd be so scared. Then we would lay next to you while we napped. That was nice. Faith wasn't like that. She was kinda cold."

"Also, I think I pampered Audrey because she had asthma," her father said. "I would get scared when she had those breathing attacks, couldn't catch her breath. That was frightening. Even after her asthma situation was under control, I still thought of her as fragile. I guess I felt guilty because of her illness. I don't know why."

"You let her get away with murder. Faith did too."

"I knew people could die from asthma. Maybe I did wrong because Audrey started to think she was sickly and different. I just wanted to protect, to nurture her. But she was always headstrong and stubborn. When she was a baby, she had a way of turning her head when she had had enough. It was like you were dismissed."

His daughter laughed. "She's still like that, uppity. Like she's from royalty."

He took a deep breath. Reliving the old days was all right, but he was hungry and wanted his food. What was the cook doing? Where was the fucking food? He didn't want to hear this shit. He didn't want to know who Alicia was fucking. He did want to know whether Audrey was whoring and if she was on crack.

"Too much information can be destructive," she said. "Like Faith was a junkie and a whore. That was my mother, for God sakes. When Grandpa told me that she was streetwalking over Park Avenue under the railroad tracks, I cried and cried for days. I couldn't believe it."

"I didn't want to know about that," her father said.

"Yes, I know," she replied. "You didn't even want us to know she was dead. You didn't want us to know how she died. You didn't want us to know what you did for a living."

"What do you mean?"

"That you were one of the biggest con men in Harlem. A big-time crook."

He took a long look around the restaurant. There was no sign of the waitress. "I felt like this. I felt that I shouldn't tell you girls anything that I didn't want you to blab. You girls had big mouths. You could have shared the wrong things with your friends or their parents. In fact, I figured what I did was none of your business."

The conversation was interrupted by the appearance of the woman again, with the drinks and the cup of coffee. She informed them that the food would be ready in a minute. Almost as soon as she left the beverages on the table, she came back.

"You did want a *fitfit* salad, right?"

Alicia gave her polite smile and nodded, then she turned back to Cootie. "So where was I?"

"I don't know." He was eyeballing the swing of African woman's round ass.

"I know. Audrey has a grudge against you. She feels that you left us. She thinks you abandoned us, left us, betrayed us. Maybe this is why she doesn't trust men."

He grew pensive. "Do you think that as well?"

"Yes, kinda," she replied. "You could have done a better job as a father."

"So you're saying that you like your life as it is now and there's no room for me in it whatsoever?" He was afraid of this very moment, the chicken's coming home to roost. The bitter consequences of spending so much time in the streets.

"I guess that's what I'm saying." There was such finality in what she said. "You did a shitty job as a father. You just didn't have much time for us. We wanted to be a family, but you wanted to find that excitement out there hustling. Audrey hates you for it. That's why she thinks black men are bastards."

He balled his hands into fists as he became frustrated. "I thought a lot about what I've done with my life. I thought a lot about us. I know I fucked up."

Alicia leaned across the table toward him. The tension was mounting. She could see he wanted to knock her on her ass. "Do you have any idea what you did to this family? Do you?"

But there was no excuse. "I know what I did was wrong."

His face was deadpan. He thought of how beautiful her mother, Faith, had been. He thought about how lame she was before he got her involved in the street life, a square girl from a square family. She loved him for him. Before somebody turned her on to the needle, before she started hustling her ass, she was righteous, pure, uncomplicated. Dark fudge-brown, little-girl pixie features, tall and sweet. He thought about the first time he saw her naked, luscious curves in a tub of suds. They had gone hiking upstate, their third date, her idea. Sweat was pouring from them as they sat in the car driving back to the city. She had teased him about how funky he smelled, holding her nose. In fact, they both were pretty foul from the day's exertion on the hills and the rough terrain. Once back at her apartment, she had called to him from the bathroom to join her, and he did. In the large tub in her tiny apartment on St. Nicholas and 147th Street, they took turns washing and holding each other, her full breasts pressing against him, his dick swelling in lust. And when they finished their love play, she quickly dressed in a tight black leotard that displayed her marvelous figure to full advantage.

"Don't explain to me," Alicia said firmly. She didn't want to hear it. "You need to explain to Audrey."

But he was only half hearing her. He was there in that golden moment with Faith, her bathroom drama, and her water magic. She could stay in the bathroom for hours, her refuge. She loved "long, hot soaks" as she called them. The sandalwood incense burning. Her feminine items all about: sweet-smelling soaps and shampoos, creams and the pink razors for her underarms and legs. He missed her badly. What was it that his grandmama used to say: "You don't miss your water till your well runs dry."

"Cootie, I'm talking to you," Alicia said in a raised tone. "Earth to Cootie, earth to Cootie."

"Why don't you call me Dad?" He hated when she used his street name.

"You haven't earned that right to be called Dad or Father," she said quietly. "Both of you, our parents, failed us. She killed herself and you weren't there."

He was silent. It was like a hard slap in the face or a solid punch in the heart.

"What were you thinking?" his daughter asked.

"I feel badly about how I treated you," he said. "I was selfish."

"Not only that, I agree with you, but you are a weak man," she said. "When I think about those early times with you and Faith, I realize how much of life I missed. I didn't really develop as a woman. In some ways, I'm still a little girl. So emotionally crippled, I went from your house to the house of a man who didn't love me, only used me. Then the kids came. Damn right, you as our parents failed us. Neither of you could nurture us. Both of you were emotionally unavailable. You were too locked up in yourselves."

He was shell-shocked. He held his coffee cup in mid-air. "I tried to be there for you girls. I really did. Don't give up on me. Please."

"Cootie, even when we were all together, we were so alone so much that it was the same as being alone." She spat the words out. "I remember Audrey coming over to my place the week before she went underground. She was so depressed. She spent most of the time talking about you and our childhood. I wasn't shocked when she said she didn't have a single happy memory of all that time."

"Not one, not one at all." He felt like crying, a father's nightmare.

"She said she was tired of being good and that she was going to be like her mother, a whore," his daughter said. "Getting fucked and having a good time. She said she was going to commit suicide, but in a different way from Faith. I didn't know what she meant, but I knew what she was feeling and how deep her hurt was. She said don't try to find her."

It was hard to sit and listen to Alicia express her anger and disapproval of him and Faith as their parents. He felt a pang of guilt and regrets, wishing he could do it all again. But there was nothing he could do about the old hurts of his girls' early life. Nothing.

"What can I do to make it better now?" he asked, almost pleading.

"I don't know," she replied harshly. "Maybe it's beyond repair."

"I've changed, really changed," he said eagerly. "No more streets, no more streets. I mean that. I'm going to walk away from that life. I feel it's useless to attack me for old stuff I can't change. I can't change the fact that your mother overdosed nor can I change the fact that I did time."

"You'd say anything or do anything to get us back, wouldn't you?"

"No." He glanced around the tiny restaurant, watching the other customers eating their food. There was no more fight left in him. His daughter wanted to smash him over the head with her new life, her new man, her new body.

"Get it, we're over. Ain't no more us, no more father and daughter. You're a damn stranger."

"I've changed," he repeated. "Getting shot was probably the best thing that ever happened to me. It made me realize a lot of things."

The food finally came. The woman and a thin man in a white outfit laid the dishes out in an attractive arrangement on their table. She apologized to them for the delay.

"Is Audrey on crack?" he asked.

Alicia pushed the food away from her, staring at him with tears brimming in her eyes. "You bastard. Goddamn you."

Suddenly, the woman reappeared at their table. "Earlier, you asked about the vegetarian dishes. We have *alitcha timtimo, shiro, tsebhi hambhi,* or maybe a *messawa* salad for the mister."

"Go away and leave us alone," Alicia hissed. The customers looked in their direction at the ruckus.

"I won't let anything happen to either of you," Cootie insisted. "Not you or Audrey. I guarantee you that. I will find her."

42

COLE RILEY

"You're a fucking loser, and you can't guarantee a damn thing," his daughter shouted. The woman and several of the restaurant staff came out of the kitchen, poised to intervene if things got out of hand.

"Believe me, nothing will happen. . . ." He never finished his sentence because a hard slap from her, closed his mouth and rattled his teeth. He rubbed his bruised cheek in shock.

Alicia rose to leave, sending her cup and saucer falling to the floor, shattering. He seized her by the shoulders, held her close, but she resisted. She began to laugh, softly at first, the more and more loudly. The woman and the staff came over to offer their assistance. She kept on laughing, almost hysterically. Cootie waved off the people who offered to help. He would handle this.

"If something happens to my sister, you're a dead motherfucker. . . ." The aggressiveness of her voice stunned him.

Alicia yanked free of his arm and started for the door. He gave the Ethiopian woman a wad of bills, more than enough to cover the cost of the meals, and ran after his daughter. But when he got to the curb, she was gone in a gypsy cab, speeding downtown to her old place in Chelsea. She was a creature of habit when she got upset—the first thing, she would run home. He watched the cab recede in the distance, then walked along Lenox Avenue, past the dingy funeral homes and stately churches toward 125th Street, and the looming shadow of the old Theresa Hotel where Castro once stayed when he came to America in the late fifties.

A man in a dark suit and open overcoat, possibly a black Muslim, walked past him. It was still chilly, but the snow had stopped. Behind the man was a young Latina dressed in a clinging short skirt with a bolero-fur jacket, shaking that ass. She was smoking a cigarette, Newport

43

menthol. Cootie hated menthol cigarettes, he preferred Pall Malls or Luckies, but he bummed one from her anyway.

Cootie lit his ciggie off hers. A ribbon of smoke eased from the corner of his mouth. He felt dead tired.

The Latina whispered to him, "Papi, you got some change, need a dollar for the subway to get home to my hungry baby. She with a babysitter in the Bronx." He gave her the dollar, and she planted a wet kiss on his bruised cheek. That made his day.

FIVE

The last time Cootie had seen his father was three years ago, when he gave him a tall, silver urn containing his mother's ashes. His mother left his father over a decade before after a square, working stiff offered her a life where she would not have to spend her days working. As for her children, they resented their father, for he was a heartless, cold bastard. In many ways, Cootie was like him.

He was still in an old folks' home off Amsterdam Avenue and 146th Street, wheelchair bound, suffering from senility. He was dressed in a dark blue robe, with flip-flops on his swollen feet. Both of Cootie's girls visited him often, taking him his favorite treats, a bag of Oreo cookies and a thermos of Seagrams. Their father thought they were trying to get back at him somehow by lavishing their affections on the old man instead of him, but Cootie wasn't a bit jealous. Although grandpa's mind wandered, he could be quite entertaining and sometimes enlightening.

Cootie never thought he would die like this, bit by bit. Nibbled away with all of his excesses and vices. He frequently would be shot by one of his women or his rivals or the cops, but not like this. But then Graham—that was his father's name—always said, "Life is a gift and we don't do anything to deserve it." Believe this, he had had a good life, a decent marriage, a nice home, great women, cool friends, and a profession that he loved: pimping.

The whole thing started about four years earlier after he was bounced around hard, and tossed to the pavement in a hit-and-run involving a mail truck. He was treated and released at a hospital in the Bronx, but something wasn't right. The brain disability increased in seriousness, one of his arms sometimes suffered paralysis, and he started forgetting things. In a few months, his father's condition worsened until he and Barbara put him in this home for the aged in Harlem. Cootie felt he should visit his father, just for old times' sake. He tried to forget his father treated him like shit.

"Hey, Pop. Whassup?" Cootie greeted the old man who was wearing dark glasses on top of his bald head. "How are you feeling?"

"Barbara said you was shot and dead." His father seemed surprised to see him.

"No, I'm still here." He hugged the ailing man and grinned. "Why are you sitting near this drafty window? You should be where it's warm."

His father's left arm hung limply against his chest, and the left side of his face lacked life, but he could still speak. "You know what I was thinking. I was thinking about God and religion. I was thinking about the power of miracles."

"That's a subject that I don't know much about," Cootie said.

"Do you believe in miracles?" His father tried to face him, even with his flimsy neck. "Do you, boy?"

"I guess. I guess it's a miracle I'm still alive." Cootie smiled insincerely.

"I can't believe in miracles somehow," the old man said. "You know why? If God is supposed to be responsible for both the good and bad, good and evil, then why is the world more evil? Innocent people dying, babies dying, all kinds of shit. I think it's the luck of the draw."

"I wouldn't know about that." He humored him.

"Is God responsible for evil?"

"I guess so," his son answered. This visit was going to be shorter than usual.

"Do you believe in the free soul and the power of moral choice?" The old man probably had been reading something. It wasn't like him to be talking like that on this subject.

"Who the hell knows?" Cootie didn't like to think about such things. He always wanted to keep it simple. These were things better thought of in churches, mosques, and temples.

"Both of us are evil people, bad people, and we have devoted ourselves to a life of crime," the old man said. "I was a pimp, a bad person, and you are a con man, a damn good one if I must say. But we are bad. Our souls are evil and bad, if the soul is the character of our personality. You know what I mean?"

Cootie really didn't like this line of talk. "I guess so."

"Do you believe in the afterlife?" the old man asked. "In heaven and hell?"

They both were crooks, life-long criminals, and he hated to see serious felons trying to find salvation on their last breath like the thief who was nailed to the cross next to Jesus. You lived your life and that was it.

"I don't know about all of that," Cootie replied.

"I'm almost eighty, and I'm ready to die," his father said, his face clouding over. "Do I care about dying? Hell yes, I do. Still I want more life, but I don't want to be a vegetable. All crippled up and wasting away. That's not a life, that's an existence. I told the docs I don't want to go out that way. I don't know if they heard me. Shit, I'm an important person. I was telling the nurses and orderlies that I used to be one of the most important pimps in Harlem. I knew all of the cats there. I was somebody."

"Yes, you were important." Cootie sighed.

The old man sagged under the weight of all the years as he thought about all of the time that had passed. Cootie didn't feel grief or regret at his decline. Their relationship had gone through more than one rough patch, although they were closer than they had ever been. His father finally let him talk to him without having his sister, Barbara, act as the intermediary or referee. She often served as the buffer between the two men, probably because they were so much alike. Perhaps that was what drew Barbara emotionally closer to her father.

"I wanted you to follow in my footsteps and create a dynasty of gentlemen of leisure, and even maybe your son would follow your lead," his father said. "You resented me. You wanted no part of it, and I never could figure out why."

"So what are you asking me?"

"Why didn't you try to build on what I tried to pass on?"

"I didn't like pimping," Cootie said firmly. "I didn't want to be a crook."

"But you did choose the street life, and you know why," his father replied. "But it's in your blood. It was the only life open to us where you could make some money. Hell, the white world didn't want us to succeed. I never humiliated the women. I treated them with respect, even though I learned the pimping game from an old-style pimp. I had a different style, so I didn't treat the girls like slaves."

"Shit, you treated them like shit. They had to submit and obey."

"Damn right. I learned early on from my father the power of pussy," the old man said. "Women love to control a man, but you got to control them, because all men are natural tricks. A little piece of ass can make guys do some stupid shit. I learned to dominate women so they can give me money. The goal was to turn the females out."

"That's what you did to my mother," Cootie said. "She didn't want to be a whore. She was the daughter of a minister, a Baptist minister at that."

The old man grinned. "Yeah, I turned your mother out. She wanted me to be her boss. She wanted to be dominated. Her father dominated her and her mother. She wanted me to boss her."

"You fucked over her and us too," Cootie snarled.

"That's bullshit," his father said. "We made an agreement. She wanted me to love her, but I told her she must obey me. And it wasn't about sex. She wanted to be under me. She wanted to serve me. She wanted to sacrifice for me; to do anything for me."

Cootie thought about their relationship, his parents—the pimp and the whore. After his mother's death, he didn't really feel sad for her; didn't grieve for her. She chose her life. He was angry about the evil of his father, the black man with no heart, no soul. For the longest, Barbara and the rest of his family were not on speaking terms with him or his father, as if they felt that Cootie was somehow involved in his mother's miserable death.

"Your mother could come and go if she wanted," the old man said. "She knew it was just business with me. She always accused me of breaking promises and shit. I told her if she wanted to build a separate life from me, that I would let her go. I said it. I promised that I would let her go."

"You're lying, and you know it," he retorted.

"No, I'm not," his father said, waving his thickly veined hands. "Even though I didn't say I loved her, she knew it. I treated every female equally, even my wife. But you must remember, sometimes it's hard to control black women. White women can be difficult but, by and large, they will go along to get along. Wives-in-law—my stable—could be a pain in the ass."

"I don't want to hear none of this."

"You should hear it," the old man said. "You don't know how to treat a female. That's why you have so much trouble controlling your women, even your girls. See, my stable of girls worked hard for me and gave me all their money, because I was their man. Your mother chose me. I tried to make a woman of her. When she was knocked up with you, she got arrested and I bailed her out. She didn't tell you about that, right?"

"No, but I'm sure she wasn't proud of that."

"Your mother was a freak," his father added. "She worked turning tricks right until she had you. Some tricks love a female who's about to pop. They get a nut behind that—a full belly ripe with a kid. Anyway, your mother never made the adjustment to being a mother like she made to being a whore. Yeah, your mother was a freak, and so is your daughter Audrey."

"Shut the hell up," he cursed him, his lips tightening.

"The apple doesn't fall far from the tree." The old man grinned, allowing his son to see that his dentures were missing. His father was very conscious about his smile—or lack of it.

"Where are your teeth, Pops?"

"I was a sweet mack," his father proudly proclaimed. "I loved the females; loved to be clean; high style in everything. So many girls, so many cars, so many vines. I wanted you to follow in my footsteps. You had to fuck it up, a damn con man."

"Where are your teeth, Pops?" Cootie repeated.

"A cat wanted to cop-and-lock a bitch, try to be sweet and sour on a female's ass," the old man said. "But you had to be slick. I could pimp a girl and turn her out, and she wouldn't even know she was whoring. I was that slick. But some of them bitches could stink. Like your mother. Damn, she would come home and her pussy stank like hell. I know why some niggas won't go down on bitches. I never did."

"Stop talking about her like that," Cootie said calmly. "Where's your damn teeth?"

"I raised a punk, a faggot," his father said. "You're weak. A damn chump. You ain't one-tenth the man I am. None of this generation is."

"Maybe so."

"See, love ruins people. Love has a short shelf life. The mistake I made was when I let love enter the relationship between your mother and myself. We would have been better off if we had just kept it strictly business. I know this. If a female wants to be with you, she'll stick. If not, she'll go. Your mother decided to go, and that's why she got killed. If she wouldn't have left, she would be alive today."

"You killed her," Cootie said. "And I will never forgive you for that."

His father pivoted, oddly dazed and confused suddenly. His mind could switch gears at a drop of a hat. Cootie couldn't figure out if it was an act, but it seemed real. The old man stared at the nurse approaching him with a cup of water and pills. "You're not my wife. No, you're not her."

Cootie turned to the nurse and asked her where his dentures were. She shrugged.

"We think he has Alzheimer's. His mind is going, but sometimes he has good days," the nurse said, handing his father the pills. "His memories are muddled together. Sometimes he thinks he's in the past, and other times

51

he's in the present. Often the memories and reality are piled on top of each other."

"I've got to get my transmission fixed on my Cadillac," his father said. "The thing is slipping. The mechanic said it was fixed but it's not."

Cootie remembered the car, a Cadillac Seville with all of the accessories, but that was more than fifteen years ago. A gold antique of a car. It was the old man's pride and joy. He recalled his father, with his conked hair, sharkskin suits from the pictures, before his mother was his mother. His father pimped girls in Harlem and on Times Square's Minnesota strip in the 1960s and the 1970s, in his heyday.

"I got to take a piss." His father pulled out his dick from his robe. Some of the other patients, especially the women, gathered around the frail man, watching the thing he had between his fingers.

"Put that away," the nurse said matter-of-factly. "You're scaring the natives."

Cootie tried to put his father's dick back into the robe, but the old man yanked away, making a slow motion as if he was pumping it, gradually getting it hard.

"You know I had a big dick. You've seen it enough." The old man laughed. "Oh baby, I would make the bitches scream. But you can't get them addicted to sex. You can't let the sex hold them, no matter how good it is."

"Your father thinks he was a pimp, a big-time pimp," the nurse said. "That's one of his fantasies. He's a successful pimp; a playa with a lot of women working for him."

Cootie didn't say anything. His father *was* a big-time pimp, that was true, but his mind was going. That was back in the day. He was nothing any longer, just an old man with his mind playing games on him.

"Please put your privates away," the nurse said. "Please. Can you do something here? You're his son."

"No, I can't." Cootie walked away, shaking his head. His mind was on Audrey and how he would not let her be swallowed up by the streets. Seeing his father like this provided him with the desire to not let her come to such a sad end. He would save her.

Standing on the corner, he watched two black girls— shapely and ripe—lean into the passenger side of a black BMW, talking to the three brothers inside. He could see one of the young men slip his hand onto the rounded curve of the female nearest him, rubbing her ass as he talked to her. Possibly the usual jive. Talking up a storm trying to get the coochie. Audrey was out there in a small dark room; a crackhead trying to fend for herself, opening her legs for anyone with the price of a rock, waiting for her pops to rescue her from her private hell.

S I X

From the nursing home, Cootie went to the Crispus Attucks Projects, the six-building public housing development that runs from 126th Street to 131st Street, between Broadway and Amsterdam Avenue. It had been a truly shitty day. Seeing his father like that was the icing on the cake—totally out of his head, a nut case. He figured he would go over to Aunt Monie's apartment to get a little dinner; some soul food and Kool-Aid, and maybe a slice of her world-famous coconut cake.

"Cootie, I've not seen you since you got out of jail," his fat aunt said, waddling around the kitchen. "Are you doing all right? Got a job?"

"Trying to find some work," he said, sitting down at the kitchen table. "I went to see my father at that place. I hate to see him like that. His mind is shot. Is that what happens when a person gets old?"

"Not necessarily," she said, heating up a plate of food in the oven. "If a person takes care of himself when he's young, they don't have to worry about bad health when they get old. And you know your father didn't take care of his health. He ran the streets, drank, caroused, and went with different womens. You know that."

"I know that."

"Do you ever think he'll get out?"

"No, I don't think," he replied. "The nurse says he has Alzheimer's, and that disease is progressive until it runs its course. They have drugs for it, but they can't prevent it from doing damage to you."

"That's a shame. I could use your help around here. The toilet needs some work. It's leaking all over the floor and on the rug. And my neighbor's pipes leaked through the ceiling, and now it smells of piss and mildew."

"Why don't you go to the Housing Authority and tell the management all your complaints?" he asked.

"I've complained and complained until I'm blue in the face," she answered. "They don't pay me no mind. Now the people on this floor are dumping their garbage on the stairs, and we got rats. Real big ones. Like cats. The gal across the hall had her little baby bitten by one."

"I hate blaming everything on the white folks downtown, because some of the blame has to be put on these filthy people who don't give a damn about the place where they live," he said. "They live like animals. That's why any decent person wouldn't want to live around them."

She reached into the oven with a padded glove, retrieved the dish of food, and placed it down before him. "And half of these folks ain't even on the lease. These are the ones who make trouble for everybody: drinking and drugging, raising hell."

He ate the chicken drumstick with his fingers, string beans, mashed potatoes then sopped a wedge of corn bread in the gravy he'd poured from its dish.

This was not in the lyrics of the rap records: the poverty, the crime, the slow deaths. He'd walked past a hill of garbage at the rear of her building around to the front, to the doors of where she lived: cans, chicken bones, broken bottles, newspapers, cardboard boxes, crack vials, and stinking trash. The odor of urine reeked from the elevators.

"Oh yeah, Audrey called me yesterday," his aunt said. "She told me that she had tried to go to Daytop for the drug rehab, but it didn't take. She sounds like she's in so much pain. I don't know what she's into, but it's not good."

"Where's the girl staying?"

"Over in Brooklyn, in Bushwick. That's all I know."

"Do you have an address?" he asked, shoveling a fork full of coleslaw into his mouth. "Did she give you somebody you could get in contact with?"

"I think I have a number. I'll get it." She walked out of the kitchen into one of the back rooms. He could hear her rummaging around in there.

Finally, after about five minutes, she came back and handed him a piece of paper. She explained that she had called several times, but there was no one on the other line. There was another time; this past Saturday, when she dialed the number and the phone was off the hook. So there was hope.

"You can try, but I didn't have much luck," she said, frowning.

"Did she say whose line this was?" he asked, continuing to eat.

"No, she didn't," she replied. "Do you think I should visit Graham up there? He'd told me that he didn't want me to visit him, but if he's sick, I think I should go."

Cootie lied. "I think he'd like that. Nobody comes to see him. He's all alone."

She cut him a slice of the cake and put it on a dish. "How did you mess up that girl's life? Alicia seems to be all right, but this younger child is just a horror. What did you do to her?"

"I don't know." He knew he couldn't blame it all on his late wife.

Another slice of cake was carved; that was for her. "I know you going to jail during her formative years didn't help. And Faith's death from drugs really scarred her as well. When a girl grows up without a father during the key parts of her young life, the effects can damage her forever."

He ate the cake slowly after finishing off the last of the dinner. "I didn't walk out on them. I was arrested for pulling a con and jailed. I knew Audrey was going to be the troublesome one. I could tell it when she was in school. She cut classes, got caught downtown in Times Square, and just hung out with the wrong crowd. I talked to her over and over, but she wanted to do things her own way."

"She needed your love, that's all," his aunt said, her mouth full.

"I gave her that. I gave it to her. In fact, I spoiled her."

"I talked to her and that isn't what she thinks," she said. "As far as she's concerned, you weren't there. Even when you was at home, she was emotionally not there. Absent. And when you got in prison, she felt abandoned not only by you, but by her mother, who was dealing with her own problems with drugs."

"I tried to give her a decent home life." He shrugged. "I really did." Aunt Monie was a sixty-five-year-old former bank teller and a recovering drunk, whose husband was killed in a construction accident. Her no-nonsense approach to life trumped any sentimentality involving family and kin.

"What you forget is that a father is so important to a daughter," she said. "Mine was to me. My father was everything to me. My mother, for the most part, was just there. I was a daddy's girl. A girl's father is the first man any woman knows, and all men will get compared to that first man. You failed on that score. You never had any time or love for her. So she's trying to get that love the best she can."

"I hate that Freud shit." He went on eating the cake, dabbing his mouth with a tissue.

"Do you know what guy she has hooked up with? Do you know?"

"No, I don't. She's probably with some thug or junkie."

His aunt smiled wickedly. "Her current beau is a snotty-ass member of the board at the Booker T. Washington Savings and Loan, on 125th Street near Lexington. She brought him by here, showing him off. I can tell he was a real phony. He was old enough to be her father."

"Well, that's good for her. Maybe she'll get off the dope."

"Audrey's a good girl despite her problems, and this guy is just using her," she added. "I wouldn't be surprised if he's supplying her with drugs. I felt he was controlling her. There was something not right with them."

"Why do you say that?" he asked, bowing his head.

"She did whatever he said. He told her to scoot the chair under him, and she did. He told her to get him a glass of water, and she did. He told her to sit, and she did. He told her to shut up, and she did. It went on just like that from the moment they arrived until they left. It was like she was his puppet."

"What else did he do?"

"I didn't recognize Audrey," his aunt continued, getting the last coconut morsel on the dish. "She was so clingy, so submissive. He bragged that she wouldn't let him leave the apartment unless he let her know when he'd be back. He said she calls him five, six, seven times a day sometimes. He told me she was just going through a phase, but I could tell he was feeling smothered."

"That's not like her. She was so independent, so feisty, so headstrong."

"But in a way, she might let him stay around, because she was going through so many guys for a while, it was like a bus station. I think she distrusted men, so she figured she'd end the relationship before the man rejected her. I told her she was just becoming a whore. Just like her mother."

He drank the last of his red Kool-Aid, the cherry-flavored water, and thought over all the revelations of his aunt. Aunt Monie was a wise woman. She had been around; having a good time, partying in the wild streets of Old Harlem, but now she was the director of The Mother's Board at her local church, and the adviser to the Girls' Choir. The woman had come full circle, through the fires of hell to the serenity of salvation, struggling to redeem her tainted soul.

"I should go before it gets too late," he said, feeling sudden disdain for her hypocrisy. She wasn't a fucking saint. "Thanks for the dinner. It was very tasty. You still haven't lost your touch in the kitchen."

His aunt was putting the dishes and glasses into the sink as she spoke very quietly. "You've got to get Audrey from those people, before they harm her or she harms herself. When we talked the last time, she said the most interesting thing. She said she couldn't find any satisfaction with any of the men she was dating, but she was miserable without male company. It was like she couldn't get enough affection or attention. But every time she gets hung up on a man, he leaves her. You have a lot to answer for, Mr. Man."

"Blame it on the father," he said angrily. "At some point, you have to live your own life and stop trying to shift the blame. I don't blame my father, and he wasn't worth shit. Excuse my French."

"So you have the answer," his aunt replied. "Let's hear it."

"Do you have any more of that Kool-Aid?"

She poured him a tall glass of the colored water from the iced pitcher, and put it down on the table. "Go ahead. I want to hear this."

He sipped while he composed his thoughts. "While I was in prison, I did a lot of thinking. Sitting there in that cell, I discovered that I had to sort out my emotions and come to terms with what happened to me. I had a lot of growing up to do. I had to stop blaming my parents and the life I was dealt, and go on with my future. I looked within myself and made a list of what was good and what was bad. I didn't want to slip into self-pity, feeling sorry for myself."

"You never told me how you ended up serving time," his aunt said.

"It's a long story," he replied. "A guy set me up, but that's a tale for another time. I had the right to be angry, but I had to move beyond the rage. That was the reason I visited Pops. I always hated him. I blamed him for his treatment of my mother and how he treated us. I was so hoping to get to know him better so I could understand myself better, but he's so sick and nuts. But at least, I think I know a little more about why I'm the way I am."

"Maybe that prison did some good," she said. "Now you have to find that girl."

*   *   *

After Cootie left the Harlem projects with a chunk of coconut cake wrapped in a paper towel, he took a gypsy cab up to a building on 183rd Street and the Grand Concourse, where he would meet with Inez and DK—the eyes and ears of the drug trade. Loyal to the drug biz, they were known as the yellow pages of the hot sellers of product and their locations, the quality of the various drugs, and the amount of police surveillance on different sites. He went into the pool hall across the street, after the guy at the newsstand pointed Inez out.

"Hey, Cootie. Whassup?" Inez asked, sticking her beeper into her jacket pocket. "I heard you was shot. You all right?"

"Yeah. I'm good to go," he replied. "What's up this way?"

She was looking at Cootie's lean, muscular frame, licking her lips. He was forever the sweet she wanted to taste, even though she was around his daughter's age, but she loved old school niggas.

"Nuthin'," she said. "Waiting for DK. There's a new shipment of candy in Brooklyn. Very tasty. I have a piece. Do you want to get some?"

"No, dahling." He grinned. "I don't do that shit no more."

Inez was a ravishingly beautiful Dominican girl; long black hair, short and stocky, with ample hips. He noticed the countless rings she had on her fingers. Along with her black Air Force leather, she wore a red satin scarf wrapped around her neck framing her bubble cleavage. She smiled as if she was very happy.

"Don't worry. He's with me," she said when one of the staffers moved up to frisk Cootie. "He's a bro. Aren't you, sweetie?"

Cootie gave her a peck on her golden cheek and laughed. They stood against the wall, watching the guys shoot pool, with their girls lounging nearby. Everybody was packing heat. Some of the boys were wearing their heavy sheepskins, and all-black bombers with fox-trimmed hoods, all with telltale bulges underneath. All of these Latin hoods sported the big, gold medallions with the Spanish patron saints. There were about thirty perps in the hall. Some of them just posed with their sticks, with their cuties on their arms, or made a big deal of racking the balls. If the cops had done a sweep, they would have caught more than a few prime felons in their net.

"I'm looking for Audrey," he said. "Do you know her whereabouts?"

"In Bushwick, I heard," Inez said. "She was at a club downtown. She was totally fucked up, high as fuck. Sloppy. And that's not like her. But then she's hanging with a rough crowd. These folks are in all kinds of shit."

"Like what?"

"All I know is what I heard," she said, lighting a Kool.

"And what's that?" He bummed one from her. She lit it for him.

"Lara said Audrey was running around with Mitch and Don, these two knuckleheads who love rough sex and shit," she said. "Audrey was fucked up on rock and let these cats chain her up, arms and legs, and forced her to fuck them and give them head. Filled every hole. They had a dog collar on her and shit. They let their crew do her too."

"Oh shit." He couldn't believe it.

"They put clothespins on her nipples and beat her across the back and legs with a clothes hanger," she added. "Lara said she was so out of it that she just stared off into space. Mitch—that's the bald, tall one— was leading her around Limbo, this club in Soho, on a leash. Audrey was so high she didn't know what was up."

"Where's this Mitch now?"

"DK can't stand the muthafucka," Inez said. "Word is he's a cop snitch. But check this out. He was buying from one of the boys: one of the Licorice crew from the Lower East Side. You know Gabby, right? They say the Licorice crew came for Mitch and swarmed all over his apartment, and cats was busting caps. Shit was wild.

Two passersbys got snuffed, just on the sidewalk at the bus stop. Mitch grabbed this two-year-old boy and used him as a human shield to escape. Bullets flying all around. The dudes, these bad-asses, popped a cap into the boy's back, but Mitch got away after slinging the kid to the curb."

"Damn, I know some of those boys in that crew," he said. "This Mitch is one mean asshole. He sounds like garbage."

"Check this out," Inez added. "A week later, Mitch was pulling up near the Brooklyn Bridge on Brooklyn's side, when one of the Licorice boys drove next to him and put a nine out the window and started firing. Glass was all over the place, but Mitch shot back and hit the driver, sending the SUV out of the control, into one of the pillars of the bridge. The driver was killed. Yes, the Licorice crew is looking for Mitch, and if they find him, he's dead."

"What about this Don?" he asked, flicking an ash on the floor.

"Don's one of the major dealers of H, namely the new Columbian White, and most of East New York, Bushwick, Fort Greene, and Bed-Stuy buys from him," she answered. "He has major suppliers in Colombia who smuggle their product through Kennedy Airport through key distribution points in the city, especially in Harlem, the Bronx, and Brooklyn. They got about five hundred people working for them. Don's not to be fucked with, but I don't know how he got hooked up with Mitch."

"I'd like to know how these dudes got so heavy with each other," he said. "If Mitch is protected by Don, it's going to be really tough to get Audrey away from him. These guys don't let go easily."

"Besides, the Colombians are using the same distribution networks and the money-laundering ties they had from the coke market," Inez said. "Last month, the cops and feds busted a bunch of couriers carrying drug-filled condoms in their stomachs at JFK, but these guys write this off as nothing. This is pure shit. A lot of these dudes who use are afraid of needles because of AIDS, and would rather sniff the shit. Worth a lot of money."

DK, wearing a black leather outfit, dark glasses, and a silver bandanna, walked up with one of his underlings. He was talking into a cell phone. He slipped Inez a tiny revolver and handed her a beeper.

"El Jefe, missed ya," DK said, slapping skin with Cootie. "Punch in 4-9-3."

Inez punched the numbers, warning the other party not to come down to the pool hall. An undercover prowl car was parked outside, with two detectives eyeballing the place. DK hugged Cootie, asked him about the gunshot wounds, and told him about the new shipment of ganja being marketed by the Jamaicans in Fort Greene. Strong, potent shit.

"The Chinese are on the outs," DK said. "These Colombians know their shit. They know how the street operates, and if they feel threatened, they can deal with it. But still the Chinks deal the majority of the H being sold in the city. They have every kind of tackhead selling for them. Still, my money's on the Colombians."

"What are you doing these days, Cootie?" Inez asked. "Funny money or phony credit cards?"

"Neither," he replied. "I'm just trying to find Audrey."

"I told him about Audrey being with Mitch and shit," she said, lighting another cigarette. "Do you know where she is? Bushwick, right?"

"Yep." He called a number on his cell phone, whispering to someone on the other end. After he finished his chat, he said he thought he knew where she might be, and would take Cootie there. Cootie nodded and presented DK with the slice of coconut cake. DK had a sweet tooth. He was known for it. They walked out to DK's car, passing right by the unmarked cop car, which followed them as they did a U-turn on the Grand Concourse, heading toward darkest Brooklyn.

S EVEN

As DK drove the late-model Toyota onto the Triborough Bridge into Queens, Inez argued he should have taken the Brooklyn Bridge and got there faster, but he was trying to shake the police tail. The unmarked prowl car kept up its pace, weaving in and out of the busy evening traffic, always keeping their car in sight. Inez smoked like a fiend, one cigarette after another, nervously turning around to see if they had lost the cops.

However, Cootie was calm, looking out the window at the bejeweled scenery and the night people. The talk with his aunt made an impression: a father's abandonment, a mother's tragic loss, and the fantasy dad Audrey had created in her turbulent heart. He remembered the calls with then thirteen-year-old Audrey at the prison while he was there—troubled and whispered, asking him to come home, telling him her mother was getting high all the time. Once or twice he cried at the sound of her anguished voice, so small and feeble.

"Baby, I'm coming home," he'd say to her. "Just hold on a little longer."

"But Mama said she has a new man and she's not going to let you come home," the unripened voice had said. "She said she's going to take you to court for custody and get a divorce. What's custody?"

He recalled her tearful speech when she said the word *custody,* how it cracked with emotion like a lyric from a country blues song. No doubt the family court would give her full custody, because he would have no rights as a convict. He couldn't even vote. The courts honored the mother as the primary parent, regardless if she was a junkie. There wasn't ever a time when he was not responsible and a good provider, even if he was a con man with assorted scams.

"Honey, custody means I wouldn't be there in the house," he had said sadly, his eyes filling with tears. "It would be like I was a visitor. But the court would decide that."

Truthfully, it would have killed him to be stripped of his fatherhood. He loved his girls. Nothing could prepare him for being plucked from their lives, making them feel rejected—being disconnected from their daily existence. No way was he going to be denied access to them, even if he had to beg and plead with her. All Faith wanted was his money and the freedom to live her cursed life as she saw fit. He knew he was more than a wallet in the girls' lives. He wanted to be there for his children. He wanted to feel like a dad to them. And the girls wanted the same thing.

"Why is Audrey doing this shit?" Inez asked, pulling him back to the present.

"Who the hell knows?" He knew all right. He'd fucked up.

"I was telling Inez you was a mellow cat," DK said, smiling. "Everybody digs you. I don't understand why Audrey doesn't get with the program. If she listened to you, she would probably learn something."

Audrey was screwed up because of Faith. It was all because of Faith with her freaky self, her and her cockeyed romance with the needle, her transparent life, her need to be herself, even if it meant hurting herself. That was not to say she couldn't be nice. Sometimes after he would get a big score, he would lay across the funky bed, smoking a blunt while she licked his nuts, then she would mount him and ride him until he would come inside her. Yet she would act distracted, staring into space, her body limp as a dish rag. It was never thrilling or seductive. Zombie sex.

"My father knew you when you was in the joint," DK said, passing a chilled bottle of malt liquor, a forty, over to Cootie. "He said you was a stand-up guy; righteous as he put it. He said you did your time and steered clear of the bullshit."

"More or less, I guess I did." That wasn't true. He got in a few dust-ups with the bulls and the cons.

They argued about the correct way to get into Brooklyn. DK overruled with an alternate route, and the cop car shadowed them. DK enjoyed it, making the car take chances, speeding into recklessness. Inez was scared shitless. A cigarette never left her thin lips.

"Why do you think you'll find her there?" Cootie asked.

"This is one of the biggest crackhouses in Bushwick," DK answered. "Everybody goes here. The real G's run it. They have a great supply of product, plenty of women, ample sitting space and privacy, if necessary. They have lookouts on each end of the block to give the customers proper warning and shit."

Inez grinned. "Yeah, Fort Knox security. I'm serious as shit."

"Yeah, buddy, these are the real grave-diggazs and roughnecks," he said. "If ya go up in there, ya got to be serious. No frontin'. No signifyin'. They might know where she is. Or they might not. But one of my boys said she was by here not long ago. Fucked up as usual."

Cootie tapped DK on the shoulder. "You got a piece?"

"I don't carry heavy artillery in my ride, because the pigs have me watched," he said, producing a .38 with tape on it. "Ya never know when they might pull me over. But this will do if shit stirs up."

"Thanks," he mumbled as they turned on the street where the crack den was.

Once at the address in Bushwick, Cootie left the car and walked effortlessly across the icy pavement. He watched the unmarked cop car parked a few houses back. The crack plague wasn't anything like it was in the late eighties and early nineties, but it was still whipping ass in the black and Latin communities. In fact, heroin was making a comeback as well. Still, crack was taking a toll on the females: leading them to neglect their babies and children, or physically abuse them or abandon them. Infants were born addicted to the shit or with syphilis. Or HIV. Also, the addicted women or their boyfriends were either beating or killing the pitiful young ones at home, while they were in the drug rages. He had once seen mothers who used to maintain homes and jobs, surrendering their lives to crack or heroin and becoming homeless, or going into the city shelters.

"This is totally fucked up," he said aloud in the dirty hallway as one of the house guys patted him down. He turned around so he could feel the length of his legs, reminding him of prison. The gun was in his waistband, right above the crack of his ass.

"Ya wanna cop?" the guy with long dreadlocks and baggy pants, asked. "Or ya wan' to do here?"

"No, I want to see Rah. Somebody told me to ask for Rah."

The guy put his hand on his gun stuck in his waistband. "Whatcha wanna see him? Ya got business?"

He traded evil looks with the underling. "Yeah, business."

They walked through the first floor to a large room where a short, clean-cut dark man in an African dashiki was dispensing glassine bags of rock and powder to customers—men and women—and nodding to his henchman to collect the money. One of the regulars, thin and pale, begged for the man to give him some shit.

"I'm sick, real sick," the jittery man said, scratching himself. "Please let me get straight. I'm real sick. Give me something. I'll give you something tomorrow."

"I don't give credit, and you know that," Rah said. "What the fuck ya want?"

He was addressing Cootie, who pinched his nose at the rank odor of the house and turned around to face the master of the crack fiefdom. The stench was overwhelming: pure raw sex, piss, shit, and the biting tang of crack smoke. It got into your clothing, flesh, even your soul. The room was standing-room only, with its low roar of a collective sucking sound as the users inhaled the vapors from the pipes, which would transport them into mental confusion.

"What ya want?" Rah asked again. He sized Cootie up as not a crackhead. There was a double-barreled scattergun near his leg.

"I wanted to know if you've seen Audrey," he said, looking around. "She's my daughter. The girl's not well. Maybe you've seen her."

"No. This is not a missing person bureau." Rah laughed. "If ya see her back there, then do what ya do best. We don't hold anybody prisoner. Everybody comes to this place willingly."

One of Rah's crew explained the rules of the house to the newbies: all business conducted had to be shared with the boss, all were welcomed to come and shoot as long as three dollars was paid, all sexual tricks transacted within the building cost two dollars per session. Everything was business. Even Cootie had to pay Rah a small fee to look for his daughter. The parade of dope seekers was endless, getting their dope, going off to look for space and privacy to get off.

He wandered through the rooms, past the gaunt faces with vacant, haunted stares. His steps took him through the hall lined with lost souls: Crowds of ghosts in hollow flesh in search of the next high. After looking into two rooms on the second floor, he saw three addicts huddled around a spoon with the heated contents of a speedball: a combination of heroin and cocaine. Another fiend sold bags of groceries and meat to get enough for a fix. Two others trembled and massaged their limbs to drive away the aches and pains.

"You got money?" asked a young man with a ravaged face, dressed in jeans hanging off his hips. "Stake me, stake me. Want a piece of ass? Anything you want."

A look in another room revealed a man shooting a spike into the throbbing neck vein of a formerly beautiful girl, who stared at him as if he wanted to take her life. "Get the fuck out of here," she growled as the man smiled and patted the fresh wound.

In the darkness—blackness illuminated only by matches and lighters—he could see the rows of tormented phantoms, skeletons, eager to embrace the rush of the dope. A few locals mixed with those imported from across the bridges. Some old guy sold syringes and a bleach rinse. It took the bleach a minute and a half to kill the HIV, but sometimes it didn't work. It was the luck of the draw.

"Can you hold this?" an older woman asked, holding out a sheet of tinfoil with powder on it to him, as she snorted it deep into her nostril. "Thanks, sweetie."

At the end of the hall on the second floor, there was a row of filthy mattresses where the crack whores plied their trade—stone freaks, rail-thin girls and guys willing to do anything for a blast or chump change. Peddling their asses or mouth for a taste or cash. The regulars watched the action, staring, now and then, and nodding out. Moans and groans of fucking saturated the room: Shadows in the dark, writhing animals engaged in all manner of sexual acts. The funk was astounding. Musky, dark, and mysterious.

"Want me to blow you, baby?" a girl, possibly school-age, asked him with a mouth full of scabs and sores. "Do you have any works? I need a spike."

He said no, then he noticed a man pushing into her hard from the rear, her narrow hips glistening with sweat and semen. With a little effort, he hopped over them, careful not to disturb any of the room's occupants, when a couple of the whores lay down with a fat guy with a bag of rocks. One started to suck him off while the other chatted him up for a toke. Two men were yanking another whore's panties down, her pimply ass bare, and the first one eased his slow, moist tongue along the purple track marks on her leg to the crack of her buttocks. While he stepped around them, a withered junkie pulled out his lighter, flicked it on, illuminating the room clearly, and then it went dark; a hand yanked his leg.

"Fuck me, fuck me . . . please." Maybe it was the eerie voice of a man or a woman.

Once he reached the stairs, he threw up the contents on his stomach, almost on the heads of a couple firing up a cap, mixing in the water for the spike. The vomit decorated the wall and their unsteady hands as they shared the needle, shooting one in the thigh, and between the toes of the other. He staggered down the stairs, unbalanced legs, and nodded to Rah and the armed bouncer.

The girl with the mouth sores followed him into the hallway. She noticed the group of cops first, three officers and two detectives. Cootie froze. He knew they were there for him. The first thought was getting rid of the gun.

Turning around, he slipped her a ten and the gun. There were no words exchanged. It was as if everyone knew their role. Then he stepped out of the crack den, walking briskly, while the thin girl lingered behind.

"Come here, nigger," one of the officers yelled.

Immediately, he was thrown to the ground roughly, and the other cops began clubbing him to the body, no marks in the face. It was an expert beating, complete and professional. They shouted and cursed at him, calling him every name imaginable. A crowd gathered, but the detectives held them behind the cars, no one assisted him. They really weren't concerned about the drugs or the occupants of the house. He got to his knees, woozy, but aware of where he was, when another cop slashed him across the forehead with a club. There was a white, blinding light before his eyes and blood coming down into his face. He pitched forward, blood in his mouth, gagging. It was snowing at the time, and the ground was hard and frozen.

When he started to get up, they pushed him into the side of a car, his body causing a huge dent in the door. Again he scrambled to rise, using the car for leverage, but they dragged him back onto the pavement where two officers held him down, forcibly going through his pockets. One pulled out his wallet, dumping its contents before dividing the money between them. He had a couple of hundred bucks in twenties and fifties.

"It's him all right," the second detective said, flashing his driver's license to someone in the unmarked car.

"You black son of a bitch," the officer said to him, placing his revolver to his head, adding "he was a dead nigger." They stripped him of his coat, tore his shirt; leaving him in his tattered T-shirt in the bitter cold.

The other officer said they could take him to the stationhouse, arrest and book him, photograph and fingerprint him, and then later arrest him when he didn't appear for court. Also, that would be a violation of his probation.

When he protested, he was told to shut up. Another officer kicked him hard in the side, in the kidneys, then aimed a kick solidly into his face. But he blocked it.

"Stand the fucker up." It was Philbrick leaning on the cop car. "Face me, nigger. Stand up straight. Do you hear me? I want you to walk the chalk line. If you put a foot wrong, you'll go to prison for a long time."

He tried to stand up but couldn't. He wiped his bleeding mouth and the long scrape along his cheek.

"Do you understand, black boy?" Philbrick was snarling as he said it.

"Yes," he mumbled.

As Philbrick left with the officers, he whispered to Cootie, "We'll be watching you. One false step, and in you go. Also, you need to think about my offer to you the other day. Give me your answer in two days." Philbrick had offered to do help keep Cootie safe, and free, if he'd help them get Red.

He nodded silently, holding himself up against the car now.

"What the hell were you doing there?" Philbrick asked. "You're not a junkie."

"I'm looking for my daughter," Cootie replied. "She's in trouble."

"She's not the only one," the cop answered, then he signaled for the boys in blue to leave. After the law was gone, Inez and DK helped Cootie to the car and pleaded with him to go to hospital, but he declined. He was hurting like a son of a bitch, possibly even bleeding again from the old wounds. But he didn't want any parts of going to the hospital. The thin girl with the mouth sores came over to them as they were pulling off, and gave them the gun. Inez gave her another ten. Their battered friend lay back on the seat, fingering his bumps and bruises, while DK piloted the car and listened to the raunchy songs on Lil' Kim's first album.

EIGHT

Once Cootie arrived back to Momo's tiny Harlem apartment, after going to five crack dens in East New York, Red Hook, and Bedford-Stuyvesant, he settled in for a little CNN news and the rerun of the Knicks basketball game, which they lost in the last two seconds of the game. No Audrey. He let the night slip away from him. It disturbed him about his father's condition—the old pimp with his memory banks erased—and his daughter's wandering around in the streets, sucking up crack smoke and peddling her ass for anyone who would buy.

The phone rang in the other room. He slowly made his way to get it, wincing. "Hello."

"Hey, did you find Audrey?" It was his daughter Alicia.

"No, I didn't. We searched a few places, but they haven't seen her. I got a lead. She might be with this Mitch character. He's supposedly a bit roguish: Mean, violent, and freakish. Do you know him?"

Alicia cleared her throat, then spoke, "Audrey brought him around once or twice. I didn't like the looks of him. He was always primping and stuff. He didn't deserve her."

"Did you know he sold drugs?" he asked, reaching into the icebox for a bottle of beer. "In fact, word has it he's a fairly big dealer, with all sorts of connections. If she wants to get away from him, she's going to have a tough time, because he's not about to let a good thing slip through his fingers."

"She wanted to leave him," his daughter said. "I know. She told me."

"What else did she say?" He drank from the chilled bottle instead of using a glass.

Alicia inhaled deeply. "She's afraid. She thinks he might do something to her if she tries to get away. You're right. He's violent. She told me some of the things he's done to people who owe him money. He thinks he can do anything."

"Somebody told me he has some crooked cops behind him. Did you hear that?"

"I don't know about that," she replied.

"How did she get on drugs?" he asked. "She was such a good girl."

"Audrey's a wild child, and you know that," she said. "Also, drugs are plentiful where she used to live. All you had to do was go out your front door, and there you could meet somebody selling drugs. Then she made friends with those guys. I would go over to her apartment, and there would be all these roughnecks and outlaws. She loved that. I thought she would have stayed away from drugs, especially after what happened to Faith."

"Exactly," he agreed. "Maybe it's in the blood." All the feeling was gone from their chatter; it was as if they were talking about a grocery list. No emotion.

"In many ways, Audrey's like Faith; same outlook and same everything," she said. "She can be a real bitch, just like Faith. She tries to sell this image of this pretty, troubled black girl who's into blowjobs, vast quantities of drugs, sleeping around, nervous breakdowns, and suicide attempts. She cries wolf all the time. And I'm tired of her and her shit."

"Nervous breakdowns and suicide attempts?" Cootie was taken by surprise.

77

"Yes. She supposedly went nuts for a while when you were in prison," she said sullenly. "They hospitalized her for about three weeks, drugged her up, and put her back out on the streets. She did two overdoses, shot a gun that she got from Kashir—DK, at herself and missed, and stood in front of a cab on Broadway. Like I said, I'm tired of her shit—'the nigger gal as waif' bullshit."

He took a sip and thought he had really screwed up his daughter's life. "Where was I while this was going on?"

"In jail." Alicia said it like a knife aimed at his heart. Cold and steely.

"And now she's in this freaky sex shit with Mitch," he said, disgusted. "She's totally out there without a net under her. It sounds like you hate her."

That took his daughter by surprise—him saying that. He looked around the cramped quarters of the boxer's apartment: the unmade bed; the pine floor, which was covered with piles of clothing—not his, stacks of books, CDs, a torn leather jacket, and two or three girlie mags. Around the walls of the two-room cell, old fighters posed stylishly in black-and-white photographs, a few greats, and no, so greats.

"I don't hate her but she gets on my last nerve," Alicia said. "She was always your favorite. Everything revolved around her. I told you this before."

"That's not true," he said, giving a weary shrug.

"Why isn't it?" she asked. "You've ruined her for any man. She worships you. That's why she believes she can get away with anything. You really don't know your daughter, do you?"

He walked to the unkempt bed and sat down. "Aunt Monie was trying to explain to me about her. I admit I didn't know half of the things she told me. I guess most fathers don't know what goes on in the minds of their daughters."

"Well, she called me up and said 'I hate myself and I want to die.' "

"When was this?"

"About five months ago. She has no friends—no real friends. She tried to sleep with my old man. I asked her about it, and she told me that she wasn't interested in him, but she thought she could get with him. She wanted to tempt him. Every guy I know is leery of her. She's a real whore. If a guy really tries to get to know her, she sabotages the relationship by doing something stupid, or she becomes so clingy that the guy backs off."

"Is it the drugs that are causing this?"

"No. I think she's damn crazy. When we met for lunch, she just cried the entire time. And the outfit she had on was worthy of a stripper. Her jeans were ripped all over her crotch and on her ass. I'm serious. You could almost see everything. She didn't care. She loved the attention from the guys at the café. I told her to order anything she wanted. All she did was order drinks, so she got so loaded that she threw up in the hallway, near the women's bathroom."

"Damn." His baby girl needed help and fast.

"It's like this, and please listen to me," she spoke slowly. "Don't put yourself out trying to find her. Maybe it's for the best. The only thing that interests her is her, and that's all that does. You'll get hurt by looking for her, or you'll end up in jail. These guys she's running with are loco and very mean."

There was a moment of silence. He listened, and he could have sworn somebody was twisting the doorknob. He peeked out of the room at the other space with the front door to the hallway. A damn break-in. Some voices.

Very quiet—then a screwdriver or a chisel going at the metal plate on the door lock.

"Sweetie, I've got to call you back," he said calmly, but inside there was the start of fear churning within him. He hung up the phone and turned off the light in the rear room. He left the light on in the front room, picked up his coat, stepped inside the closet, and pulled the door closed behind him.

Within minutes, the door's two locks gave away, and the footsteps of the intruders could be heard in the front room. They were whispering, not sure of what they should take. One of them could be heard packing a plastic garbage bag with CDs, DVDs, a radio, and the DVD player. The other one stepped toward the rear room. Cootie could hear the man's breathing as he cut on the light. His heart was running frantically in place. He was scared shitless. Maybe some of Red's crew was coming for him. Maybe they were going to finish the job. Maybe they would off his ass. Through the crack in the closet door, he could not see a gun, but the other man with the garbage bag could have had one.

"Did you find any money?" the first thief asked.

"Hell no. This nigga ain't got shit," the other man snarled. "Not a damn thing."

"I got everything we can use. Let's split."

"Hey wait, hold on." The other man spotted a camera, a Polaroid, on the dresser and some photos sticking out from a book. "Check this out." He scooped up the photos and walked out to the front room, waving them. They were of naked women, probably some showgirls Momo knew, in provocative poses.

"Wow. Look at that one," the first thief exclaimed. "Look at the ass on her. One of them onion booties. Oh yes, I could play with that."

"Check this one out," the other man said as they walked toward the door. "You can see all the way down inside her. So pink and shit. I bet she's got a big pussy. Probably you could fit two hands in that bad boy."

"Or two dicks." The first one laughed as they closed the door.

Cootie got out of the closet, and he could hear them talking with one of the boxer's neighbors, telling them that somebody broke in the apartment and the police had been called. He crept closer to the door and opened it as the two men, carrying their loot, trotted to the stairs and walked down them to the ground floor.

"Can you remain here, please?" he asked the old woman and what appeared to be her grandson. He was about eight years old, very neat with close-cropped hair. "Those men just robbed the apartment right there." He pointed toward Momo's door. "I'm going to call the police."

After he entered the apartment, he looked around and checked what they had taken, then he called the police. The old woman stood in the open door. He also called his daughter and told her what had just occurred. She asked him if he had a gun or something with which he could have defended himself. His answer was no. He'd given the .38 back to DK. It was a violation of his probation. No way. He didn't want to let Philbrick get his hooks into him and send him back upstate. A convict with a gun. A weapon would have surely brought trouble, and he did not want to go back to prison.

NINE

Cootie's father died that Thursday in the nursing home, a week after the burglary of Momo's place. His heart just stopped. Possibly the Alzheimer's squeezed all of the life out of him. He wanted to think the old man was just tired and wished to go home. Tired of life. Two days before word reached him of his father's death, he visited him, taking him some Mounds candy bars, two diet Dr. Peppers, a pack of Luckies, and a beer. He seemed to know the end was in sight.

One of the nurses said his father was holding out until he could see Cootie for the last time. The old man had been dying a long time. His mind had long quit before his body or the spirit of his flesh, had resigned to illness and pain. After years of doctors, nurses, social workers, welfare workers, social security staff, and nursing homes, he often said it was his wish he was not to linger around on machines if it would be easier to die.

"Don't let me be a vegetable," his father had told him. "Promise me."

"We had this conversation before, and I told you that I won't let you stay on this earth any longer than you want to," Cootie had said. "The doctors know what to do. They're not going to experiment on you. I told them that."

"Now they're saying I have advanced heart disease with chest pains," he had said. "My mind is starting to go. I don't know what the hell I'm talking about most of the time. Sometimes I get these shooting pains across the chest, that just take my breath away. And the doctors won't give me anything to stop the pain."

"The doctors said they discussed a morphine drip with you."

"What's that?" his father had asked, his memory having another gap.

"So they can kill the pain."

"But the nurse, the Jamaican one, said to me that if they use the drip, it will shorten my life by days or weeks," his father had said, suddenly remembering. "I don't want to die if I don't want to. The docs have no right to kill me if I'm not going to die. What is that called? They have a fancy term for it."

"Euthanasia," Cootie had answered. "That's what it's called."

"I want to choose when I want to die," he had said. "That's final."

One look at him in his frailty, underscored how old age could ruin a man who used to be in good, robust health, battling to turn back the clock on his life. He had been without his wife for years. He had spent the remaining years alone. Even when family members invited him on outings or reunions, the old man declined, saying he was ill or busy. Apart from doing laundry, grocery shopping, and maintaining the small rituals of life, he never left the apartment except to go to a bar or tavern, drinking himself into a stupor and dragging himself home. Cootie's sister, Barbara worried about him with the years of isolation and withdrawal, thinking if he didn't find another woman or even a friend, he would drink himself to death.

"I think he's grieving over Mama," she had said. "I really do. His life literally stopped when he buried her. All he does is drink. I tried to tell him that he should make friends and go out and meet people. He needs a hobby or even a part-time job."

"You forget he was a pimp," Cootie had retorted. "How in the hell is he going to find a job with that on his résumé?"

Barbara had ignored that. She never wanted to see her father as he was, but what she wanted him to be. "I even introduced him to a woman who was a widow, a church woman, who was very kind and considerate. He agreed to meet her, but nothing came of it. He would say yes to everything, and then he would go on drinking at the bars and all."

"Do you know what he told me during the last visit?"

"What?" she had asked, frowning a bit.

"He said he thinks of Mama as if she was still alive, like she was still living under his roof," he had said. "He has her clothes in the closets and the trunks in the hallway. He even has her makeup—lipsticks, mascara, and powder—on the bedroom bureau."

"Damn." His sister was stunned by that revelation.

"I told the old man about his grieving over Mama and that it had to end," he had said. "Or it would kill him. He should confront it and let it go. If he doesn't do this, he'll never move on with his life. Now he needs the grieving as much as the bottle and the booze."

"If not more," she said. "It's choking away his life."

"He's fooling himself by keeping her alive," he said. "I believe he likes to suffer. I believe he feels by holding on to the image of Mama that he can do away with the regret and guilt he's going through. That's what I believe. He won't face the hard facts . . . shit . . . his wife and our mother is dead."

"That's true. He is definitely in denial."

"Shit. His whole life has been in delusion and denial. He's a dinosaur. He didn't want to understand that selling ass to people, who can now get it free, was in past. Time's changed, and he didn't want to make something else with his life. He just clung to that damn memory of what he once was."

Barbara had grunted. "He was a bastard. He ruined a lot of lives."

"Yes, he did. He ruined us. That's why I'm fucked up like I am."

Mr. Graham, that was what Barbara called their father when his back was turned, was never home. He was always in the streets. The kids cooked the food, washed the dirty dishes, folded his clothes, and shopped. Their mother had no privileges around the house. In the language of the streets, she would be his prized lady, but she had lost her throne a long time ago. They didn't sleep together; instead they rested on twin beds. The old man forever talked about how their mother had let herself go.

"You can't blame it all on him," Barbara had retorted. "You've done your own shit. You could have been anything you wanted to be. You had potential, even the old man said it. You're wasting your life. And now you're wasting the girls'. Maybe you should leave them alone before you drag them down with you."

He had closed his eyes. "Pops sees our mother as a whore."

"Well, she was, and she was proud of it," his sister had said. "She let him kill her. But I'm not going to let you off the hook that easy. Why don't you leave the girls alone and let them find their own paths? They can do it if you just walk away."

"She knew he was fucking around on her," he had said. "He fucked everything in a skirt. I remember going to her once and complaining to her that he didn't hide anything. She sat down after pouring her tea laced with scotch, and said real politely, that men will be men, pimps will be pimps. Oh yeah, he was working out some sexual problems he had from his childhood. She never told me what she meant by that."

"I know how she was hurt by his madness," she had said. "Probably she did too."

"She was a good-looking woman when she was in her prime," he had said. "I've seen the pictures. The old man said she was a money-maker."

"But why did he have to marry her?"

Cootie had paused at his sister's bitter question, his eyes red and itching. He didn't want to let her see him cry, but he felt sad for the whole bunch of them. Pops and Mama, the kids, and his kids. The entire lot of them, the cursed bloodline. "Sure she was. She loved him. That was her downfall. She loved him too much."

*   *   *

Following his father's funeral and the gathering at the chapel, Cootie watched all of the old crowd who had known his father, file out: retired pimps and whores, burglars, Murphy men, car thieves, addicts, two preachers and a group of deacons, hot-sheet hotel clerks, the nurse from the home, and even a detective from Vice. He collected his old man's ashes in a Chinese urn, bagged it, and took it home to the mantel. At the farewell ceremony, they all shook his hand and embraced Barbara in a farewell, mumbling how Graham was a bad nigga back in the day. Old school playa. He hugged Barbara and whispered he would call her the next day. None of their family or close friends had shown up— nobody. One young woman, the daughter of a business associate, approached him as he left the chapel and found his car in the parking lot.

"Hey, Cootie, wait up," said the woman; dressed in a yellow pantsuit that was inappropriate for such a grim gathering. "Can I get a lift?"

It was very cold outside. He was having trouble turning the door key. "Yes. Where do I know you from?" His memory was not that bad. He recognized her, but the name eluded him.

"Paula." She waited for him to let her into the car, still not answering his question. He held the door open for her, and she scooted into the vehicle, careful to let him inspect her body up close.

"So where to?" he asked, while she fired up a cigarette.

"Let's drive around," she said, inhaling a plume of smoke after winding down the window. "Is that all right with you?"

They rode in silence along the Henry Hudson thruway, going south on the paved road along the deserted marina and the frozen river. There was no reason to chat. Or to make small talk. Still, he wondered what she was doing there. Who had seen her? Was it a police trap? Philbrick wanted him awfully bad, even to the point of setting him up on a crime so he could pry open Cootie's mental address book, get himself a rat, and get some of the big crooks in Harlem.

"Paula, huh?" He saw how she had the quick step of a woman in a hurry; her jiggling breasts and perfectly round ass. He'd seen her rolling and twisting her hips when she walked up to the car. A bitch on low flame. Once he smelled her breath, he could see she was half drunk. Maybe bourbon or possibly scotch. She held her hand up to her mouth self-consciously, hoping not to let him get a good whiff. And smoking didn't help.

"It was a nice ceremony, don't you think?"

"I guess. The old man would have liked it: seeing some of the old faces in the church. Hell, they probably haven't been on holy ground in their lives. He would have gotten a laugh behind that."

He passed a truck, weaving wildly, but soon gaining control. She noticed his prowess behind the wheel, and commented on it. "You're a pretty good driver. Heard you got shot."

"Yeah. Everybody knows about it. *The Daily News* must have run a piece on it. I got shot, but I'm all right now. I've been out of the hospital for a few weeks now. Who sent you? The cops or what?"

She spoke with a slight lisp, very sexily, and he noticed she had a small metal stud in her long tongue. "Who do you think sent me? Guess."

"Hell if I know." He pulled into one of those rest stops along the highway where small cars and trucks were gathered. Sometimes you could see whores giving head to drivers at dusk before they went across the bridges to their Jersey homes in the suburbs.

"They say you was a mean bastard before you went to jail," she said softly. "Is that true? Were you as mean as they say?"

"You'd have to ask someone else about that," he replied. "All I know is that the state would love to lock me up and throw away the key. I'm just trying to live my life. That's all. I want to get back there in the real world and go on with my life."

"How was prison?" she asked, arching an eyebrow.

"Prison is hell. It can wreck you. I'm not the same man I was before I went to prison. I'm a changed man. Now, who sent you?"

She looked at him quizzically. "Does it matter?"

"Yes, it does," he answered. "It matters very much."

Yet there was a grace about her, sleek and beautiful. Cream-colored. Hair in tight black curls. Luscious, in her yellow form-fitting pantsuit. She was a very closed-mouth woman, speaking only when required, no idle chatter. He liked that in a woman; speak only when needed.

"So you're not going to tell me?" he asked. "What do you want? Everybody wants something. Especially women."

"You don't like women?" she said. "I forgot you were in prison. Do you like boys?"

"No." He was getting tired of her bull. "What do you want?"

"I want you," she said sweetly, smiling quietly.

With the old man dead and burned to ashes, Cootie worried about becoming a prisoner to his father's wretched memory and the bleak past, possibly depriving himself of the possibility for happiness and a fulfilling life. There was some time left. He wasn't old. He grieved the loss of his wacked-out father, wrapped him up in the warmest of remembrances, sealed off the old days, and tried to walk on into the future. The choice of opening up his life to living once more in the present, was his and his alone.

"You're not going to tell me who sent you, are you?" he asked once again. "I haven't been with a woman since I was in prison. That would be nice."

"No, I'm not going to tell you," she said. "And yes to your other request. Maybe we can work something out." Her gaze moved about restlessly as she grew more silent and thoughtful.

"This was not a chance meeting, was it?"

"No."

He squeezed her shoulder, looked into her brown eyes, and kissed her. His mouth completely covered hers, enticing but polite, and she yielded to the kiss, totally submissive. He remembered the way his wife—his dead wife—used to kiss with a mashing of the lips, abused and bruised. They say no two people kiss alike. No two folks fuck alike as well. But Paula was a helluva kisser. She laid one kiss on him that almost took his air away, his breath coming in short spurts, the kiss sneaking up on him when he wasn't looking.

"Why don't we go to my place?" Paula asked. "It's quiet there."

He made great time driving to East Harlem where she lived, amid the battered buildings where the Ricans and Dominicans were packed like sardines in tiny rooms. After he parked his car in front of the apartment, they walked up to her room, a blue cubbyhole with a bed, a tape player, and a small black-and-white television. Everything was in blue. She said it was peaceful and serene. There was one color photo of her with her father, former Mayor Davis, both smiling like they'd won the lottery.

"Is that your father?" he asked. "He looks like you."

She giggled. "You mean I look like him. Yeah, that's the source."

He looked to the other room, a very small bathroom, barely big enough to hold a bathtub, immaculately tiled. His view took in some clean towels, also blue, and a row of scented soaps and bath oils. A photo of Billie Holiday was positioned near the sink, with her showing her big teeth and the tiny toy dog in her grasp with her swollen hands.

No sooner than they were inside the door, they locked mouths and bodies, some more—the excitement mounting—and her hand finding his stiff Johnson, stroking and fondling it. She grinded herself against his leg, pressing his lean flesh against her crotch, and a very hot feeling of pleasure surged through her. Stronger than she looked, she shoved him back on the bed and began unbuttoning his shirt. He thought he was in heaven. She opened the shirt and started tracing her long tongue along his neck, the length of it, then to his chest, stopping at his nipples. Her mouth played with his muscular skin, along his ribs and stomach.

"Who sent you?" he asked with a rasp.

"You have a one-track mind," she said, laughing. "Anybody ever tell you that?"

Her hands went under his buttocks as she found his dick with her mouth. It didn't take much time to stand erect. Her tongue slid over its length, at the root, the balls, and between his forbidden crack. Finally, her lips swallowed the fullness of him, down to his groin, until it reached his man-scent and the thick thatch of hair. She heard him panting, anticipating in lust, with short, breathy gasps. There was a sweet liquid at its tip, but he had not come as yet.

"Who sent you?" he repeated.

"Damn, you're like a broken record," she joked, drawing him close until the head of his sex pressed against the back of her throat.

She positioned herself over his leg, so she could wiggle, and make herself wet for him. Her head moved up and down, slowly and methodically, properly gauging his manic thrusts. It was obvious that he had not screwed for a long time. His desire seemed to overtake him as he wanted to place her on top of him. Her face, luminous with passion, reared up to look at him quivering, until she removed her mouth from his rod. Quickly, she moved up his bulk and straddled him, reaching around with her fingers to guide his throbbing sex into its rightful place.

"Who sent you?" he asked once more.

She laughed and laughed and laughed. "You're a nut. Do you know that?"

He didn't know how he was going to get inside her, for she was very small, her tan opening almost engulfed in curly hair. Twice she lowered herself on it, but it only accommodated the bulbous head. She whispered that she wanted him inside her, at all costs. He lifted her long, shapely leg and placed it over his shoulder, and with one hand, he slipped himself inside her, more and more, to its silky limit. The movement between them was like an exquisite dance of the senses—rhythmic and spontaneous, measured but tantalizingly good. He moved in her expertly, and her sex came to life, and they pounded each other, making sounds like newlyweds in heat. He came with her, lying across her belly, moaning in her ear in rising ecstasy, before his warm fluids filled her to the brim. And he gave out one more shout, shuddered between her moist thighs, then collapsed beside her.

It was quite a while before he moved. His limp sex made a popping sound when it came out of her. She wiggled out from under him, started putting on her clothes, and opened the top drawer on the bureau in the small room. She located a revolver, a .25 caliber Glock, holding it at her side. Moving quietly, she found his clothes, first going through his jacket pockets, then his pants.

"What are you doing?" he asking, watching her go through his clothes.

"The truth?" She smiled cheerfully, her gun pointed at him.

He sat up on the bed, his legs tucked under him. "All I ever wanted was for you to tell me the truth. Who sent you? I just don't want you to shit me."

Her gun was still aimed at him, at his head. "You're not going to get angry. If I tell you the real deal, you won't fly off the handle, will you?"

"I won't get pissed." He was puzzled. He wondered what she meant.

"I have a message from Mitch, and he wants you to give up the search for your daughter," she said snidely. "You've been asking too many questions. He wants you to go away. Don't bother her. All you can do is stir up trouble."

"Whose idea was it to fuck me?" he asked her.

"Mine." She laughed. "And a damn good fuck it was. You're no slouch."

"So what's next?"

"I can offer you some money," she said, pointing to an envelope on the dresser. "If you let the matter drop and go away, the money will be yours. I hope you do that. I don't want to kill you."

"I'm to let him pimp my daughter or whatever he's doing for some chump change?" he said, and before the words could leave his lips, he dived for her. She got off one shot, and it went wide. He knocked the gun out of the way, and it went clattering across the floor, under the bed. She took a swing at him. The blow went high above his ear, yet the blast didn't pack enough punch to make him lose his balance.

"Damn bitch," he shouted when he put his hands around her throat.

"It was business—strictly business." She gagged as he let go.

He stepped back away from her, and she slapped him hard on his face. He twisted out of her reach, her flying fists, but she was on him again, flailing like a woman would do. He grunted and hit her in the chest, solidly and efficiently, so she flew against the wall and slid down it. She clutched her chest with both hands painfully, and curled up.

"I hate hitting a woman," he said, "but you gave me no choice. Tell him that it's no dice. I want my daughter back. If he harms her in any way, he'll answer to me."

"Go to hell," she said in a spent voice.

He slipped on his pants, shirt, and jacket, and pocketed the gun. Walking over to her, he gave her a kiss, said: "Thanks for the fuck," and patted her head. She spat at him. He strode over to the pack of cigarettes, took two—one for now and the other for later.

"Don't forget to tell Mitch what I told you," he said, smiling. "I'll be visiting him . . . very soon. Also, tell him don't fuck with me. I'm not a man to be fucked with."

He closed his eyes, wishing he could blink all his troubles out of his life, but knowing he could not. He had to face them dead on. Or otherwise he was dead.

T EN

On Friday, Cootie went to the track to watch the ponies. He drove out to the Aqueduct—Big A—in Queens, and although it was the middle of winter, there were the regulars, about the amount one could find in a church during a big snow, placing their bets on the jockeys and horses on the frozen track. It had been a while since he had been there, since he had gotten out of stir. He mingled with the trainers and riders and touched some of the four-legged winners for good luck, even watching the assistants hot-walk them before going back to the paddock.

"Hey, Mike. Whassup?" he asked one of the riders leading a promising nag, the cloud of warm breath issuing from its nostrils. "You riding today?"

"Yeah. In the third race," the midget-sized jockey said. "Bet on him. Dark Fudge. He's a good one; loves a hard track."

"Will do." He walked off toward the crowd of security, tellers, stewards, and gamblers. He stopped to chat with Stella, a buxom doll in concessions, tending her hot dog and soup stand.

"What ya know? What ya say, Toots?" Stella said, forking some of the franks into the boiling water. "You look cold. Wanna borrow my scarf?"

"No, thanks," he said. "How's tricks?"

"Slow. Real slow. I heard your father died. There was a real gent. He used to always come out to the track, bought gifts for the jockeys and the girls. Real gent. What he die of?"

95

He drew a deep breath and spoke softly. "The old man died of a heart problem. He was in a nursing home. Hated it. I was sorry to see him go like that. I guess we all got it coming."

"Old age's a bitch," Stella said, holding up a bun. "Wanna dog?"

"No. Too early," he said, touching her shoulder. "Thanks."

Weaving his way into the main building of the Big A, he walked through the herds of die-hard fans who huddled in front of the TV screens. The pale-faced horse addicts allergic to the cold, the suit-and-tie boys with their beers, the blue-haired gals with their racing forms, the old geezers betting at the windows and the machines. He laughed at their rituals and their habitual wooing of Lady Luck.

"Cootie, Cootie," yelled one of the bookmakers who shuffled along with the regulars. "What's shaking, baby?"

"Nuthin'. I just buried my father." He opened a pack of cigarettes and offered the amputee one. The Cuban, a long-time pal of his old man, had lost a leg from sugar. He was forever fly, dressed in nice threads, and had a constant sweet tooth.

"Time marches on. Ain't that the truth?" the bookmaker said, adjusting his binoculars so he could watch the next race. "The weekdays ain't shit no more. You used to get more of a crowd during the week. But now you only get the people in on the weekends. Look at those damn nags being led to the post. Two of them should be shot as dog food."

"Do you come every day?" Cootie asked.

"Damn near," the bookmaker answered, heading for the grandstand. "Speaking of your father and family, I got my wife on as a teller. I got a brother on in security, and a nephew in maintenance. As much as I hang out here, I should get a job around the place."

"Have you seen Mitch? You know the skinny brother who drives the black Jaguar. They say he comes out to the track on Fridays around this time."

"I ain't seen him today," the bookmaker replied. "I don't think you want to mess with that boy. He's a bad customer. Plus, he always has at least two thugs with him when he mixes in public. What do you want him for?"

"Business."

"He's one evil nigga. Tread lightly with that bastid."

"He has my daughter, my baby girl," he said. "Word on the street is that he's pimping her, making her do all kinds of foul shit, and got her on crack. I want to find her before it's too late, before she winds up dead."

"That's Mitch," the bookmaker said. "He doesn't give a shit."

With a lowered voice, the bookmaker told Cootie about a neighborhood activist who was killed three blocks from his Harlem brownstone, his throat cut and his dick mutilated. The man's bloody body was parked in his car and was discovered by some boys playing stickball. He was totally clothed, sitting up, and had his severed Johnson in his lap. There was money in his wallet, two credit cards, cell phone, and an un-cashed check, so robbery was not the motive. The activist, who had been trying to shut down two of Mitch's massage parlors because of the unsavory characters, drugs, and prostitution going on in the location, had taken the hoodlum to court and tried to get an injunction.

"Are you sure it was Mitch who did this?" Cootie asked.

"Oh yeah. Everybody knows, including the cops," the bookmaker replied. "Nobody can touch him. And his wife knows a congressman, who is afraid to take him on. Mitch is totally plugged in with the cops and everybody else."

He shook hands with the bookmaker as he gimped away. "By the way, I got a hot tip. Dark Fudge. Somebody said he's a long shot, but he'll take the race."

"The only way they get that nag to win will be to juice him," the bookmaker said, turning away. "Save your money. I'm betting two hundred dollars on the daily double."

"Good luck," Cootie said, walking up to the betting window, then stopping. He watched the gimp move to the stairs leading to the grandstand. The thought entered his head that he should save his money and not toss it away betting on a broken-down chance to break even.

Trying to stay straight and not do some bullshit was tougher every minute. He knew this Mitch asshole was going to have to be confronted. Everything he learned about this thug was bad. He'd learned from a brother convict on parole from Downstate Correctional at Fishkill that Mitch had served a long time on a beef of raping and sodomizing three teenaged nieces under his supervision with another psycho. He was released on appeal due to a legal technicality, and was soon up to his old tricks.

As Cootie drove back from Queens, he was trying to unravel the riddle of Audrey and how she had fallen from grace, slipped up so badly. Did he do something to screw her up like that? Or was it her mother with her drugs and highs every hour on the hour? He remembered when Audrey was little and she'd climb into his lap and wrapped her small arms around his neck, and said she loved him. If he was lying down on the couch, she'd put her head against his chest and plant a wet kiss on his heart.

Sometimes, she would come in from riding her bike and run into his strong arms, crying, "Daddy, Daddy." She would make him little gifts—homemade, but crude and heartfelt—and present them to him while he was watching a baseball game on TV. He would slowly undo the tangle of ribbons from the boxes, act like she was surprised, and embrace her for her thoughtfulness. The little girl with her trademark dimples, would just beam with joy.

"I love you so much, Daddy," she would say, tears in her eyes. "So much."

Something happened along the way to young adulthood. It happened in high school with peer pressure, during the time Cootie was in prison and her mother was floundering from one fix to another. If he could have only been there for Audrey, maybe he could have saved her from herself. In high school, Audrey joined a gang of young girls, Latins and blacks from broken homes and dismal futures, and soon she was tossing other girls down the school stairwells, robbing them of lunch money, and beating them down. She started smoking because the gang smoked. She ditched school because the gang ditched school. She boosted clothes and jewelry because the gang did it.

On one visit to the prison, Faith, his wife, sat in the visitor's room and told him through the wire mesh window about the little darling's current troubles. "I'm tired of your daughter giving me lip. She acts like I'm supposed to do everything she wants. I tried to tell her about staying out late on school nights, but she flipped me the middle finger. All the neighbors say she acts like a prima donna. The other night she came in with blood on her clothes and she wouldn't tell me where it was from."

"Was it her blood?" Cootie had asked.

"No. I tell her that I won't be treated like a doormat. Alicia's a perfect girl, loyal and loving, does her schoolwork, and even has a part-time job at the Loew's Cineplex. But Audrey ain't worth shit. In front of people at the grocery store, she yells at me, calling me a drug addict and says I fuck anybody who will give me money. I was so humiliated."

He knew both of them were unstable, but he wanted to pursue whether Faith was fucking around. "Is she right? Are you screwing around?"

"No, I'm not," Faith had said, offering a cherubic smile.

"Are you still using? And don't bullshit me." He had leaned forward to inspect her eyes, to see whether the pupils were dilated or not—A sign of usage.

"No. I'm off the shit. You need to be worried about your daughter. Not me. I can take care of myself. Audrey is your child too. Be a father to her. Her boyfriend was shot and killed in a drive-by shooting at the school, and she hasn't been right since then. I found a .38 gun when I went through her purse. She lied. Told me that it wasn't hers, that she was keeping it for somebody. The girl is going to get herself killed."

"What do you think?" he had asked. "Maybe you should have her visit me at the prison."

Faith had covered her face with her hands. "I don't think she would like that. I know we were talking, and she said that she hated for you to be locked in a cage like some animal. She's right. I hate it too. I know she wouldn't come."

When the visit was over, Faith had left, but his mind was racked with how he was going to reach Audrey. The guilt of being a miserable fuck and a worthless nigger was upon him. He'd failed his wife and the girls. He'd failed his own life. Faith never came back, and when he got out, he had to find her—and he did, living with a boozer in a flophouse. The girls were faring for themselves, doing a shitty job of it, but they tried. Audrey was robbing people on the trains and walking home in the dark with her gang friends. Welcome home.

*   *   *

Uptown, Cootie was eating fried chicken in Copeland's Restaurant with his friend Guy and some broad who fiddled around with a Caesar salad and corn bread. The waitress wiggled her fat ass every time she passed his table and seemed to be trying to entice him with each stop.

"That bitch's checking you out," Guy said, drinking a sip of wine.

"I didn't notice," Cootie said, acting as if he was absorbed in the cutlery.

The broad Tammy made an ugly face and chewed the roughage. "Why doesn't she just bend over the table and pull up her dress so you can get busy?"

Cootie whispered to Tammy, "Do you think she wants me?"

Tammy wiped her ample lips with a napkin. "Oh yes, definitely."

Cootie smacked on a drumstick, tearing the tender meat off the bone. "Tell me, Tammy, you know women rather well. How does a girl get like that, off on the wrong foot? How does a girl go bad? What happens to her? What makes them do the shit they do?"

Tammy loved to be the center of attention since she thought she was the best-looking female in Harlem— pretty face with a well-proportioned package, the supreme feature of her long, long legs. She fluffed her hair, which fit her like a frizzy helmet. The wonderful thing Cootie liked about her was she smoked cigars, loved them, and the Cuban ones were her favorite.

"I wish I had some pig feet," Tammy said, giggling.

"Answer the man," Guy told her, sucking the sauce from a demolished rib. "He asked you a question. He wants to know what you think. Black men usually don't know what black women think. They usually just want them to fuck or cook or keep house. So let him know what he asked."

"I'm not representing all women, let me say that from the git," Tammy said. "As a girl, born and raised in Harlem, my folks were proud to be black, and nobody was a maid or butler or Pullman porter either. I had two parents all my life. I was really proud of my father. We were never evicted, and we always had enough to eat. My mother was always there when I got home from school. I never had a door key around my neck. I never saw my father drunk or hit my mother. So what are you asking me?"

"What did your father do?" Cootie asked.

"He was a bus driver," Tammy said sadly. "He was killed by a mugger at Easter. I remember it so well. My father was bringing home a hat that he had bought for my mother. The damn thug shot him in the head. The cops found the hat in the Bronx in Hunt's Point."

Both men said they were sorry. Cootie returned to the original question of how young black women could go so wrong, turn their backs on their families and turn their backs on what they knew to be right.

"I've got three sisters, and we were all pretty," Tammy said, licking her fingers. "Nobody dared to fuck with us. My father would have killed them. He was our protector. He was our friend. Thank God we were almost young women when he was killed. I don't know what I would have done if we didn't have him in our lives. Guy said you was in jail for some of your girls' lives. Is that true?"

He was embarrassed by being a con. "Yeah. It's true."

"What were you up for?" Tammy asked. "Did you kill somebody?"

"That wasn't Cootie's question," Guy snapped. "Answer his question."

"Maybe the girls were embarrassed by you being a jailbird," Tammy said. "Maybe that was why they acted out and shit, if that's what you're asking. Is it?"

"I guess it is," Cootie said. "It's only one of the girls. The other one acts normally. But one is flirting with the rough street life. I don't know how to reach her. Even if I find her, I won't know what to do. I'm afraid that I've lost her forever. The streets can gobble you up."

"When I was young, I remember I used to get off the subway at 116th and Lenox and, oh man, there were junkies, dealers, pimps, and whores around," Tammy said. "The place was always jumping. It was the drug and sex mecca of Harlem. I was always scared when I had to go over to my aunt's house, which was near there. If she sent me to the grocery store, I was afraid that somebody would rob me and beat my ass. It seemed like every black girl around there was a whore, and they were pretty too."

"But you kept your nose clean, right?" Cootie asked.

"Maybe it was because our family belonged to a church," she said, watching the shapely waitress roll her hips as she walked past. "We belonged to Abyssinian Baptist Church, you know, where Adam Clayton Powell used to preach. I think God steered me through all of the bullshit I could have gone through in the streets. I was a good church girl."

"We didn't go to no church," Cootie offered. "Faith and me didn't go for that. Where did you live in Harlem?"

"Edgecombe Avenue," Tammy said. "It was a decent neighborhood. Everybody knew everybody. If somebody saw me doing something, all they had to do was to tell my father and he would whup my ass. Or my sisters. My father was real strict."

"Other than church, what other things kept you in line?" Cootie knew it was too late for the girls to benefit from good upbringing, but he wanted to know where he had failed as a man and a parent.

"When the drugs hit their peak in Harlem in the late sixties and seventies, my folks moved us into a nice house on the hill and warned us not to go to the valley where all the crime was," Tammy said. "They got us outside of Harlem every chance they got. We went to plays, operas, even summer concerts in Central Park. They took us to Jazzmobile, fixed us a picnic, and listened to the music. It was fun. They got us to join Jack & Jill, where we got more culture and into society. We could dress up and go to cotillions with boys in tuxedos. Did you ever do that, Cootie?"

Cootie hung his head. "No. My wife just let our girls run wild."

"My father used to tell me Harlem was real safe when he was a kid in the forties during the war," Tammy said, turning around to watch the men watch the waitress's big ass. "They had clubs like the Savoy where they featured two bands every night, and even the Renaissance where they had good entertainment. He told me he and his brother used to go to see plays at the LaFayette Theatre. Real class. But nobody had cash money in Harlem so everybody used to have rent parties to make the cash to pay the landlord. That was probably fun. Dancing, good times, and such."

"Man, they also had riots in Harlem at that time, because the white folks wouldn't let the black people work the stores and shops on 125th Street," Guy said, remembering how his father and uncle got arrested during the ruckus. "The cops bust heads, but the brothers gave them all they could handle. They turned over cop cars and trucks and smashed windows."

"It was summer of 1943, hot as hell at the start of August," Guy explained, "when the 'cullud' exploded and took to the streets. Blacks plundered and pillaged the dark ghetto until the sun rose, but not before four lost their lives, and forty policemen and 155 civilians were hurt. It was a lawless, wild night. Cars were flipped and set afire. The cells in the four police stations of Harlem were filled to capacity. And still, several hundred were housed in detention in the armory on 94th Street and Park Avenue, as mob violence and looting broke out in one place after another. It was open revolt. People threw bottles, rocks, and bricks from windows and roofs on cops who tried to bring them under control."

Guy didn't stop talking. "One of the black men killed was my uncle, who was shot in a grocery store by a cop. He'd been out of work since the fall, and he was desperate to get some food for his family. The cop blew him away."

"I never could figure out that shit," Cootie said. "They fucked up where they lived. Tear up something where they lived. That didn't make sense."

Guy sipped the wine. "Sure, it did. The blacks didn't own the stores, so they wrecked them. All the money was going out of the neighborhood to Staten Island and white Brooklyn, and upper Bronx. White folks got the cash. Niggers didn't get shit. Reckon the old man got about forty-three dollars a week, while the old lady got about thirty-five dollars—and that was no money. That's why every black person played the numbers before the honkies got the Lotto approved."

Guy's father was a retired number runner who operated from Sugar Ray's tavern; worked the regulars for years. Sugar Ray Robinson the champion fighter. The numbers game was said to have been brought up from the West Indies in the twenties. Some said the numbers was Harlem's biggest business, with almost seventy-five percent of black folks playing it in its heyday. The white East Harlem mob, and another gangster faction from across the bridge in New Jersey, took it over from a group of Harlem policy barons. All of the big number boys went into the bars along the 125th Street, such as: Pompez, Miro, Francis, and even the Ison brothers. And Guy's pops was in there with them.

"Man, you know that's right," Cootie said, staring at the waitress who gave him a sly wink. "My father hit a few times. He got that red Cadillac for his thirty-fifth birthday. He knew he was King Shit, driving around with all his ladies on the boulevard."

Guy gnawed a rib before tossing it on the plate. "Cootie's old man was one of the biggest pimps in the city. Lots of ladies, fine wines, great cars. Plenty bread."

"Is that true?" Tammy asked Cootie.

"Yeah. He was real big, a real big playa," Cootie said. "He just died."

"I'm sure Mr. Graham wanted Cootie to follow in his footsteps, but he just wasn't cut out for the pimping life," Guy said. "Cootie was more of a confidence man. He was too slick for the sporting life. He liked the big scores. Right?"

"I guess," Cootie said.

"At one time, Mitch lived in Lenox Terrace," Guy volunteered. "But that was quite a while ago. You'd see the long black Caddie pick him up with his girls. I think he's moved downtown on the East Side. But he still goes to his usual haunts."

"I tried to look for him at the racetrack today," Cootie said. "Nothing doing."

"You should go and look for him at one of the massage parlors or those porn shops in the Bronx," Guy said. "He goes by there regularly."

Cootie was eager to get this business over with Mitch. He said they could drop Tammy off at her apartment, then continue on to the Bronx. When they asked her if it was all right, Tammy was cool with it, shrugging her shoulders. Guy paid the bill, like the big man that he was. He held hands with Tammy as if they were young lovers, real cozy and hot to trot. Once they were all in the car, they sped off up Amsterdam, passing a lit joint among them.

E LEVEN

The car pulled up into a gas station on the upper end of Madison Avenue, so Guy could put ten dollars of fuel into the tank. It was well into the evening. Cootie told them to wait for him because he wanted to take a piss. They had dropped Tammy off at her aunt's house after getting a bottle of castor oil, two cans of ginger ale, a big bag of potato chips, three onions, and a pint of gin. The plan was to refill the car with gas, pick up a couple beers, and drop in all of the Mitch's parlors and porn shops until they found the elusive criminal. When the attendant took the money from Guy, Cootie came back out of the building, then he noticed the unmarked prowl car and a white man waving to him.

"What do you want?" Cootie asked the man.

"Come here," the man said, showing a detective's badge. "We're supposed to pick you up. There's been some trouble. We have to run you in."

Cootie thought of his options: badmouth them, resist, or run. "What in the hell is this about? I've done nothing wrong. I don't get it." But these Harlem cops would shoot a nigger as soon as breathe. They didn't give a shit. One less spook.

"Get in the car, goddamnit," the white man growled. "I don't want to tell you another time. It's routine. We want to ask you a few questions and that's it."

With a wave of his hand, Cootie walked over to Guy, told him that the cops were taking him down to the stationhouse, and to let Barbara know where he was. He would call her from there. Guy asked if there was anything else he could do, but Cootie said no, he'd wait to see how the hand played itself out.

Slowly, he walked over to the cop car, and the white man let him in the backseat. The cop eased himself next to him. They didn't cuff him. The driver pulled off. There was quiet all the way to the stationhouse.

They pushed him into a seat in a small interrogation room. He borrowed a cigarette from a cop, and they let him have a cup of black coffee. The room smelled rank. One of the detectives left the room, the papers of the complaint exposed, and he saw them, narrowing his eyes at the first page. No doubt the law wanted him to see them.

"Don't worry. Everything's routine," the uniformed cop said, trying to reassure Cootie. "They're pulling in everyone, no matter if you do this kind of thing or not. Guys on probation and parole. They just want to chat them up and see what you know. So don't worry."

"What is it I'm supposed to do?" Cootie asked, smoking nervously.

Neither cop answered his question. They left the room, talking between themselves about perps, motives, crimes of opportunity, and rape. The last word, *rape,* was significant because Cootie told himself that he would never get involved in such a crime. The long con was his ticket. Scams were his thing, so he stared at the complaint sheet and tried to see something that would connect him with this case. There was a constant game going on between cops and cons. He knew they were probably watching him that very moment to see if he was responding to the folder. He didn't touch it.

HARLEM CONFIDENTIAL

NYPD FORM UQ41
INITIAL REPORT OF CRIME

COMPLAINT # 3869

DET. T. QUINN
RAPE/STABBING

1. AT 2050 HOURS, THIS DATE, NOTIFIED BY PATROL
SUERVISOR OF A POSSIBLE DOA AT THE NORTHERN END OF
MORNINGSIDE PARK.

2. AT 2125, ACCOMPANIED BY DET. LOPEZ OF 26 PDU, I
ARRIVED AT ABOVE LOCATION AND OBSERVED THE BODY OF A
WHITE FEMALE, APPROX 20 - 25 YRS., UNCONSCIOUS AND
PARTIALLY CONCEALED IN FOLIAGE.

3. UPON ATTENDING OF VICTIM BY EMS UNIT, I FURTHER
OBSERVED THAT THE VICTIM HAD APPARENTLY BEEN SEVERLY
BEATEN, RAPED, AND HAD SUFFERED MUTIPLE STAB WOUNDS.

Another big, burly Irish detective returned, quickly
closed the file and stared with burning eyes at the black
ex-con sitting at the table. Two more detectives joined
him. The cops smoked continuously as they hammered
away at him with questions. The air was blue with stale
cigarette smoke. Cootie listened when they recounted the
crime, keeping his face calm, but directed at the video
camera that they had brought into the room. It was not
turned on—not yet, they said. They told him they wanted
to go over a few of the facts before they switched on the
machine.

"You play fair with us and we'll play fair with you." One detective gave a Ken doll smile at him and offered him a cigarette. He kept assuring him that this was not an interrogation but an interview, and that the contents of his wallet would be returned before they let him walk.

The cops went over the tale of the poor white girl supposedly raped, sexually assaulted, or whatever you wanted to call it. The victim, a young Jewish girl from Connecticut, was a student at Columbia in the business school, working on her Masters. From the pictures they showed him of her, she was not bad looking—full body, nice legs and all. Healthy pink skin with freckles. She was really fucked up, but she would live. All of the bones in her face were severely battered; her body carved up real bad, but she possessed a real will to live.

"Why are you sweating, jig?" the other one said with a snarl, curling his thin lips angrily. He was a tall, thin man with big, furry hands. There was very little hair on his head, but he combed the few strands over to hide the bald spot. His eyes couldn't be seen because he wore mirrored sunglasses.

Cootie put the cigarette on the table and stared at it. He had seen this routine on *Dragnet* once—good cop, bad cop. But he felt he had nothing to hide. What had he done wrong?

"Testing one, two, three . . . four." The cop who had given him the cigarette was testing a tape recorder. He said a few things into the mike on the table which was placed not too far from the black man's perspiring face, pressed a button on the machine, and the words came back to him.

"Quinn, why doncha just use the video for the dinge?" the bald detective asked, still glaring at Cootie. "Shit, why waste good tape on this son of a bitch?"

111

"Cool it, DeStefano," Quinn shot back, then spoke softly into the mike again. "This will be a recording of the questioning of Harry Chambers, and his responses made this fourteenth day of July at ten thirty-one A.M. Asking the questions of Mr. Chambers will be Detective Thomas Quinn of the New York City Police Department."

"I don't know why we're wasting the camera on the nigger, Tom," Baldie said again. "Come on, we're wasting time with this prick. He saw some white trim so he figured he could just take it, right, boy?"

Quinn motioned at him to cool down, and continued his spiel into the mike, pausing only to take a deep drag off his cigarette. "You have been informed of your rights, Mr. Chambers, but I should repeat them. As the Miranda v. Arizona statute states, we cannot ask you any questions unless you have been warned that anything you say, can, and will be, held against you. Also, you have waived the right to counsel, isn't that correct?"

"Well, yeah . . ." Cootie sputtered. "You said this ain't official or nothing, so I figure I don't have to retain any lawyer. Just some questions, right?"

"Sure, right, Mr. Chambers." Baldie snorted. "Get on with it, Tom. I've got to get home so I can take Timmy to the dentist. Don't have time to be drawing this out with this fucking perp."

"You sound like I'm a suspect," Cootie said. "Wait, hold on a minute."

Both of the other white detectives in the room ignored his remark, and Quinn went on with the opening statement for the tape, stopping to insure that Cootie understood what was involved. He was led to believe that the proceedings were only a casual questioning. That would put him at ease and make it easier for him to slip up. Quinn asked Cootie his name and age.

"Thirty-eight," Cootie said quietly.

Baldie moved up behind him so that he couldn't be seen, but his presence could be felt in an intimidating way. He put his lips close to the black man's ear and whispered in a hiss for Cootie to speak the fuck up.

Cootie shouted his age this time.

The white men laughed. Baldie winked over Cootie's head at his partners, starting to crack the nigger already. Piece of cake.

"Have you got a wife?" Quinn asked gently.

"Wife's dead and two daughters."

"How did your wife die, Mr. Chambers?" the cop asked.

"Drug overdose, a few years back." Cootie wasn't saying anything about that. That was his business.

"What are your daughters' ages, Mr. Chambers?"

Cootie folded his arms, his body stance stubborn and adamant. "I don't think that's any of your business. I thought we were here to get to the bottom of the crime, and my whereabouts on that day. I don't want to go into my past history."

"That's all right," Quinn said, pointing to a binder. "We have all of that right here. Do you have a record?"

"Yes, but its not violent crime," Cootie said. "And yes, I served time but you have that information right there too. I've kept my nose clean since my release."

"Sure, Mr. Chambers. Can you tell me, please, as best as you can remember, where you were last night?"

"Detective, I was at a restaurant with some friends most of the evening. When your men picked me up, I was at a gas station getting some gas."

"Do you remember what you had at the restaurant?"

Cootie laughed. "Soul food, the usual stuff."

"We have your friends, and they will be questioned," Quinn said. "Do you recall what you talked about?"

"Not really; love, life, and kids but other than that, my mind was on other things," Cootie replied. "I just buried my father, so that was what I was thinking about."

The officers said nothing about his loss, but Quinn continued his questioning. "What was the woman's name? Was this woman a romantic acquaintance of yours?"

Cootie was becoming angry. "No. Her name was Tammy. She was a good friend of a friend. No, I have not known her socially or any other way. She was just joining us for dinner."

"Was this Tammy a working girl?" Quinn asked with a smirk.

"Hell if I know," Cootie replied. "I've never seen the woman before. That's the truth."

"Did you know she has a prison record?" Quinn asked.

"I don't know. And I don't care." Cootie stared at the pale faces of the policemen.

"You like the working girls, huh?" Baldie mouthed the words close to the black man's ear again. "You like to buy white pussy, huh, nigger?"

Cootie wiped the sweat from his brow with a forearm and answered with a firm voice. "I said I didn't know her. I don't know her history. She was just a friend of a good friend of mine. You're trying to make something out of nothing."

"But this white pussy wouldn't be bought, so you had to pull her into the park and rape her, isn't that right?" Baldie kept on with his menacing talk.

"Why don't you shut the fuck up . . ." Cootie snapped at the bald detective, and the cop slapped him hard along the side of the head, just above the ear, sending a blinding white flash across his vision for an instant.

"Watch your mouth, boy," Quinn barked.

"Can you make him stop?" Cootie asked politely and turned in his chair to face the bald cop.

"We're not trying to trick you or put words in your mouth," Quinn insisted. "This is a particularly brutal crime. We will get to the bottom of this. If we find out you did this, we're going to throw the book at you. We're going to clear our books of every unsolved rape committed in the last five years. Do you understand what I'm saying, Mr. Chambers?"

Baldie smirked. "Don't worry about the camera. It's off."

"I didn't do anything," Cootie said.

"You never answered him, you sick fuck," Baldie shrieked. "You like a little white nookie on the side. Raping white coeds. Let me tell you something, Mr. Black Buck. They have a chemical that castrates you where you'll never get it up again in life. You might as well become a faggot, because your screwing days are over. We'll put you in the joint, and you'll spend your time catching, because you damn sure won't be a pitcher."

The other cop, a Hispanic, laughed low in his throat and mumbled something about the nigger taking some hot dick up his Hershey highway. All of the other detectives broke up at the remark.

Cootie visibly flinched. "I never raped no damn body."

"Then where the fuck were you last night and don't give me that friends-and-the-restaurant bull," Quinn said angrily. "Because we're wise to you."

Cootie looked from man to man to man, the sweat soaking the back of his shirt now. The room was getting ever more hotter. He said nothing.

"Let me tell you what happened, Mr. Chambers," Baldie started with a sense of malice in his voice. "It was dark, and you had been following her for blocks. You stalked her, that sweet young coed, her long blond hair swinging over her shoulders. You could just taste that tight pink pussy, couldn't you, Mr. Chambers? She sensed you behind her and tried to walk on a street where there would be security patrols. She says she saw someone she knew walking his dog near the park, so she crossed over to him. When she told her friend that she felt she was being followed, you ducked behind a row of cars parked across the street. They couldn't see you, so you waited for her friend to leave before you trailed her again. You waited until she was alone—totally alone before you struck her from behind with a large rock. We found it a few feet from where you dragged her into the park and raped her. You beat her good before you fucked her. Did she scream?"

Cootie jumped up, shouting, "How the hell do I know? I wasn't there. You're making this up as you go along. You're trying to ruin my life."

"When you put the knife to her body, did she scream then, Mr. Chambers?" Quinn asked, smiling cruelly.

The Hispanic detective leaned forward. "What hand did you have the knife in, Mr. Chambers?"

"Stop it . . . stop it . . . you bastards," Cootie shouted.

Quinn again. "How many times did you stab her, Mr. Chambers?"

"Stop it," the black man screamed, holding his hands over his ears.

Baldie snatched Cootie's hands away and was about to shout something at him when the black man punched him in the face, the hard ridge of his knuckles crunching solidly on the detective's hawklike nose. Blood flew everywhere. Cootie remembered very little about what happened after that. The blows seemed to rain on every part of his body. He tried to cover his face, but there were too many fists, too many cops. He welcomed the warmth of the blackness that soon enveloped him like the comfort of his mother's arms.

*   *   *

Cootie awoke in a holding cell with a group of other men, mostly black and Hispanic. He never remembered being booked, fingerprinted, or photographed. His head and body ached like hell. One eye was swollen shut, and there was the rusty taste of blood in his mouth. One guy, a Dominican, told him he was in jail for holding his daughter down while a crack dealer fucked her in exchange for a day's supply. The little Negro huddled in the corner had raped an eighty-three-year-old grandmother and carved her tits up some. Another man—looked like a hillbilly—had robbed a gas station on Eleventh Avenue, put a gun to one of the attendants and made him suck the other one's Johnson.

There were twelve guys in there with Cootie, each crime worse than the one before it. He sat quietly in a corner of the cell, watching the others, not saying a damn thing. Several hours later, the cops allowed him one call, and Barbara bailed him out. Their case against him was flimsy. However, he'd been held almost all night.

In the newspapers, the picture of the victim showed her laughing with her family—all smiles and pigtails— looking as pure as Rebecca of Sunnybrook Farm. When the work with the bondsman was behind them, he was finally allowed to go home. His neighbors whispered as Barbara and him got out of the cab in front of Barbara's building. Some were holding newspapers and pointing at them.

Later that night, Barbara couldn't sleep with him in the apartment. She lay awake in the dark, thinking over everything that the papers and the man on the TV said her brother had done to the girl: the vicious beating, the sadistic rape, the ruthless stabbing.

"Cootie, I didn't ask you this, but did you do this thing?" Barbara asked, sitting on the edge of the couch where he had been sleeping.

"No, I didn't." He yawned and stretched his limbs.

Cootie sensed her anxiety, but he couldn't explain everything to her. He wanted to talk about it—the whole thing—with her, but she didn't speak about the matter. At one time, he was very close to his sister, but time had eroded their love. Never before had he felt so estranged from her, so alien, so separate. Most of all, he needed to be comforted, to be assured that she would remain by his side. He needed to know she would be with him through the entire ordeal.

"I need to talk about this with . . . with . . . you," he blurted out. Her gaze was focused on his hands. She seemed genuinely frightened of him, of what he might do to her.

"There's nothing to talk about, Cootie. Nothing," She said it in an odd way.

"I've got to talk about this frame-up with somebody," he complained. "I didn't do nothing. Everybody's treating me like a damn criminal. Do you believe me?"

There was a long moment of silence.

"Do you believe me, sis? You don't think I would do some shit like that. I'm a lot of things, but I'm not a rapist. Do you believe me or not?"

Silence again. She kept her eyes on his face, trying to read him. Finally, she cleared her throat and asked him in a strong, calm voice, where he was that night. The night of the rape.

"I'll tell you like I told the cops, that I was eating soul food with Guy and a broad named Tammy," Cootie said.

"That's it. I think Philbrick's behind this. He wants me to roll over on some dudes I know, and he's going to great lengths to make me do this. He says he'll send me back to prison if I don't cooperate."

"You were always a good liar," Barbara said. "Even when you were a kid, the lies would just roll off your tongue. Daddy used to hate that about you."

"I'm not lying," he said. "I swear to God. I ain't done nothing."

"I don't believe you. I think you did it."

"Barbara, I need you to believe me," he pleaded. "I really do. You know how hard it has been trying to go straight since I got out. The old friends trying to make me do one last score, the cops trying to get me to rat, and now this mess with Audrey. I need you to believe in me."

A few seconds later, she stopped staring at him and told him she never wanted to see him again. She laughed coldly, saying she hoped the cops put his lying ass under the jail. She also said she wanted him to go in the morning. After she left for her bedroom, he laid there in the darkness, trying to undo the damage to his shattered life in his mind; trying to imagine how his existence would improve. Eventually he fell asleep. When he awoke, he found her gone, probably to work, and he searched her closets for a gun. He knew she had one. But it was gone. She knew him like a book.

For several minutes, he stood at the kitchen sink, looking out the window at the street-sweeper truck pushing the trash around on the roadway below him. There was something symbolic in that, but he couldn't put his finger on it.

TWELVE

The phone rang in the boxer's small apartment. Cootie knew it was Philbrick, probably gloating about how he'd set him up to be hassled for the rape beef. At first, he didn't want to answer it, but he decided it could be Momo calling to check on him. The boxer always wanted to avoid trouble if necessary. Cootie was in his sweats, dressing a shot of gin and smoking a cigarette when he picked up the receiver.

"Hey, Mr. Chambers. How did you like the little rumble you had with the boys in blue?" Philbrick asked. "I can make your life a living hell. I can set you up with a weapons charge or a robbery charge or even a rape charge, and get you sent back to the big house. You know that, right?"

"You know I didn't do any of that shit," Cootie said.

"But the detectives didn't know that," the lawman replied. "You see how easy it is to go back behind bars? One-two-three and that's it. Once you got a record, you're a cinch for some more jail time. We had to break you down. I didn't like your uppity attitude."

Cootie took a full swallow of the booze. "Did you find out who did rape and stab the girl? It wasn't me."

Philbrick laughed. "I knew that from the start. The DNA from the semen showed that she had been raped by more than one guy. And also, the knife wounds indicated that there was more than one assailant. But you have to admit that the boys shook you up. They definitely had you going. Shit, you'd probably have confessed to the rape if they hadn't blown it."

"Why don't you like me?" Cootie asked, putting a little childish whine in his voice. "I'm just trying to go along to get along. Why can't we just get along?"

"I hate liars and thieves and criminals," Philbrick said softly. "And you're all three. Mr. Chambers, you're a fucking blight on society."

"Are you sure there's nothing racial about this whole thing?"

"Oh no, you're right. On top of it, you're a nigger." The lawman snorted.

"Well, now that we got that out of the way," Cootie said. "Did your boys catch the guys who did this awful thing to that precious white girl?"

"Yes," Philbrick said with a grunt. "The four teens, who were from Coney Island, laughed and joked as they were charged with the stabbing, robbery, and rape of the white coed. One of them was only twelve. The baby-faced teen, the youngest, told the cops they needed her money to play video games, and one of the older boys suggested rape after they found that she didn't have enough money.

"The fifteen-year-old held a gun to her head while the boys took turns. They dragged her through the park, kicking and screaming, to the secluded area where they raped and beat her. An elderly couple walking by saw what was happening, but they scurried away and didn't phone the police.

"The girl was trying to get up, but two of the boys kept knocking her down, the youngest one said. She was in shock. Blood covered her face and chest, between her legs. She wanted to get up and walk home, but they continued to punch her. They gave her a beat-down. They said they wanted to hawk somebody, but it got out of hand."

"When did the cops catch them?" Cootie asked. His question was aimed at finding out if they had falsely arrested him; if the boys were already in custody when he was pinched.

"I don't know." The lawman sounded disgusted when he explained that all of the boys were students in junior high or senior high schools.

"Will my arrest get cleared up?"

"It's gone," Philbrick answered. "But your people are animals. Fucking savages."

When Cootie asked him why he said that, the lawman told him they chased her down and caught her, then stripped her naked. They raped her, and two sodomized her. One of the older boys held the gun to her heart and warned her if she told anyone that she would be killed and her family too.

"Then the fucking mother comes in the stationhouse and keeps yelling about her boy is innocent," Philbrick said, his voice angry and tight. "She knew he was damn guilty—guilty as sin. He even said he was guilty. He was one of the ringleaders who thought up the rape and the beating. The boy even returned to her, and started kicking and beating her after she was unconscious. His mother shouted the police were just rounding up young black boys, although they didn't do nothing."

"The cops sometimes go overboard, and you know that," Cootie said. "I saw the pictures of the girl. The boys really worked her over. She was messed up. Add to that, she was a white girl . . . oh, man."

"They were bragging about what they had done. They were proud of it. This girl will have to deal with this terrible thing for the rest of her life. Imagine if she was one of your girls. Her mind is totally screwed up. Nobody wants to talk about that."

"No, I know."

"You think you know. That's why I refer to them as animals. Savages."

"Did you talk to my parole officer?"

"Yes, I did. He knows what we had to do. We pull everybody in with a record. That's routine. Once a fucking criminal, always a fucking criminal."

"Will there be any fallout from this?" Cootie asked.

"No, there won't," Philbrick replied, but he was still keyed up by the crime. Turned out that two of the older boys were wanted for setting homeless people afire on the subways and doorways after dark. The one who was laughing when he said this, talked about how they tossed matches on the men and women, ignited newspapers under their bodies, and doused their clothing with flammable liquid. The two older boys had records at Spofford Juvenile facility.

"What did they do it for?" Cootie didn't understand it. The boys were from Coney Island, an area not necessarily rolling in wealth, so they had to know how it was being poor. It was the poor striking out against anybody in reach, and loving it.

When Philbrick told him one boy said:

"We doused the guy with gas and lit the fire and he screamed like hell. It was a crowded subway car and he took off, trailing the flames behind him. We didn't mean him no harm. We didn't want to kill him. Some of the kids yelled, 'Burn, nigger, burn,' so when some riders risked themselves, we made sure that they wouldn't. People see men or women sleeping under a blanket in the rain or snow, they step over them, they don't feel shit. Even the ones who say they're Christians. They don't consider them humans or people. Nobody gives a damn about them or us."

"Not all of those black and Latin kids are bad," Cootie said. "I was one of them. Sometimes you get off on the wrong foot, or crumble under peer pressure and go astray. Hey, that's why I'm telling you. I know how I did wrong. All I want is to go straight."

Philbrick gave a mean laugh. "Shit, don't con me. You're a damn thief and a crook. All you know is breaking the law. When I walk through the neighborhood, I feel the hatred toward me and the law. The grownups see some shit go down, and they don't call us. They know their kids are thugs. Damn mutts. I have no pity for them."

"Then why are you a cop?"

"To keep the peace in the fucking jungle, that's why."

"Maybe if you would treat them like human beings, then your job would be easier. Folks know your rep. Take me for example. You were going to put me out to dry, fuck me up, bring me up before the *man*, so your hate for me could get satisfied. That shit wasn't right, and you know it."

"And you still ain't off the hook," Philbrick joked. "You still can go down."

"Do you believe in redemption?"

Philbrick snorted again. "So you read a book in prison. So what? Hell no, I don't believe in it. I think we are born in sin and we die in sin. And some of us just wallow in it like yourself. You don't have a good bone in your body."

"I'm going to prove you wrong," Cootie said.

"I know what I'm talking about. My grandfather was a cop. My father was a cop. My two brothers are cops. My cousin is a cop. My uncle was a cop. And I'm a cop. I know human nature. The job runs in my blood. Believe this. Niggers and spics are animals, for the most part. If they took them away, we wouldn't have a justice system or prison or courts. Listen, you have nothing against me.

But I have plenty against you. I'm the law and you're a damn crook."

"But you don't believe in change?"

"Hell no, you can't change. It's in your blood. Half of your damn race is crooks. Your parents were crooks. Lawbreakers. How are you going to change?"

"By the force of my will. I know how I fucked up."

"I'll believe it when I see it," Philbrick said. "Until that time, stay out of my way. If you hiccup the wrong way, you're going back to jail."

"What do you know about a Mitch character?" Cootie asked.

"I don't know him," the lawman replied. "What do you want with him?"

"I thought every cop knew him. He's one of the biggest smut and drug peddlers in the city. I hear he has juice. All he has to say is something is so, then it becomes that way. He's a very bad man."

"What do you want with him?" Philbrick was probing.

"Do you know him or not?" Cootie knew Philbrick was in the pocket of Mitch and his cartel. A few of the folks in the know had seen them together at one of the Bronx strip clubs, but he decided not to press the lawman.

"Hey, I got to go. Don't fuck up. And we still have to talk over some business. I know you just buried your father, so I'll give you time, but we still have to do that. I'll take only one answer and that's yes. If I want you to snitch, you'll snitch."

Cootie heard the click, and the phone went to sleep.

*   *   *

"So I'm a bad father and a failed husband," Cootie said aloud to himself, thinking over the conversation of the previous night with his sister.

He lay on his back on the sofa, listening to CDs with music by Charlie Parker, John Coltrane, and Miles Davis—good jazz, the music his father gave him as an inheritance. If his friend Guy, the jazz buff, was there, he'd turn sage and quote The Bird:

"Listen, baby, it ain't how long you live that matters, it's how well you live that counts. What you do with that life matters. Dig it?"

His life had spun out of control. Everyone he loved was destroyed or in the process of destruction. Maybe he should have stayed in the joint. As the Bird classic, "Cheryl," was warming up in those smooth alto sax lines from the CD player, the telephone rang. He didn't want to talk to anybody. Especially after that chat with Philbrick and the lies he told about Mitch.

The phone rang again. He picked it up. Whoever it was hung up.

It rang once more. He stood and watched it ring.

"Hello. Who's speaking?" Cootie asked.

"I'm sorry that I doubted you," Barbara, his sister, spoke, gulping her words. "I really didn't think you did it. I don't know what came over me. Forgive me for calling you a liar and a thief. I didn't mean it."

Cootie laughed slyly. "Yes, you did. You meant everything you said."

"I guess so, but I'm sorry."

"Sorry for what? You know me, but I've changed. I'm trying to get my life on track. Still, it's hard because nobody will give you a chance. But I'll keep trying."

"Is there anything I can do?" his sister asked.

"We've got to find Audrey," Cootie said. "That's what we've got to do."

"I know that," his sister said. "When I saw in the papers that the cops found the boys that did that thing, I felt like such a fool. I cried and cried. Everybody in the family had called me, telling me that they had thought that you had done the rape. Now nobody has called. I think they're embarrassed to admit they were wrong."

"Fuck them. All I wanted to believe me was you. To hell with the rest of them."

Her short burst of laughter was the first sign the crisis was over. "Will you keep me posted on your search for Audrey? I'll tell you if she calls. I'll try to get an address from her or a phone number. Keep me informed, okay?"

"Sure."

With the phone call over, he went back to listening to his jazz, and thinking about how fatherhood was a privilege, a responsibility that he had thrown in the towel early on in his marriage, by choosing the streets over his family. That was what his father had done as well. Pimping.

Cootie continued beating himself up emotionally over the loss of Faith, and the ruin of Audrey. If only he would have focused on family life and being a loving, devoted father. But like a lot of black men, the streets and its temptations proved to be irresistible. What was the new modern dad all about? Maybe doing his own thing, still sending cash home to Mommy and the little ones, yet he could be absent, with no direct hands-on involvement in the home. Just be a breadwinner and provider.

He brought out the other bottle of scotch. It was going to be one of those nights. Maybe a family didn't need the daddy there. Women were better at raising kids anyway—more emotional, more open, more nurturing.

Men were too locked up inside themselves to be of any real use as caring parents. In the end, Faith didn't seem to need him there anymore.

When you looked at the big picture, men didn't really seem necessary to anything much, especially in the family situation. Women gave birth and took the primary role as the main, nurturing parent. Nurturing, there was the word again. It was the woman's duty to love and nurture the brats. The man would be the authority figure, the one with the discipline, and he would show the kids the ropes when it came to knowing about life. He could remember when his father ruled the roost, ran everything. His word was the law. A kid's blood would run cold if his mother said: "Your father's going to hear about this when he gets home."

Cootie respected and feared his father. The old man could stop your heart with one cold, mean look on his face. He took another sip and savored his memories of his early years at home. It wasn't like that anymore.

The phone rang again. He sat there on the sofa, watching it ring. Why couldn't they just leave him the fuck alone? Why couldn't they just let him get fucking drunk in peace? He gulped down another fiery mouthful of the scotch, and reached for the phone. As his fingers neared the damned thing, it stopped making noise, and he laughed for a time at this little head game.

He was having a real pity party and wanted no one to interfere with it. *Oh man, Faith and her addiction.* Thinking about it, he couldn't remember how she got hooked, whether he gave her the needle as a gift, because he was afraid that some other man would lure her away from him. But that was not the case. Her uncle turned her out shortly after they met and married; gave her the legacy of dirty needles, hepatitis, abscesses, and periodic overdoses. She had a death wish. Everybody could see it.

"I need my medication," Faith would say to him, preparing her works.

The phone rang again. He threw a sofa pillow at it and missed. It kept on ringing. He staggered over to it, picked it up, and shouted "fuck you" into the receiver and slammed it down.

What was it that his nana used to say? His grandmother, an old, wizened Geechee, had a million sayings that she could pop out at a moment's notice:

"As we go up, lift everyone you love up along with you. We must be responsible for ourselves, or we will hurt the ones we love. We choose our fate."

We choose our fate. He thought about that for a moment, and the tears came again to his eyes. He wiped them away with the back of his hand, took a deep breath, and poured himself another drink.

THIRTEEN

Cootie and Guy were sitting outside one of Mitch's Bronx porn shops near Hunt's Point, watching the near-naked girls walking over to the cars of the male patrons, offering hand jobs, oral or anal sex for a fee. Nobody craved for anything without kink. The place wasn't much from the outside, but once inside, it was a sex palace of the first order. There were many cars and SUVs parked in a lot adjacent to the building. Also, there was a constant parade of cars patrolling near the shop on the street at the front entrance—indecisive customers who couldn't make up their minds whether they should go and partake of the pleasures of the flesh.

"Cootie, are you going in or not?" Guy asked.

"I don't know. I hate to think my baby girl would end up in a damn place like this. I just can't believe it."

He looked across the street and saw the sign announcing the X-rated films, sex toys, and other marital aids. A sign of a nude woman, tan and healthy, was on a large billboard, illuminated with colored lights and stars, strategically placed over her nipples and genitals. A few men walked through the electronic doors into the inner sanctum, where the others surveyed the girlie mags, dildos, vibrators, penis pumps, and erection creams.

They crossed the street and entered to a man who handed over a fistful of tokens for their hard-earned money. The attendant pointed to the sign, which read movies on the lower level and the girls upstairs. Guy wanted to walk around, check out the aisles of booths and the short snippets of hardcore porn. He stepped into the booth, closed the door, and the sound of tokens

BOOKOFF USA INC

49 W 45th St., 500
New York,, NY 10036
(212) 685-1410
bookoffusa.com
@Booko

Feb 28, 2020
2:11 PM
JESSICA

PURCHASE

Receipt DRLd

96 Thin Comics	$1.00
Clearance $1	

Subtotal	$1.00
Sales Tax(NYC)	$0.09

Total	**$1.09**
Cash	$1.10
Change	$0.01

We buy your Books, Blu-rays, Electronics,
Figures and more.
please bring in your items to our store

Return Policy: Items found to be defective
within 30 days may be
exchanged or returned with the receipt.

could be heard. After a time, he came out and was almost shouting.

"Damn, this bitch took two dicks in her ass, holy shit," Guy yelled. "And the other nigga was in her snatch, all the way. She was loving it. These boys were built like horses down there—long and thick. Oh shit, shit, shit."

Cootie didn't want to see any porn. He wanted to visit upstairs so he could see the girls, see the performers on the mini-stages on the second floor. But Guy wanted to press on through the booths.

"There was an ocean of come under the stool," Guy said. "I wouldn't like having the job of cleaning that shit up. Who knows what kind of diseases that mess could hold. The smell up in there was fierce."

An attendant watched them and reminded them that only one person could enter a booth at a time. Guy laughed. The attendant, a young Haitian, explained that gays used the booth to suck off the customers, and the street whores spread their legs over the Johns who fucked them, until the films concluded. He peered at the shadows underneath the doors to see if the rooms were in violation, and then he was gone.

In an adjacent booth, they watched a woman with her breasts almost exposed, and a short skirt she hiked up, placing it on her full ass, revealing her hairy sex. The customer licked his lips and smiled, then closed the door, as he put one hand on her smooth butt. Other men walked past the booth, unaware of the sex play going on inside. There was no sound coming from the booth other than the moans and sighs of the porn film, the wet smacking of lips on flesh, and occasional footwork.

"Oh damn," Cootie said, thinking of his daughter doing something like that.

He read the large sign posted near the stairs, listing all of the benefits of the shop: PRIVATE VIP ROOMS, ALL NUDE

DANCERS, COZY HUG AND SQUEEZE ROOM, EXOTIC TABLE DANCING, AND LARGE-SCREEN PORNO TV. More customers poured into the shop, bought their tokens, and filled the booths. Three voluptuous Latin dancers adjusted their tight-fitting leather outfits and walked upstairs, trailed by horny, panting customers who looked like they could wrestle them down and mount them right on the steps.

"How late do you stay open?" Cootie asked as Guy disappeared into another booth.

"Till two in the morning on weekends and till four on weekdays," the man at the token booth said. "At Mitch's Fantasy Lounge, you get more for your money."

Cootie fished around in his wallet, dug up a photo of Audrey, and handed it to the token man. "Have you seen this girl? I'm trying to find her."

"No. I've not seen her. How long has she been missing?"

"About seven months. She's a young kid. Good kid, friendly, smart, decent."

"Well, you're not going to find any decent girls around here," the token man said. Something about his eyes tipped Cootie off. He wasn't telling what he knew.

"Who hires the girls?" Cootie asked.

"Mitch himself, but we run the shop," the man replied. "But we have real girls, natural, not the false silicone, fake tit jobs." He lied. "Boob jobs. This is a fetish heaven where customers can know they can spend a wild night, safe from crooks or cops. Real girls. Some clubs don't hire black girls. They go for white, blond, tall and skinny chicks. The customers love that. And Asian girls are in season now."

"That's why I want you to look at the picture again," Cootie said.

The token man inspected the picture closely, looking at the facial features of the attractive black girl. "I don't know. Maybe I've seen this girl. Like most of them, they use stage names. You never know their real names."

"So have you seen this girl or no?"

Lotus, a dark Vietnamese female full of curves, walked up and took the picture away from the man. She was probably mixed with some African or European blood, possibly French. "Don, you know this girl. Remember Sam? Used to work here, but she left quite a while ago."

"I still can't place her," the token man said. "Maybe I was over at the other club."

"Mitch used to hire porn stars for shows, but the regular girls hated it because we would have to compete with them to get tips," Lotus said, tweaking her nipples into hardness. "These women were pros. A lot of girls bitched to Mitch. The porn stars would do anything to get customers, give private shows, take Polaroid's with the customers and even suck dick. Mitch was always on us to be creative. We became freaks."

"And was this around the time Sam quit?"

"I don't know," Lotus said, after hearing Cootie's sad story of his search for his young daughter. "She had nothing against fucking. She loved sex. We should go upstairs and talk to Kelly. She was her roommate for a while."

They walked up the stairs, through a pair of large velvet curtains, and stepped into darkness. Lotus was accustomed to the pitch blackness, whereas, Cootie had trouble adjusting to the lack of light; careful where he was placing his steps. The odor was stronger than the booth; one of sweat, sex, dampness, and a peculiar sourness. A narrow hall lighted by yellow Christmas bulbs along its length, opened to their left.

A voice, husky but slurred, sounded behind a barred window. "Two tokens. Two tokens for entry. Do you have them?"

Lotus spoke up. "The guy's with me. Have you seen Kelly?"

In the dark, Cootie saw nothing. For a second, Lotus's Asian face was lighted by an amber glow, then it disappeared. A hand fell quickly on his leg, moved upward until it caressed his crotch—dick and balls—and soon it vanished. The sex odor grew more potent as they neared the dimly lit entrance of the small performance cages where the girls danced and gyrated to music. There was a group of men watching the performers wiggle their asses and shake their tits, while the men slipped them precious tips through slots in the walls.

There were booths along the cages. Cootie's forehead was sweating, and the back of his shirt was sticky with perspiration from the heat of his overcoat. It was hot there, like a hothouse nourishing tropical flowers. He stepped into one of the booths, which was in total darkness, but there was a lit screen and a slot for tokens only a reach away.

"I'll find Kelly, and I'll find you here, okay?" Lotus said, touching him on the arm.

He nodded, depositing the tokens into the slot, and the large screen slid back, opening up a soft, passive vista of a female pair of thighs, chocolate colored but as inviting as a sensuous tongue flickering around a belly button. Rhythmically, the woman swayed back and forth against the glass to the throbbing beat of Sir Mix-A-Lot's unholy hymn about big asses. Her fingers probed down underneath the shaven nether lips, as smooth as a tyke, moving in tender circles of lust, before pulling them to reveal the pink throat of her sex.

"Oh shit," Cootie said, moaning. He couldn't take his eyes off her pussy.

He shoved in two fives as a tip through the slot. No response. Suddenly, the woman bent over, parting her ass cheeks to give him a view of her anus and sex. The rhythmic circular movements continued, bumping and smashing her moist flesh into the glass as he unzipped his pants, found his stiffened penis, and began touching himself.

"No, no, no, wait," the woman's voice said, deep and seductive. "I can see you. Don't waste it. Lotus said to take care of you. Here, put your hard dick in the hole and leave the rest to me."

He did as he was told. He pressed himself against the wall, his groin through the opening, the air soft on his sensitive skin. Her mouth was wet and simmering, taking it between her lips as her tongue flitted across his thick meat. She kissed it, nibbled and played with his Johnson, until they were interrupted by a quiet knock on the door.

Cootie's heart skipped a beat, pulling his pants back up and making himself somewhat presentable for company. He opened the door to Lotus, who seemed alarmed that Kelly had gone home sick. Stomach flu.

"Get your friend, and I'll go there with you," Lotus said. "She doesn't know you, and she might think you're a stalker or something sick. In this business, you can't be too careful. Is that okay with you?"

"Yeah sure." He was very disappointed that the woman couldn't finish with her sword-swallowing act. She was definitely a pro in her field.

"I've got to pack up some things, and I'll meet you in the parking lot," Lotus said, starting toward the dressing room. Cootie nodded and looked longingly at the woman's delicious lips, which still remained in the square of yellow light in the booth. Now he was turning down sex. Damnit. He went to find Guy, who he knew was having a good time in the booth, and probably setting up some dates for later that night.

In the car, Guy was the driver, which allowed Cootie to talk with Lotus about her line of work: the pay, the tips, the benefits. She was in the front seat next to Guy. He was distracted by the panoramic view of her surgically enhanced breasts, bursting to get out of the very tight silk blouse; stylish with the long black leather coat almost going down to her ankles.

"How big are your tits?" Guy asked.

"I don't know, but do you like them?" Lotus bounced them up and down while Cootie's amorous friend licked his lips. She then explained to Cootie why she wanted to help him to find his girl—because the sex business had a way of chewing up its young, and usually they ended up strung out, crazy, or dead. And Cootie's girl was a nice kid.

Now it was Cootie's turn to ask some questions. "What does Audrey—uh, Sam—see in Mitch? From what people tell me, he's a fucking asshole who really doesn't care about anybody or anything."

The car moved over the dark Bronx streets to the radiant glow of the Manhattan skyline, toward the FDR roadway to downtown. Guy wasn't fooling around, his lead foot was riding the gas pedal, regardless of speed traps or police roadblocks.

"Mitch is a bad boy, an outlaw, a thug," Lotus said, smiling. "Women like bad boys. And they're experts at wild sex. I guess when you get older, the bad boys don't appeal to you so much, but when you're young like Sam, they can twist your heart around. When you're young, sex is everything."

"But when you get to be an old fart like me, sex is when you can get it or get it up," Guy said. "I do too much blow and booze to have a good sex life. The desire is always there, but the flesh is weak."

"Is sex so important?" Cootie asked.

"Hell yeah, most folks say sex is the real monitor whether a relationship is going well or not," Lotus suggested. "It's probably true. When my old man suddenly lost interest in sex, I knew something was up and we better talk. I knew he had problems with my job. But I told him that he shouldn't be jealous, that I was making money for the both of us. We couldn't communicate, so I had to leave."

Guy piped up. "That's the way your wife did too. She got on the needle and really didn't give a shit about you or the girls. A man needs loving or he'll act out."

"Act out?" Lotus sounded surprised. "I didn't know you had been married."

"That was long ago. My wife died." Cootie looked out the window at the lights on the bridges.

"His wife died of drugs," Guy blabbed. "That's why he's looking for his girl."

"Oh Sam, right?" Lotus turned around and watched Cootie staring at his friend. He wanted to kill him. Guy could be a gossip at all the wrong moments.

Guy's gaze went sideways to Lotus. "Why are you staring at my dick?"

"I did check it out, and it seemed like a nice hunk of meat, but don't get crazy on me," Lotus said, shrugging. "Should I get embarrassed? Women check out men's dicks and asses all the time. Just like the fellas. Isn't that right, Cootie?"

"Yes," Cootie mumbled and continued watching the dark eddies of the river.

"You don't say much, do you?" Lotus asked.

137

"If there's nothing to talk about, I keep quiet," he said. "Sometimes Guy can talk too much. I hate chatty bastards."

"Do you like foreplay?" she asked.

"Sure do, and I can lick with the best of them," Guy announced proudly.

Lotus snapped Guy's head off with a loud roar. "I was talking to Cootie. You talk too fucking much. Let him answer it. Do you like foreplay, Cootie?"

He laughed. "Yes. Foreplay is always good."

"Do you like quickies?" Lotus quizzed him.

"Yeah." Cootie reached into his pocket for a pack of cigarettes.

Lotus caressed her soft cheek. "Well, I like a guy or a girl to start my engine, get me warmed up, touching, kissing, playing, and everything that doesn't seem sexual at the time, but it is. It's all always about sex. I used to hate my body, but I've been doing some work on it."

"Do you mean by work, having your breasts done?" Guy asked, turning onto the on-ramp of the overpass.

"I used to run marathons when I had smaller tits, but I want to strip, and you got to have big breasts for the customers, especially White men," Lotus said. "But being athletic can be a drag when you have fuller tits. They can get in the way. Sometimes when men stare at them, when I'm dressed up on a date or something, I feel self-conscious about them."

Where is it?" Guy asked, coming out at Fourteenth Street, overlooking the projects in Alphabet City. "Do I turn right or left?"

"Go right, and I'll tell you to stop when we get there." Lotus smiled broadly at Guy, wiggled her eyebrows, and winked at Cootie. All he could do was shake his head. Women. You cannot figure them out.

FOURTEEN

The car parked outside of the projects in Alphabet City on Avenue B with the trio smoking cigarettes, waiting for the lights in Kelly's apartment to come on. Guy looked at the long, thin, lipstick-smeared cigarette he'd borrowed from Lotus and wondered what kind of fuck she was. There were only two cigarettes in the pack Lotus had in her purse. After that, they were out of luck. Cootie worried they had missed Audrey, or maybe she had gone to a nearby bar or a friend's apartment. The calmest of the group, Lotus, seemed to be used to waiting; very patient, almost serene.

"I've known Kelly since we were in a juvie pen," the stripper said. "Remind me to get a box of detergent before we get out of here. There's a bodega across the street. I know she'll come this way. She won't stay out all night. She loves her cat too much."

"What kind of cat?" Guy asked, handing the cigarette back to her.

"It's just a tabby cat, a mutt, I think," Lotus replied. "But she loves it madly."

"What time is it?" Cootie asked.

"Three-thirty," Lotus said, checking her watch. It was totally dark, and the absence of a few streetlights didn't help the forbidding ambience much.

"Tell her about Sam—uh, Audrey," Guy said. "If she gets the lowdown, maybe she can help to locate her. In this kind of business, there's a million places to hide, and nobody would find you."

Lotus winded the car window down and flicked the butt out. "That's true. A lot of the sex trade is completely

139

private with a secret clientele with clubs that you have to get on a list to get into. But we were talking about Mitch before. Maybe I should explain more about him. Mitch is a young thug, sex peddler, pimp, and killer. He'll fuck anything that moves. Anything that's moist and smooth."

"Is he bi?" Guy asked. "Some of these thugs are, you know. AC/DC."

"I don't know, but he has a big rep with the ladies," Lotus said. "When I was with him, he used to say getting a nut made him feel powerful and dominant. Like he could whip the world. He has raped a lot of women. A lot. He tries to act gangsta and Mackish, but he will tap another dude's booty and or use a homie's mouth to get his nut. He was in the joint for a stretch. He's an animal. Women know this about him, but they don't care. They just like being around him, being seen with him. It's a power thing."

"Do you think Audrey would be attracted to this nigga?" Cootie asked.

"Sam—uh, Audrey—is no different from any other girls," Lotus said. "Girls love power and flash. They love glitz. The nigga could be John Wayne Gacy if he had cash money, a fine ride, and clothes. They love that shit. Hey, he pulled Kelly when she came back from juvie. She had been on the street, peddling her ass. She had no pimp. She was walking on the East Side, hooking the white middle-aged business types."

Guy peered up at the dark windows of her place. "How much did she make back then? Did she rake it in?"

"Kelly was young—real young, seventeen—so she made two grand a night," Lotus said. "She once joked with me that it only took fifteen minutes to make a hundred dollars. These White guys who are married and got a little bit of cheddar in their pockets, love the rough trade, especially if they're into the kinky stuff. They get down with girls like Kelly, wipe off, and go to the commuter train, then go home to their wives."

"And Mitch saved her from this?" Guy asked.

"Yes, he did and put her in his Bronx clubs," Lotus said. "If he hadn't done that, who knows what she would have become, crack ho or anything. He did that for Sam—uh, Audrey—as well."

"Is Audrey using crack?" Cootie asked.

"No, I don't know about that," she replied. "Hey, I know that nigga. Wind down the window on your side. Honk the horn." She instructed Guy.

Lakisha, a very skinny, dark girl with tight pink pants and a yellow winter coat, stepped up to the car. She recognized Lotus from their project days. In her arms, she carried a small cat, which was shivering from the cold.

"Hey, girl. Whassup? I just came from Kelly's, but I don't think she's home. I knocked and shit, but no one answered. I was taking her one of her kittens. My old man don't want the thing around the house. He says she cries all the time and pees too much. If I had my way, I'd keep her."

"Sha, when's the last time you saw Kelly?" Lotus asked.

"I talked her tonight, but she said she had to make a run to this spot," Lakisha replied. "That was hours ago. She said she would be home before long and bring the kitten by. Hey Lo, are you holding?"

"What do you need?" the dancer asked.

"Anything . . . I need to get my head bad," Lakisha said. "Anything, rock or weed, anything. My old man is totally acting a fool. He's coming down from a bad trip and is grumpy like hell. I can't stand him when he's like that."

Lotus reached into her bag and passed her a joint. "That's all I have."

"That damn cat doesn't like the wind," Guy said. "You need to get her out of the cold. She's trembling like a leaf. You should put her close to your body so she can stay warm." Lakisha tucked the kitten in her coat, under her arm with its head poking out, and walked away the way she had just come.

"So where to now?" Cootie asked.

"I know a place where Kelly and Mitch might be, up at this Elks Hall in Harlem," Lotus said, lighting another cigarette. "Do you want to try this place? They might be there. And then maybe not."

Guy looked at Cootie, shrugged, and said why not. He started the car, pulled out into traffic, and headed back to Harlem. Along the way, Lotus hopped out of the car to get a box of detergent, cigarettes, beer, a bag of Fritos, and a *People* magazine. To spite Guy, she also bought Cootie a pack of cigarettes—wrong brand, but Marlboros would suffice.

Whether or not Guy wanted to annoy Lotus, he kept asking the most ignorant questions about her, sex, and her stripping profession. The woman answered him as if she was on a talk show, being polite and candid, even giving the most explicit replies to his stupid queries. Cootie smoked and sipped his beer, shaking his head at the dumb-ass remarks his boy was making.

"That's why you don't get the women," Cootie said. "You talk too much. You ask too many questions. Women don't like a man who asks so many questions. Right, Lotus?"

"It's all right," she said. "Maybe he just wants to know more about the birds and the bees. It's good when you find a man who knows how a woman thinks. But it's rare. Men are usually only concerned with themselves. Maybe he's just lame and shit."

It was a relief when they pulled up in front of the hall in Central Harlem. One after another, women came to the doors of the brick building, two big guys checking out their purses, and waving them to enter. After the trio parked, Lotus led the men inside, following a brief pat-down to check for guns and other weapons. These burly boys didn't want a robbery or shootout on the premises.

"Where's Mitch?" Lotus asked.

"He was backstage with some of the dudes," one of the bouncers said. "Man, these sistahs act like they haven't seen dick before. They trying to tackle the brothers on stage and trying to pull the dicks off their bodies. It's crazy. We need more security and shit."

"Bitches fighting over dick," Guy said, moaning. "It's like real life."

"Word." The bouncer laughed. "The biggest dick wins."

"Have you seen Kelly tonight?" the stripper asked, not paying attention to the banter. "Sometimes she rolls with him on his stops."

"Not tonight," the bouncer said. "But you can go around to the back. Take the steps, they come out to a row of dressing rooms. You should find him there."

Cootie walked to the men's room, opened the door to find three buff black studs doing some blow and jacking off to get their meat ready for female inspection. A lovely sistah was squatting near the urinals, fluffing up the fellas who need help with their snakes, a little oral assist. Another muscle man, bald with bulging biceps worthy of Arnold in his prime, entered the room, waving a porno mag, attracting the strippers like flies on sugar.

"Anybody need a dick pump before they go on?" one stripper asked.

"Hell no," the men yelled in chorus and laughed.

One of the veterans, a tan Adonis with an anaconda between his thighs, was schooling a newcomer about a trick of the trade, near a sink, holding a length of pantyhose. "You tie your dick up with this. You got to have it erect so the honies can get excited. If your meat is soft and limp, you're not going to get any money, and that's the name of the game."

The rookie stretched out his Johnson and let the veteran secure the long penis with the elastic hose. "Show me how you do it. If you tie it wrong, can't you cut off the circulation, and then it can go down?"

"Yes, it can. That's why you want to go on and get off quick. Get the bills thrown at you and run off, so you can untie your shit. You want to flash that big dick and let them go wild and run off. One of the crew will pick up the money, so you don't have to worry about that."

Cootie found an unused urinal, took a leak, and walked out into the corridor where he could see the hundreds of women, black and Latina, screaming and shouting for the hunky bucks coming on a makeshift stage in the main hall. The females—bachelorettes and girls on the prowl or in need of thrills—huddled around the ramp, sliding their seats for position to see more. Since Mitch's father opened the first male strip shows in the early 1980s, women had been flocking to eyeball the muscle boy's strip, beef up, and pull it out.

"We may need more security up here," a bouncer shouted. "The girls are more randy than usual. We don't mind them putting their hands on the guys, but when they try to take the merchandise home with them, that's a problem."

The second dancer, a tall, lean joker, spun a heavyset woman, opened her legs, and pretended to hump her. She wrapped her thighs around him, getting all into the act, and the ladies roared. The following dancers were welcomed with a loud chorus of approval, even the men became more daring and risqué—and the crumpled-up bills showered on the stage.

"Where's Mitch?" Cootie asked. "Do you have an idea where he is?"

"He was here a moment ago," the bouncer said. "He was dealing with one of the strippers who wanted to shake his dick, and then part his ass cheeks. They were arguing whether the ladies would consider that a gay move. Nobody, especially these girls, wants to see a guy's asshole."

Cootie laughed. "Do you think he could be down there in the rooms off to the left?"

"Who knows?" the bouncer replied.

They watched the dwarf announcer introduce the next dancer, Ajax, a former pro football linebacker, with massive arms and steroid-enhanced legs. Ajax did a series of cartwheels, flipping high above the stage before coming down into a split. The speakers blasted Prince's antique ditty "Head." A short, buxom Latina hopped onstage and tossed bills upon him, but the stripper took her hand, grabbed her around the waist, and pumped the woman against his crotch. Then he slid her on the stage, crawled behind her legs, and buried his face into her sex. The crowd was delirious, going amok, barely restrained.

"Go on, girl," one of the audience bellowed. "Show him how it's done."

Ajax unsnapped his tear-away shorts, kneeling as he pulled out one of the woman's large breasts, then sucking the nipple and licking his ample lips. He soon did the other as a bouncer handed him a banana, and Ajax positioned the half-peeled fruit against his groin. The woman flipped him over on his back and straddled

145

him with her face and mouth near the slightly curved banana.

"You know what you got to do, you know that, baby," the dwarf hollered. "Put your lips on that big thang. Do it, baby. Give her some encouragement."

The room was bursting with excitement and noise as the woman lowered herself toward the banana. The dwarf egged her on, shouting, "Do it, do it." She gulped down the fruit while the stripper surprised her, revealing his large dick near her lips. It was only a micro-second, but it sent a shudder of erotic heat through the girls. Wisely, he stopped before the act of the kiss helped her up, and smacked her on her big behind. The women jumped to their feet, screaming and yelling, surrounding the stage. Bills flew in his direction from almost every seat, piling up nearly ankle deep. The security held the ladies back as Ajax bowed and blew them kisses when he exited.

"Damn, that bitch almost sucked his dick," one woman yelled. "Too rude."

"Point Mitch out to me," Cootie said, walking back through the curtains. "Is that him? In the dark suit?"

"No," the bouncer said. "It's the Valentino standing near the dancers."

When Cootie walked to the handsome stud, he found Lotus, Guy, and a couple of the male strippers talking. Mitch was holding class, spewing out orders and instructions. They stood around the "great man" as he held court to the lowly and the faithful.

"You know the rules, you know them," Mitch barked. "What are they? A dancer always wears garter belts around his thighs for tips. A dancer always wears tight shorts with space for his bare butt. A dancer always humps at least three members of the crowd. And his act always ends with a slow, sensuous R&B number, so you can strut your stuff—grind with the woman like you're actually taking the pussy. You want every woman to feel like she's being seduced and fucked. That's the hallmark of the show."

"I understand," the young stripper said, his head down.

"See that you don't forget the rules," Mitch added. "Don't forget to untie your dick after the show, because I don't need any unnecessary medical bills. And the other thing is, you leave your woman at home. We don't need your lady getting stressed because these other broads are grabbing at you. Do you understand?"

"I understand."

"I don't usually hire guys like you. The only reason that I hired you was because Ajax said you give a good show, but we don't need complications. You have to make your woman understand it's a job. When she sees you on stage naked, on top of another woman, she has to get used to that. She can't be shaky. It's just a job."

"I'll make her understand. It's just a job."

"One more thing, you can't let these women get into trouble," Mitch said. "Last night, someone said a customer had on a dress and your fingers were in her crotch, and you were humping dangerously near her sex. You're not allowed to have sex with the customers. I don't care how good they look, how big their asses are, or how large their tits are. No way. If they get aroused, you still have to remember that it's just a job."

"I wasn't going to do anything. I wasn't going to fuck her. I swear."

"Now, what do you want?" Mitch turned and asked Cootie, hearing a thunderous roar of female shouts for an entertainer behind him. "What can I do for you?"

"This is the brother I was talking about," Lotus said, indicating Cootie. "He wants to ask you some questions

147

about Sam—uh, Audrey. He knows she worked for you some time ago."

Cootie introduced himself and Guy, and shook hands. "I was wondering if you knew where she is. We've not heard from her for some time. I knew she must make a living, but I just wanted her to know that I was thinking about her."

"You're the jailbird," Mitch said. "She told me about you."

"Do you know where she is?" Cootie asked.

Mitch kissed Lotus on the cheek, frowned, and motioned with a snap of his fingers for the bouncers to throw Cootie, Guy, and even the stripper out of the hall. That was the end of the pow-wow. Cootie was pissed that he had not learned any more about Audrey's whereabouts, than when he came in. There was one thing, and that was Mitch was hiding something. He didn't trust him; he didn't like the man who controlled so many lives. When the men tossed them out in the Harlem night, they started planning the next skirmish in this ongoing war, for they were determined to find Audrey and get her to safety.

FIFTEEN

A short time after their eviction from the hall, Cootie, Guy, and Lotus walked down the block to a beer joint, where some regulars and stragglers watched a Yankee classic game, courtesy of ESPN, with Whitey Ford on the mound. The bartender had his thumb on the scale, meaning he was serving powerful and plentiful drinks. Folks were getting loaded and rowdy. He didn't give a shit. It seemed he was pissed at the boss, so he was going to make him pay one way or another. The trio wandered up to the bar, but there were no seats.

"Everybody's out tonight," the bartender said, asking them what they'd have. "We have a little agreement with the cops. They let us stay open longer, and they look the other way. A lot of places in Harlem have this agreement, but you have to know the right folks."

The joint was jumping. Five guys, casually dressed and totally zonked, watched a shapely girl with slim hips pounce around to the tune of Sisqo's "Thong Song," trying to catch a peek at her panties and possibly some pubic hair. They cheered and urged her on as she spun and twirled recklessly, sending her dress higher and higher.

"Hell, she should stand on her hands and give them what they're looking for," Guy laughed. "She ain't going to get anywhere just teasing them. Especially if she wants to loosen the purse strings."

The bartender pointed to a table near the window as the occupants were leaving. Guy went over, ordering a round of drinks, and Cootie and Lotus chatted about Audrey's whereabouts, and the futility of getting Mitch to tell anything about her location. Cootie wanted to fuck Mitch up. He made a mental note that if he got a chance, he would do just that.

"Mitch's hiding something," Lotus said. "He doesn't want you to know where she is. Sam—uh, Audrey—is a cash cow for him. Young, pretty, and kinky. That's a combo that's hard to beat. And he knows that. These bitches don't age well in this business. Every dick they swallow tells on their face. So slick niggers like Mitch are always on the lookout for fresh faces and young bodies."

As Cootie pulled the chair out for her. Lotus explained how Mitch and the big boys worked an unending parade of attractive young girls to their advantage, in the network of topless bars, porn shops, massage parlors, and hot-sheet hotels in their sex-for-pay scheme. The stripper said she used to be a recruiter going into such cities as: Los Angeles, San Francisco, Seattle, Denver, Kansas City, New Orleans, Washington, Chicago, Detroit, Baltimore, Philadelphia, Atlanta, and even Miami. She was paid handsomely for every girl she got into the pipeline.

"Yeah, flesh is cheap," Guy said, returning with the drink. "Pussy is a dime a dozen. Girls are nothing but a product."

"He's right," Lotus replied. "Yes, you see how many girls were there just in that one club. Mitch has several clubs like that. He has about thirty massage parlors in the tri-state area. When the business uses up one girl, there's always another to take her place."

"Why do they do it?" Cootie asked.

Lotus's answer was most of the girls came from broken homes, families where drugs or alcohol played an important role, or they were fleeing from abuse or brutality. Others just left home, seeking adventure and the glitter of the fast life. Once on the streets, they fell prey to slick-talking men who convinced them they could still get jobs, although they were underage and unable to secure employment. All they had to do was sell their bodies to survive and get a better life.

"Like Audrey, these girls probably have a good reason why they're peddling their asses," Lotus said, drinking her beer. "There's always a good reason for following a wrong path. Were you a good father, Cootie?"

"I guess so," he said. "Better than most, but not as good as many."

"But did you care about your little girl?" Lotus asked. "All these girls want is love. They think if a guy pays them a little attention then he loves them, and they'll do anything for him. And I mean *anything.*"

Guy was his usual chatty self. "But you've told me that you didn't really feel like a father. Remember you even had trouble touching her—hugging her. You had trouble being affectionate with her. Even Faith said that."

"Who's Faith?" the stripper asked.

"My wife. She died kinda young," Cootie said sadly.

But Guy wasn't finished. "But you told me that you had problems with the whole thing of being a parent, providing for a family, child rearing, self-esteem, especially after you got out of stir, the man-woman thing, and even the job market. I remember you telling me that you just fucked Faith, just getting a nut, and you couldn't believe a kid could come out of that. You had problems attaching feelings to fucking her."

"Why don't you shut the fuck up?" Cootie shot back. "You talk too damn much."

"To tell the truth, nobody gives a shit about black fathers anyway," Lotus said, tracing her slender thumb around the mouth of the bar glass. "Probably most of these girls have daddy issues. Some girls were abandoned by them or some seduced by them, but all of them are frustrated with their family situation."

"You should be a counselor or some shit," Guy said. "You have the lingo down. I bet all the girls go to you when they want advice."

"They do. I'm good at giving advice, but I need to take some myself."

"Did Sam—uh, Audrey—come to you for advice?"

"Yes, she did, Cootie. She said your wife hated you for getting busted—said you was no good. Said you was a bullshit nigger always trying to do a scam on somebody. Told her to not to trust black men, no way no how. Said your wife said anything was better than a nigger, or somebody black for a lover or a husband."

Cootie stared at her as if she had stabbed him in the chest. Right in the heart.

"Thank God you didn't have any sons," Guy wisecracked. "Shit, they would have been faggots for sure. They'd always have a dick in their asshole, trying to recover from the old lady cutting their nuts off. Faith was a serious ball-busting bitch, that's for sure."

When Cootie met the stripper's gaze, he was forced to look away, back at the drink in the glass. Statistics and white folks told him that the black family was in trouble, and that black women had taken over the head of the household. Nobody needed to listen to the black man because he was useless and obsolete. Black kids were out of control and crazed because their parents had failed—and failed miserably. And he, Cootie, had failed miserably by choosing a worthless, junkie wife; by fucking up and going to jail; by abandoning the responsibility of being a father.

"How old are you, Lotus?" Cootie asked.

"Twenty-three. In the prime of my life," the stripper said. "Why do you ask?"

"Faith was twenty-one when we got married, young and pretty, and willing to do anything that was necessary to keep our love alive," Cootie said, taking a drink. "Everything went fine until our first baby came. She became depressed and anxious when she first learned she was pregnant. The doctor told me he was giving her some pills, so that her mind wouldn't race; wouldn't see such horrible images. I had a helluva time getting her to take the pills, and she kept saying that she couldn't take care of the baby."

"Was she using drugs when she had Alicia?" Guy asked.

"Yeah, but the pregnancy had nothing to do with the drugs," Cootie replied. "No. The docs called what she had a *prenatal depression,* and said I had to watch her so she didn't do something to the baby, or try to abort. She kept saying she didn't feel like a mother and that she felt ashamed of having those feelings toward her pregnancy. We had to rush her to the hospital after she drank iodine. I yanked it out of her hand, or she would have taken a big gulp."

"Did it hurt the baby?" the stripper asked. "Iodine is poison."

"No. Thank God for that," Cootie said, holding up his glass after finishing the brew.

"I remember that, and we almost didn't get to the hospital in time," Guy said. "The traffic along 125th Street was incredible—bumper-to-bumper—and we had to zip down some side streets. Faith was fighting all the way. She was out of her head, said she wanted to kill the baby, and the baby would kill her if she didn't do away with it. Remember that, Cootie?"

Cootie leaned back, frowning. "Yes, I do. Faith was determined to kill the baby. She smoked and drank until she blacked out. Alicia was lucky to survive. Sometimes I wonder if the girls weren't affected by Faith's anxiety and depression. A doc I saw on TV said that babies of depressed mothers can grow up and be sad, lonely, and have panic disorders. So it could have affected the girls. I really believe that."

"Audrey said her mother was a sad person," Lotus said.

"And it was worse with Audrey. Remember, Guy?" Cootie asked. "I was so proud to be a father the second time. I guess I should have focused more on Faith's happiness, especially after the difficulties she had with Alicia. I should have concentrated less on below the waist, and more above the neck. I didn't see that Faith was slowly going crazy."

"Damn, she was a mess," Guy said. "She tried to get run over by a bus when she was carrying Audrey, in her seventh month. Remember that?"

"I don't understand why you didn't get Faith more help," Lotus said, wiping a lipstick smudge off the glass with a tissue.

"I know, Lotus. I felt guilty, but I didn't know how to help."

"Didn't she have any family? A mother, father, sisters or brothers? I don't know how you thought you would cure her by yourself. Did you think about signing her into a nuthouse before she did the baby harm?"

"No, I didn't, because I thought I could've helped her," Cootie said. "All of the signs were there: loss of appetite, lack of sleep, tiredness, feeling hopeless and helpless, thinking about dying and death, worrying about little things, and obsessing about the baby's health. And yet, she said she didn't want to take medication in her condition. She had taken pills before with Alicia, but it didn't help."

"I don't know why Audrey is so mad at you," Lotus said. "It seems you did the best you could under the circumstances."

He thought about how they fought with words, never with fists, but Faith always seemed to get the last lick in on him. Sometimes he couldn't talk or shout. Sometimes it seemed she wanted him to strike her—every nasty word or phrase was used to get him to release his anger. One thing his old man taught him was, the art of walking away before the situation could escalate.

"The girls won't forgive me for not being there during the lean years, when I was behind bars," Cootie said. "Faith, I guess, did her best. But it would have been better if I was there too. Audrey doesn't say anything about it, but Alicia reminds me that I was absent when they were growing up, and every Tom, Dick, and Harry was competing to replace me in bed. Faith was not good with men."

"On the streets, people respect and honor Cootie," Guy said, almost proudly. "Cootie knows the streets—everything about them."

"Still, the girls think I killed their mother, and they fault me for neglecting and abandoning them, when they needed me most," Cootie said. "They think I'm to blame for their mother being a junkie. They don't understand that she had a jones way before I was with her."

"Cootie, she is so furious at you," Lotus said. "She thinks you're a bastard."

There was an image that haunted Cootie, that of Faith holding both girls in her lap, stroking them, cooing to them, kissing their foreheads and hugging them against her breasts. She talked softly to them with their faces lovingly turned up to hers. Faith was crying—tears running hotly down her tan cheeks, sobbing as she fought to explain his absence to them. He was in jail for the first time. He would be released for lack of evidence, but the damage was done in terms of the girls.

"What was your relationship like with your mother, Cootie?" Lotus asked. "I'm curious. Did you like your mother?"

"She was all right. She was my mother, and I didn't think anything of it."

"Did you like your mother?"

"What do you mean? Do you mean, like a girlfriend, sexual?"

"No. Not sick like Oedipus, who married his mother, or Norman Bates, who wanted to fuck his mother and killed folks," Lotus said. "Did you like your mother as a person? The reason I asked is because I just wanted to know if you liked women. Your mother is the first woman a boy has as his own, and she can turn his world upside down."

"I never really thought about my mother as a woman or anything," Cootie said. "She was just my mother. I saw how she catered to my father; the way he used and abused her, and I often thought she should have left him. But then a lot of black men treat their women like shit. And the thing is, they take it without question."

"Is your mother dead?" Lotus asked.

"Yes, she is. I'd rather not talk about my mother. Okay?"

"I just asked, because your mother spent the most time with you, especially since Guy says your father was out of the house," Lotus said. "I know that a woman can't raise a boy into a man. And your father wasn't around, so I was wondering whether your mother gave you what you needed from her. Whether or not she taught you the things you needed to be a human being."

"Hey, what the fuck you trying to do with me?" Cootie shouted. "You're just a damn whore, and you're trying to take apart my life. What gives you the right to stick your fingers into my life? The fucking conversation is closed. You're getting too damn familiar."

Instantly, Guy and Lotus looked at each other as if she had pressed a button that endangered Cootie's soul. She wanted to speak, but decided not to. They drank their beers quietly and watched the patrons, and the TV airing the antique ball game. When they finished, they filed out of the beer joint, found the car, and started to get in.

"A woman said to hand this to you," an old man with dark glasses, a derby, and shabby clothes, said, handing a note to Lotus. "She said I was to put it into your hand. And that you would give me two bits."

Lotus placed a crumbled five into his palm and got into the car. "It's from Kelly. She knows where Audrey is. I know where this is if you want to go there."

But Cootie was exhausted. All he wanted to do was to go home and rest. He'd go to the address and find Audrey the next day. The thought that he could save her was evaporating, because he realized that she might not want to be rescued, and her current life might be all she needed.

SIXTEEN

That next afternoon, a dreary Sunday, the phone rang. Don, another cousin on his father's side, called to tell Cootie about the murder of Aunt Monie. He felt around for a chair to sit down—his legs shook badly. His aunt, an eighty-three-year-old woman, was walking to her local Baptist church when two young thugs robbed and beat her to death, after taking her purse. A few church members chased the assailants and held them until the cops arrived.

"Man, why would some young assholes rob and kill a nice old lady like that?" Don sobbed. "I don't get it. She always went to the church. My wife said she had the flu last week, so this was the first time she could go. How could anybody do this to her?"

Cootie was in a state of shock, his face ashen in grief. "These bastards are animals. She never hurt anybody. She was always trying to help. Probably if they would have asked for some money, she would have given it to them. She was like that."

"You know how much money she had?" Don was very angry over her death.

"What?" He knew she never kept any significant money in her pocketbook.

"She had ten dollars—ten fucking bucks," Don fumed. "Can you believe that?" He went on to say that the boys were going to be charged with second-degree murder, first-degree robbery, and criminal weapons possession.

Don was crying when he hung up.

But that was not the only call on that Sunday afternoon. Another one came from Momo, the boxer who was fighting some exhibitions at some Indian casino in Western Pennsylvania on Wednesday. He asked if Cootie would be at ringside.

"No, I can't," Cootie said. "My aunt was murdered."

"Oh shit," Momo said. "The one I met up in Harlem that time? The one who gave me the blackberry cobbler? I hope that wasn't the one, because I really liked her. She was so funny."

"Yes, that was her. The pie lady."

"How is the place holding up?" Momo asked.

"It's great. Thanks for providing a roof over my head. I'll get my own place once I get a job. My parole officer supposedly has some leads for me. I go back to him this week. He's a cool guy. Likes jazz."

Momo wanted to talk about more things than that. "The press wants me to score another sensational knockout in my next bout, but I'm totally distracted by everything that's happening to me now. The only time I ever go to a nightclub, and there's trouble. Some skank says I groped her, grabbed her ass on the dance floor. She filed a lawsuit, charging me with sexual harassment."

"Do you know this woman?"

"Hell no. I don't even know this bitch. Never met her before. Wouldn't know her if I saw her."

"What does your lawyer say?" Cootie asked.

Momo cleared his throat and emitted a low groan. "My mouthpiece, Guttman, says it'll blow over; for me to not to worry about it. After all, I'm not like Tyson or some of these other guys. I'm happily married with kids. My lawyer also says he knows you from the old days. Do you know Stephen Hurt?"

159

"Yeah, I do. That's the cat who got me out. He knows his stuff."

"So anyway, Guttman says she went to the papers, hoping to blow this thing up all out of proportion, so she could get some big bucks. The bitch wants green. She'll lie, cheat, and steal to get it. I work hard for my money, and I'm not going to give it away."

"I agree with your lawyer," Cootie replied. "If you never saw this woman before, then you wouldn't have to fight this scam artist. She's just hoping to raise some stink, then you'll have to pay. I guess she figures if you get a little dirt on your reputation, then you'll fold into her blackmail. When did all of this break into the news? I must have missed it."

"The day before yesterday." The boxer paused, then continued, "The bitch is now telling the press that she's getting death threats, that she's afraid for her family. Even my manager Tommy, says she just wants to get some notoriety. She's a gold digger. Everybody knows that I've never done anything like this."

"Does she have any witnesses?"

"She says she does. Some bogus friends of hers. Even her sister told the reporters she was full of shit. Said all her sister wanted was money and that she'd do anything for it. The woman's a bitch if there ever was one. And I'm not going to let her rip me off."

Cootie walked to the window and watched a group of kids riding their bikes in the dwindling sunlight. "I wouldn't let this bother me. You got the fight to think about, and you can't afford to fuck that up. You've got to be sharp. You don't want to mess up a big payday."

"You sound like Tommy," the boxer said. "All he talks about is the fight and how I have to stay focused. He keeps lecturing me on how I can't let anything get in the way of that."

"He's right. Listen to him."

Momo chuckled. "You're an all right brother. Anything I can do for you? I know you're still looking for your daughter. Any new leads?"

"Something, but it might not pan out. Who knows?"

"Coming to the fight? I'll send a car for you, and you can ride down with my wife on the jet, if that's cool with you."

Cootie was watching two brothers hawking counterfeit CDs and DVDs out of a garbage bag. "I'll be there. By the way, whatever happened with the feud between the managers?"

There was a strange silence on the other end of the line, then the fighter spoke slowly and deliberately, as if talking to a child. "Yeah, they're still trying to put the screws into me about that. I keep telling them no dice, but they're getting nasty. We can talk more about this at my party on Saturday. Coming?"

Cootie didn't press the issue. "Hey, that's cool with me. See you on the weekend. Take care of yourself. Say hello to Guttman for me."

After the call, Cootie ran some bath water, poured himself a glass of scotch, and slipped in a video, *Independence Day*. He could never finish the damn thing. It reminded him of the old 1950s outer-space invasion flicks, the black-and-white duds, except the classic 1951 *The Day the Earth Stood Still* with Patricia Neal and Michael Rennie. He loved that movie when he first saw it in the theater, and still loved it.

"Klaatu Barada Nikto," he said, laughing. There was one other thing. He had nothing against Will Smith, the Fresh Prince, but he was rooting for the hostile aliens against the earthlings.

He dozed off in the chair, arms going limp, spilling his drink onto the floor. *His father pulled him up by his ear, yelling for lying. The boy doesn't talk much, but when he does, he often lies. His father, a towering shadow, shouted he doesn't know whether to trust what he says. Maybe he doesn't know the difference between a lie and the truth. The boy cowered between the sofa and the wall, tired, but fighting sleep. He can see his mother has a slip on, and he can see the form of her body in it. She plunked him out of his hiding place, hummed a tune to him, and placed him on the bed, fast asleep. The boy heard himself ask the woman: "How do I pay you?" The woman slapped him. "You don't owe me a fucking thing." The boy, with his eyes closed, explained to her, "You fed me. You were kind when I needed kindness. Please let me pay you."*

With his arm turned under his body, he shook the flesh, which felt like it had a swarm of stinging wasps inside it. He tried to get comfortable, draping his arm over the chair. *The boy said to the woman, "You is one pretty woman. I don't see how a man could not treat you right." She watched the man, his father, take off his shirt and fold up his clothes after he washed up in the sink down the hall. Times were hard then, before he turned to a life of crime. Hunger made men into wolves. She turned off the light after checking on the boy. The man carried the boy to the couch and returned to the woman on the bed, where they thrashed around under the covers and sang songs of lust.*

Still, he savored his dream, wrapped his dream around his body like a comforter. *Once when the boy was in a school play in the role of a drunk, he prayed for his family to come, but neither parent attended the production. They had no excuse since they were not working. Only Aunt Monie came. She clapped loud enough to shake the rafters, and shouted her approval every time the boy came on stage. His sister understood his parents' lackluster attitude toward them—their children, their kids—because in them, they saw their own decay. One thing he learned from his sister was the need for magic, sorcery, and myth in one's life. She forever made things up. She created worlds. She conjured every event with a supernatural bond, taking her themes and plots from bits of conversation heard from the street. The ordinary events. The stars lied to them, hinting that so much more awaited them than the loss, suffering, and pain accumulated with each passing breath. None of them under that roof were fully human. It was the first truth they accepted about themselves.*

A knock sounded against the door leading to the hall. He stirred from his sleep full of images and visions, and concentrated on the thump. There it was again. He crept toward the door, but then turned and retrieved his gun. Finally, he looked out through the peephole cautiously, carefully. Nothing and nobody. He held the gun at his side as he turned the knob, pulled back, and opened the door, revealing a gift-wrapped box.

"What the hell? . . ." he said, walking with the box to the kitchen table.

The phone rang once again. He decided that the phone was designed to worry man to death, a messenger of bad news and grief. Nothing good or positive was ever transmitted over the hellish instrument.

"Hello. Lotus speaking. Did you get the gift?" She was probably calling him from the street.

Cootie smiled, thinking of the outlandish outfit the stripper wore that night. "I just got it. I haven't opened it. But I'm unwrapping it . . . right now."

He fumbled with the box while he was trying to balance the phone against his ear. Man, he could be clumsy. The old man said he was not a thief who could use his hands, for they had no poetry in them; instead, he had to use his mind. The receiver went crashing down on the wooden floor, and skidded along it until it landed between the icebox and oven. When he reached for it, it clicked off, but it rang again.

"This is Nathaniel Gangi, an officer for the New York Division of Parole," the man said with a light, musical voice. "I'd like to speak to Mr. Chambers. Is this he?"

"Yes, this is him. What do you want?"

The man spoke in warm, pleasant tones, like he was trying to sell Cootie surplus land on the moon. "You didn't keep your appointment with me. I have to maintain constant supervision over your case. If you don't cooperate with me, you know where you will end up. We don't want that, do we?"

"No, sir." He tried to sound submissive and humble. All of his time was consumed with the search for Audrey. It seemed nothing else mattered to him.

"We did you a favor by letting you out," Mr. Gangi said. "We could have let you rot inside there. You're a fucking criminal. Don't try to get cute."

"I'm not, sir. When do you want to see me?"

"The day after tomorrow. One sharp, Mr. Chambers. Is that clear?"

"Yes, Mr. Gangi," Cootie said, placing the receiver down. He squatted against the wall, staring at his trembling hands out in front of him. Damn them. All he wanted to do was live; live his life his own way.

His foot hit the phone, knocking the receiver off the hook. A female voice. It was the sweet, seductive voice of Lotus. He guessed she'd been talking all the time while he was gabbing with the parole officer, getting his nose rubbed in shit—holding out his wrists for the chains and bondage.

"I was saying I liked you from the first time I saw you," Lotus said. "I like tall, skinny guys with big lips and good cheekbones, long arms and narrow asses. Big men are a turn-off. I've had plenty of those, who all want to paw me. Plus, I like that you're quiet and sorta peaceful. Unlike your Mr. Chatty friend."

"What's in the box?" Cootie asked.

"Open it and see. It won't bite you."

He removed the red ribbon and unwrapped the box, exposing an expensive layer of gauzy tissue paper with gold trim. He held a small brown teddy bear with a white T-shirt with the words: COOTIE BEAR and a smoochy pair of lips.

"Like it?" Lotus asked. "It was a spur-of-the moment thing."

"Why?" Cootie held up the bear, examining it to get some manner of symbolism. Women were totally a mystery to him. Why would she do this?

"Maybe I bought it because I was impressed about your concern about your daughter," she said. "My father was never that concerned about me. You really care. I know your friend wouldn't be as concerned. He was trying to get fucked all night. All he was concerned about was pussy, and getting his dick wet. But not you."

"Guy's okay," Cootie said. "I think you misjudged him."

"I don't think so. His fly was unzipped all night. Two of the girls said he wanted to fuck them on the floor; said he'd give them a big tip if they would go down on him. He acted like a pervert. I don't like guys like that. You just played it cool."

He didn't say anything about offering himself to the girl in the booth. He was as guilty in his actions as Guy. Possibly Guy was more obvious. Some men go all to pieces when sex and lust are introduced into the mix.

"Do you still want to find your daughter?" she asked.

"Yes, but I've had a shitty day," he replied. "I'm going to chill out now. Tomorrow I'll resume my search. I need my rest. The phone has been ringing off the hook."

Lotus was breathing hard. He wondered what she was doing. "We're going to be friends. I can tell. And you need friends. Everybody needs friends."

"I guess so. I wouldn't mind having you as a friend."

"By the way, Kelly sends her love," she said. "She has a crush on you. I had to tell her that it was hands off. I saw you first. The girl's greedy."

"What is this Kelly like?" He just liked to hear Lotus talk.

"Kelly's a spoiled brat. She's from a rich family. Her father's a big-time criminal lawyer. He ran for the Manhattan Borough President once upon a time, but he was defeated. Kelly's cute and stacked. She loves to fuck. She loves getting her kicks. Kelly loves to get high. That's where Mitch comes in. Mitch furnishes Kelly with her highs, so she stays with him and fucks whoever he wishes to be fucked."

"Lotus, what's her drug of choice?"

"Coke and crystal meth—fuck drugs," she said. "When she gets up on that shit, she can fuck five to ten guys a night. She's like a bitch in heat. I don't fuck with meth. That shit can make you act stupid. You don't know what you're doing. You just want to fuck."

"This damn Mitch is a virus, isn't he?"

"I dunno. But getting back to Kelly, she's married, but separated. Her hubby neglects her as all significant others do. She needs somebody to dote on her twenty-four/seven, so that's where Mitch comes in. He knows she's a total freak, so he fulfills her needs."

"What does her husband do?" Cootie asked.

"Real estate; married him for his money," she answered. "He's Cuban."

Cootie didn't remember how Kelly had seen him, but she had. "Her old man must give her a blank check as she wishes. I know men like that. Rich guys with trophy wives. But the Cuban must be pissed with her running around with Mitch. That bastard will use her up to nothing."

"Kelly loves excitement," she said. "Gals love cash and kink. You know that."

"Do you have a man?"

"I did have one once. But it ended. He was crueler and meaner than Hitler, Genghis Khan, and De Sade combined. Much more evil than Mitch. I was in love with him. I did anything for him. Since I met him, there has never been any other man for me."

"What did he do? Business, politics, entertainment, or crime?"

"I never knew what he did," Lotus said. "He was very yellow, tall, muscular, and smooth skinned. A Korean man from old money. He had the most remarkable dick I've seen. That thing he could have tied around his ankle. When he met me, he told me that he had plenty of bitches, and that I would have to wait in line. I was furious. But once he touched me, I thought I would die from desire. He fucked me from sunset to sunrise. I thought I had died and gone to heaven."

"Do I know him?"

"I doubt it. His name is not significant, but the important thing is that he exists. I wouldn't give you his name, even if we were good friends. He loves to give pleasure to women. That's what he lives for. He lives by the power of his dick."

"As do most men," Cootie said, scowling. "Why did he leave?"

"He got arrested and convicted of sexing some young girls," she said. "The guy loved to see himself on video.

The cops caught him with pubescent girls, advertised as barely legal, but not quite. Also, he got addicted to amphetamines."

"Have you been married?" he asked.

"No—well maybe. I was for a minute to this bean counter for The World Bank," she replied. "But he wasn't important. Just a footnote."

"Damn. A footnote, huh?"

"We got our marriage erased because it was a joke," she said. "We got drunk on rum. Went to the church and asked the pastor to marry us. He did it, and then we spent a honeymoon pissed out of our minds. When we sobered up, we knew it was a mistake. After that, I almost married a Trinidadian, a cameraman. Trinny men are nuts. They're really strict with their women, but they love to screw around—like most West Indian men. This Trinny guy had all kinds of kids by outside women. He wanted me to live with him, but he told me that he was very jealous, and that he would kill me if he ever thought I was sleeping with another man."

Cootie sniggered at the jealousy bit. "Guy's father is Haitian. They don't go for that kind of thing either. If a woman slept around, they would kill her."

"Do you believe in love?"

"I don't know. I thought I believed in love with Faith. But then we started having all kinds of trouble. Love can be a dreadful thing. Sometimes you can care too much. I tried to rescue her, but I couldn't. Something died in me when I lost her. I probably haven't gotten over it yet. I don't know. What do you think about love?"

"I don't trust it," she said. "Sometimes I get it confused with sex."

"Men never do," he said. "If they do, they're fools. Pussy is pussy, and love is love. And never the twain shall meet."

They laughed. "If more women felt that way, the marriage rate would plummet," she remarked. "If a man lays some good pipe, puts some good dick on a woman, she will follow him anywhere. Our bodies betray us all the time."

"I think I got married too young," he said.

"What happened?"

"Faith told me that she thought she was knocked up, and said I should marry her," he said. "Plus, I was afraid of her father. Abortions weren't that available like now. I didn't want to send her to some butcher. I saw what my cousins went through with the clothes hangers and the knitting needles. Both of those girls almost bled to death, and were later sterile. They couldn't have kids, and that fucked up their lives."

"What did your parents say?" she asked.

"My old man told me to be a man, but my mother said Faith was a whore just trying to land the first man who came along," he replied. "One day, I was driving my old man's Bonneville, and Faith's pop cut me off and pulled a gun on me. He dragged me from the car and put the gun to my head and said I would marry her, or the next time I wouldn't be so lucky. Do you know what my father said when I told him?"

"What?" Lotus loved he was opening to her. Telling her all the dirt.

"He said that it served me right. He had a strange code. For him, he said Faith's father had every right to do that, because he had raised the girl right, and to be a whore for some guy. But he was a damn pimp. Still, when we got hitched, he was always trying to get her alone, trying to get her liquored up so he could fuck her."

"Guy said she was a junkie," she said. "Heroin, right?"

"Yes. That's why the girls ended up like they did. If she had been a good mother to them, they would have had a decent life. Well, Alicia is all right, but Audrey is just out there, doing everything under the sun. Smoking rock and fucking everything that moves."

"We'll find her. I guarantee you that."

"I hope so," he said, sighing from the weariness he felt.

"I should tell you something," she said. "I'm built very small. Very tight."

"Oh, down there. I'm not a pounder sexually. I wouldn't hurt you. I'm tender and gentle. I go slow. I take my time."

"Guy said you wanted me," she said. "He said he could tell just by the way you stared at me. I'm very picky. Mitch had me, and I bled for a week. He was proud of it. If I let you, you better take care of me and make me very wet. I'm very attracted to you. Don't disappoint me."

"When do you want to come over?"

"I dunno. I'm still debating. Maybe after we go out searching for Audrey tomorrow. Maybe after that. Maybe I'll fix you dinner. Maybe I'll have a little party. How would you like that?"

"Sounds like a plan," he said, chuckling. "Hey, I've got to go and make some calls. Take care."

What Cootie did was to go by the church where Aunt Monie was robbed and beaten to death. He stood in the cold and saw the bloody ground marked by yards of yellow crime-scene tape, imagining her battered corpse laying there. He wondered how her children were told by the police, who stared at the body, inspected it, and rolled it over before placing the dead flesh onto a gurney for the coroner. He wondered how many lives were touched by this senseless killing. He wondered how something like this could have happened. He suddenly felt dizzy. Then the old pain of his wounds came in a tidal wave of sensation, and his legs almost went out from beneath him.

SEVENTEEN

"Mr. Gangi's expecting me," Cootie said dryly to the guards at the security desk. "Mr. Chambers for the one o'clock sharp appointment with the officer. He said I had to be on time." The brick building was located on West 127th Street and Lexington Avenue, with a continual parade of law breakers and lawmen.

Inside, three parole officers gabbed with the guy behind the desk about their bullet-proof vests and their smugness: the stopping power of the .38 revolver against the gatling gun spray of the heavy-duty assault rifles, and the mental chess game between the officer and ex-con. They complained about their sixty-client caseload, which strained the workweek and frayed the raw nerves of the law officers.

"I'm sick of the forty thousand parolees who clog up the correctional system—a bunch of sick fucks and violent animals," a parole officer said. "I'm tired of rapists, robbers, alkies with emotional woes, murderers, child molesters, sickly cons with the virus, and scam artists. Mickey said I'm going up the pay scale to unit supervisor."

"Mickey ain't giving up raises or bonuses to a bogus city clerk like you," another officer replied. "You should go back to welfare as a caseworker, or a maintenance man at the city zoo. It's the same brand of animal."

Cootie stood before the desk, raising his voice to the man. "I really can't be late. Can you ring him up? I don't want to get him pissed."

"Officer Ham will escort you to his office," the guy behind the desk said.

The officer, with Cootie in tow, walked through one electronic door after another, until they entered a long corridor with a series of offices. Once the man arrived at a certain office, he knocked on the door, heard a loud shout to come in, and waved the ex-con through the entrance to a seat.

"Mr. Chambers, signed, sealed and delivered," Officer Ham joked. "Oh yes, he says to tell you that he was not late, that he arrived at one sharp. He thought you should know that."

It was the usual office: two desks, stacks and stacks of folders, and four rows of file cabinets. A portrait of the state's governor, looking dull and moronic, as he sat for the camera like a mug shot. There were news articles stapled to a bulletin board, announcing captures or escapes.

"Punctual, eh," Mr. Gangi said to an average-looking white woman, blond, with thick glasses. "Sit down, Mr. Chambers. Just don't stand there like a fool."

Cootie found a seat on a wooden bench running along a wall near the door. After he folded his coat across his legs, he sat back, watching the two parole officers—a couple of pale people. Mr. Gangi discussed something about a case to his assistant, the woman who seemed startled by the contents of the file.

"This is Mrs. Walters, my assistant," Mr. Gangi said. "Meet Mr. Chambers, who needs very little supervision. He is determined not to become one of these hardened felons on our roster. Lockup didn't agree with him."

The ex-con stood and shook hands with the woman, said hello. He was old school, meaning: polite, courteous, and pleasant. When he would run scams, the victims who later testified in court would all comment that he seemed like such a nice man.

173

"You know the drill, so this is nothing new to you," Mr. Gangi said. "We're running a little behind schedule. We're going to have to take you with us so we can make our surprise visits. Some of these guys need to be reminded that the long arm of the law sees all and knows all."

Mrs. Walters, dressed in a black business jacket and jeans, adjusted her glasses. "Is that all right, Mr. Chambers? You don't have to be anywhere, do you?"

"No. I can go anywhere you want." Cootie knew the last person an ex-con should aggravate is a parole officer. He smiled and went along for the ride.

They went through the maze of hallways to an underground garage where their late-model Plymouth sedan, federal issue, was parked. It had a small antenna for wireless communication. Mr. Gangi told Cootie that the unannounced home visits would take them across Harlem, Washington Heights, and Manhattan's Upper West Side. With a warm antiseptic smile, Mrs. Walters opened the door for the parolee and asked him if he was comfortable. He nodded.

Under way, the dark sedan sped off through the afternoon traffic. Mr. Gangi asked Cootie how he was doing, and if he had any job prospects yet.

"I'm getting along all right," Cootie answered. "I've got a few job options."

"You'll keep me posted," Mr. Gangi said. "I hope you're not hanging out with your old crowd. You know that would be a parole violation."

"I know that. I'm trying to lead a decent life."

The woman was quiet, but Mr. Gangi continued to talk. "Even in the afternoon, we won't find all of the parolees. Often they change addresses. Sometimes they give a fake address so they can get out of prison. They're real slick. That's why we don't like to call. It's easier to run up on them and catch them with their pants down—so to speak."

"Why do you carry the guns?" Cootie asked.

"You know why," Mr. Gangi said. "In the eight years on the job, I've not had to be involved in a gun battle, but I've often had to pull it out to get the jump on these guys. Especially if you have to make a hit—you know, pick up a violator. Frequently, we have to go in with the cops as backup, if things got crazy."

Mrs. Walters grinned. "Remember that shooting gallery in East Harlem? That was spooky. No lights. A pack of pit bulls snarling at our legs. A gun-happy Latina girl gang running the joint. One of them fired at us. The cop with us punched her clock, and that was it. But that was hairy. Still, we got our man."

"Did you carry a gun in your line of work, Mr. Chambers?" Mr. Gangi asked him.

"No. I figured if I had one, I would be tempted to use it."

"Smart," Mrs. Walters said. "You never want to get a murder rap."

The sedan halted in front of a shabby brownstone, with a group of young teens smoking cigarettes and drinking forties on the stoop. None older than fifteen. Checking their vests, the officers exited the car and trotted into the entrance, parting the crew like a propeller, churning through still water. They stayed in the building for half an hour, and were laughing as they descended the steps.

"Did you see him looking at your ass?" Mr. Gangi laughed until he turned red in the face. "When these cons get out of lockup, often they don't care anything about romance, but when he said he loved you, I thought I would die."

The woman chuckled, then scowled. "I wouldn't touch him with a garbage man's filthy glove."

Sliding inside behind the wheel, the officer in charge turned the key to start the engine. "That parolee's father called us to turn him in, but the young man wasn't home," Mr. Gangi said. "The father just said, 'Come and get him.' But he didn't want to let the boy know he ratted on him. He has the boy all packed. The boy is shooting up. You just hope the boy won't get violent. Probably he'll struggle with the cops when the handcuffs go on, but nothing more."

"What happens if they hit you?" Cootie knew what would happen, but he wanted to hear them say it.

Mrs. Walters made a sour face. "If he hits you, you can charge them with assault. You can't fuck around with them. I had this one woman attack me, slapped me and then tried to rip my hair out. She was high on reds. I busted her one in the face with my gun butt, and got her together real quick."

Cootie sized up this dame. She could probably take care of herself.

"Damn right," Mr. Gangi said, pulling up to a red light.

"If an ex-con senses a weakness in you, you're fucked," Mrs. Walters added, jotting a few notes on a pad. "You can't come across as a pushover. A sissy. They'll walk all over you. Some try to be clever and cry. I tell them the tears don't mean a damn thing to me. Crying doesn't move me. Being a parole officer is no bed of roses. You've got to be on your toes out there, because your life's at stake."

Mr. Gangi agreed. "Yep. Anything can happen."

"Wait out here," Mrs. Walters said. "We'll be right out."

Again on the road in Washington Heights, they went in a pre-war building with a doorman, on Broadway next to a Chinese restaurant. The building seemed fairly prosperous, not one that would house a low-life felon. This time they took about fifteen minutes.

"I like him," Mrs. Walters said as she got into the car. "I think he's learned his lesson, but I think we should send somebody around to check on his ankle bracelet. He says the thing is acting up, not doing the right thing with his transmitter."

Mr. Gangi explained the visit was to a lifer who got out early. "He really seems like prison shook him up. When you do a long stretch, you know how to not get back in there again. He's committed to going straight. Contrary to the other lifer we're visiting tomorrow, this joker has been in prison a few times, knows how to manipulate the system. This guy is a powder keg. He's slipped through the cracks and is waiting to do something violent. I feel it. We have to watch him real closely."

"We don't have to watch you closely, Mr. Chambers," Mrs. Walters said. "Or do we? You're not going to make trouble for us, are you?"

"No, I'm not."

"The fact of the matter is that you have too many convicts, and not enough officers to watch them," Mr. Gangi said. "Regardless of how closely you watch them, you can't predict behavior. Sometimes there's nothing in the record to indicate a potential problem for trouble. Remember the guy, the son of the state senator who had been convicted of a rape, a one-time thing? On the streets, he seemed an excellent risk, a very good parolee. That was all a scam. He was arrested three weeks ago for eight brutal rapes of old women, where he used objects to rape them vaginally. How do you foresee that? How do you get inside their heads and know what they're thinking?"

"They're animals," Mrs. Walters said. "But not you, right?"

"Yes, right." Cootie didn't want to give them any cause for concern.

"I think you're a very good risk," Mr. Gangi said.

"My boss thinks you're a very good parolee, and won't land back in the lockup," Mrs. Walters added. "It was his idea to let you go along for our little ride."

"We're always on the lookout for high-risk offenders," her boss said. "It's not foolproof. We get surprises sometimes. You might be a surprise. Who knows? See, we've had hard-core cases where they were just waiting to get out and go back to their old lives of crimes. Nothing can reach them. They're completely rotten. Mean and violent. Some say never let them out. But you can't do that."

"I'll ask you again, you're not getting back with your old buddies?" Mrs. Walters asked Cootie. "You're not going to screw up your one chance. Are you?"

"I promise I won't," Cootie said softly.

On the border of Harlem and the Bronx, they visited a mother-and-daughter team, out on parole after serving time for a murder. Mrs. Walters argued with her boss that she didn't like the look of them, that they were doing something criminal, but she couldn't put her finger on it. They entered the apartment, where they stayed for almost an hour.

"I think they're whores," Mrs. Walters suggested when they were in the car. "They're definitely selling their bodies. Did you see that apartment? All that expensive furniture, the large-screen TV, and the rows of CDs? And the outfits—the designer outfits? de la Renta and Dior? We've got to watch them. Something's up."

"You're right," Mr. Gangi said, flashing a grin. "Times are bad. It's especially bad for an ex-con because the economy is flat. The jobs aren't there. We know prison can't rehabilitate people. Prison removes the bad people from society. It contains them. Justice works best when it can restore people by returning them to the community, and working with them to integrate into society."

"So when will you get a job?" Mrs. Walters asked Cootie.

"Over fifty percent of people go back to prison at some point," her boss said. "Most people who violate will do so in the first five months. We watch them the closest during that first year. There are those who won't make it. Either they're ready to change or they go back to their old life. Which one will you choose, Mr. Chambers?"

"What do you think?" Cootie said. "I want to go straight."

"So when will you get a job?" Mrs. Walters asked again.

"In a couple of weeks," the parolee replied. "Is that all right?"

"No, it's not," Mr. Gangi said. "You must have a job by next Wednesday. That's final. You've had enough time to find work. We can't carry you any longer. Either you work or you go back to prison. Do you understand that, Mr. Chambers?"

"Yes, sir." He looked at both of them like the vultures they were.

The dark sedan pulled over at the next light, and the woman officer opened the door and said get out. The parolee was surprised, but obeyed, for they were the law. Nobody disobeyed the law, not if they wanted to breathe fresh air.

EIGHTEEN

The call from Lotus didn't come. He waited for it, anticipating the excitement of someone who could talk with him, and understand what it was to be inside prison walls. He tried to see what she'd seen in his face, his eyes, and his tall, lean body. When the call didn't come, he phoned the boxer, who didn't forget his promise to get a ringside seat to one of the exhibitions.

Faithful to his word, Momo assured Cootie got the royal treatment with a window seat on the new Lear jet, purchased from the purse of his top-ranked bout. Everyone on the jet was in high spirits: drinking, singing, and partying. Guttman and Cootie talked about the pending legal battle with the woman from the Harlem club, the sexual harassment rap, and its negative effect on the boxer's concentration.

"He has got to get his head on straight," Guttman said. "The title fight is the only thing he should be thinking of. If he's distracted with all of this ruckus, he'll get knocked out and lose."

"Well, we'll see," Cootie said. "We'll see how he does tonight."

The jet circled above a small airport, dipped a wing, then plunged through the clouds to glide into a perfect landing on the runway. The guests disembarked in the chill and met the limo driver, who sped them through the night to the exhibition at the old Norton Auditorium in Hallanville, Pennsylvania. Momo's management scheduled one more exhibition at an Indian casino in the western part of the state, and another one in northern

New York. He had to keep fighting so he could stave off ring rust.

In the dressing room, Cootie shook the boxer's hand and whispered good luck into his ear, then he was led through the crowd to his seat. There were two preliminary bouts; one quite lousy with a sudden first-round KO, and the other a barn-burner with the fighters slugging toe-to-toe for three brutal rounds, until one punch fell flush on the opposing boxer's face. The crowd, thirsty for action, ate it up and roared its approval.

"Who's this bum that the kid's fighting tonight?" some guy asked Cootie.

"I don't know." Cootie shrugged.

The gent on his left went into a full spiel about the boxer's Italian opponent. Milo Livoni. Big guy from Rome, thirty wins with twenty-two by KO. Five losses, but all to name-brand fighters. Tricky, solid chin, a vicious left and a sneaky right. Cootie wondered why the boxer would want such a tough fight just before going against the champ. It was a big risk.

"T'anks, Mac," the first guy said and filled his mouth with popcorn.

Cootie knew Momo was ready for this opponent, because he had been training for five months, sparing over two hundred rounds to meet the champ. However, he was amazed at the arrogance of the boxer with his deeply held belief that no one could beat him. But this wasn't going to be a safe fight, even if it was an exhibition. He could get hurt. He could get beat or even knocked down.

"I'm at peace mentally and spiritually," the boxer told reporters gathered on the lawn of his new home in Miami. It was only one of three homes in this country—Miami, Las Vegas, and suburban New York. "All of my demons of my past are behind me."

"That's a lie," said Guttman, who knew Momo as well as his mother.

When the bell rang, Momo walked slowly to the center of the ring, while Livoni moved out toward him with determined steps. Livoni jabbed twice, a preventive measure, and stepped away. Momo lunged forward and swung a strong right hook at the square face of the Italian. It caught Livoni flush on the face, but did not move him. The boy was tough.

With the start of the second round, the Italian tried walking through the boxer's punches, started hooking to the body. The burly foreigner bulled him into a corner where he pounded on the black boxer's ribs and arms. Sidestepping the assault, Momo unleashed a swarm of blows at the Italian, some landing solidly before an elbow from Livoni almost knocked his mouthpiece out. It dazed him for a moment. The crowd stomped its feet to boost the action. They wanted blood, so Livoni rushed the boxer, pinning him to the ropes again, where he smashed a hard blow into the boxer's privates. A chorus of boos went up. Momo, wincing, complained to the referee, who ignored him.

"Maybe this was not a good idea," Momo's trainer said.

Before the end of the round, Livoni hit him four more times below the belt. Sending volts of searing pain up Momo's spine and down his legs. The strategy behind low blows was to sap your opponent's strength. Even though the protective cup would take some of the power of the punch away, it would not stop the pain. The burning, numbing pain.

Between rounds, Momo's trainer yelled at the ref about the ongoing low blows, "That Dago bastard keeps hitting my boy dirty. I'm sick of this shit. Do your job."

The bell rang for the third round. Livoni rushed Momo again, swinging a looping right, followed by another wild punch. The crowd cheered his aggression. The second punch scored a direct hit on the side of Momo's face, rocking him again. But he showed heart and went on the offensive. He threw a series of five-punch combinations—left-right-left-right-left, *pop-pop-pop-pop-pop*. The guy, frustrated, tried to butt him but Momo pushed him off and split the tender skin above the Italian's right eye with a hook. Then he moved to his right and uncorked a savage left that spun the Italian's head almost completely around. The Italian fell against the ropes and Momo pursued him, throwing a vicious left-right combination to the guy's chin.

Livoni wobbled and punched him again in the cup, low blow once more, and took another chopping hand that rattled his teeth. The Italian retaliated by hitting him so cleanly, so precisely, in the privates. He bitched to the ref again, "Come on, do something." The ref responded by taking away a point from Livoni, who nodded politely that he was sorry.

In the fourth round, the crowd could see the Italian talking to the boxer during the clinches. Saying foul things, disgusting things. "Is that all you got, nigger?" "My sister hits harder than you, nigger." "You take it up the ass, nigger." When the ref separated them, Momo scowled and looked closely at the large square face of his foe, his broken nose, and the ribbon of blood flowing down from the cut over the eye. The cut was deep, and the guy's corner had not been able to stop the flow.

The Italian was desperate now because the blood was coming from the cut in a gush of red. It affected his vision, and he knew the ref would stop the fight unless he did something dramatic soon. He decided to force the fight, pushing Momo into the ropes again. He threw everything he had at the muscular black man. The roars of the crowd shook the building as Livoni caught him coming off the ropes with a punch that lifted the boxer off the canvas. The Italian charged him again, but Momo stayed away, piling up points with jabs and hooks. Momo was a master counter-puncher, so he made the foreigner pay for every mistake. Every time the man rushed him, Momo would hook him to the body or shoot a quick one to the head. Then there were the low blows that were coming with more regularity. Hard, sharp, intentional low blows.

"I told you that the Italian was real powerful," the man to his left said.

"Have faith. Have faith, baby," Cootie said.

The ref pushed them apart. When the ref stepped back, Momo ran to the Italian, crouched, and uppercutted him savagely between the legs. Livoni howled and grabbed himself. He was in terrific pain. The ref asked him if he needed a break, but being all macho, Livoni declined and moved gingerly toward the smiling boxer.

"This is like a title fight, not like an exhibition," the man to his left said.

"Bullshit," Cootie said. "Momo wouldn't be fucking around if it was a title fight. He would be trying to knock the block off this honky."

The boxer waited for his guard to drop. He swung twice at the guy's head, but the Italian made him seem clumsy with his evasive tactics. Momo finally caught him, and staggered him with a tremendous right-cross that could be heard in the back of the hall. Then he landed a crisp left to the cheekbone of Livoni, and a mean-spirited right to the top of the Italian's head. Now he crooked Livoni into the ropes and punched in bunches, every blow thrown with bad intentions.

Bloody and battered, the Italian would later tell reporters that Momo was growling at him like an animal—like a Doberman—as he launched his final assault. Livoni tried in vain to tie the boxer up with his arms; tried to make him miss, but every punch from the black man found their target. Another right to the temple, another left to the ribs. Livoni now understood how quick the black man was with his hands, and each punch hurt worse than the one before it. The crowd sensed a kill and yelled for a merciless finish. Livoni tried to fight back, but Momo ducked into a crouch, and the punches sailed over the black man's head. Blood covered the Italian's pale face when he backpedaled to avoid more punishment, with the ref following, watching closely for a stoppage.

Finally, the two fighters came together in a last slugfest, trading punches at a furious pace, with the swifter black man getting the best of the exchanges. The Italian fouled him again, but Momo made the guy pay with a shot that made the crowd gasp. Livoni was going down as Momo hit him three times in the face with various hooks, before he fell and bounced on his side. The ref started the count, and the Italian crawled to the ropes and tried to pull himself up. He was on his feet, staggering on spaghetti legs, and his opponent ran toward him. The ref stepped between them and waved his hands. It was all over. The fight was over.

The bruised Livoni pitched forward and toppled on his mangled face, sending a spray of blood out into the front rows. The guy's handlers rushed into the ring, kneeling next to the unconscious pug. While the doctor worked on the fallen guy, the first of several chairs flew into the ring, and fights broke out in the hall. Members of both fighters' crew struggled along the ring apron, and a photographer was hit and thrown bodily, into the crowd. Some injured fans were trampled during the melee, and robbed, and two security guards were beaten with their own nightsticks.

The mayhem lasted for thirty minutes before a wave of policemen moved in to clear out the hall, arresting the troublemakers and assisting the wounded.

In the post-fight interview, Livoni, who suddenly forgot his English, used a translator to say:

"The referee stopped it early. I could have beaten him. The black boy hit me dirty, so I hit him dirty. He doesn't hit hard. He stunned me, but I was never hurt. He never knocked me down."

The announcer showed him the video replay: the punch distorting his Roman face, his body going limp and falling to the canvas. Livoni grunted and walked away. He yelled, "He hit me with a punch I did not see. A sucker punch."

"This exhibition was like one of the bloody Philly boxing gym wars," the man on his left said. "Neither man wanted to give an inch. Sometimes boxers of quality would leave these gyms worse for wear. Did you think about that happening?"

"Not really," Momo said. "I needed a tune-up. I know the champ's going to be a real hard case. It's going to be a matter of survival."

"What about the Italian throwing low blows?"

Momo smiled. "The rules say protect yourself at all times."

The boxer raised his wrapped fist in a thumbs-up gesture of victory, when he saw Cootie enter the dressing room.

"No, I was not pleased with my performance tonight," Momo replied to a question from a reporter. "The long layoff hurt me some. I did not execute my game plan when I slugged it out with him, rather than, outboxed him. Truthfully, Livoni was tougher than I thought he would be. But I'm ready for the champ. He has my belt, and I want it."

His manager stepped into the crowd, earning a groan from the reporters, and grabbed Momo and told them all interviews were concluded. Everybody out. Cootie started to leave, but Momo asked him to stay. Cootie stood near the door as the boxer sat on the table and let his trainer undo the wrapping on his hands. He was surprised at the scarring on the boxer's hands, the swollen knuckles and twisted thumbs.

Later in a limo, en route to the airport before their flight back New York, the two men talked while the boxer soaked his aching hands in a bucket of ice.

"That Italian bastard's got a hard head," Momo joked. "I hit him with some good shots, and he didn't flinch until the end. The very end. Damn, he hit me hard down in my nuts and kidneys. I was pissing blood before the car got to the hall."

"Still hurt?" Cootie asked. "The cup didn't look like it was giving you too much protection."

"I'm used to it. Did you check the crowd out? Man, everybody was out there kicking butt. They just went crazy. You expect something like that in New York, but not here in this small town."

Cootie laughed because he didn't see a thing. He walked quickly to the exit when the mayhem broke out. He watched safely from the doorway, before pushing through the crowd to the boxer's dressing room. He wanted no part of the madness.

"Think you're ready for the champ?" he asked Momo, who looked pensive for a time before nodding.

"I've got to be sharper than I was tonight," Momo continued. "Maybe I need a different trainer. I can't be sloppy when I fight the champ or I'll get killed."

Cootie nodded this time. "That's for sure. He's a bad man."

Momo watched the lights stream past the window in the night. "They say they will hurt my family if I don't throw the fight. They say they have too much money on this thing to let it go any other way. They say the champ will win one way or another. Easy or hard. I just know that I can't do what they ask. I can't, Cootie."

"You've worked too hard for this," Cootie said.

"I know, I know." Momo stared at his clenched fists.

"Then we have to find a way to make sure that they can't do their plan. My old man had a friend on the boxing commission. Used to supply him with whores. I'll talk to him next week. We'll see what he can do."

Momo smiled broadly for the first time since they started the ride to the airport. He shook Cootie's smaller hand and muttered, "You're a good brother." Once on the Lear jet, both men napped as the plane soared above the clouds, silently heading for the long necklace of bright lights that was New York City.

NINETEEN

There was a depression that gripped Cootie. The gray, cold drizzle of gloom that enveloped his mind, sometimes haunted him like physical pain; like an arm or leg would ache and throb. Despair. There was no escape from this agony, as if knitting needles were penetrating his sick brain—his head where the rooms were stifling and smothering with heat. Guilt. Regret. He went to his unmade bed, the sheets and blankets funky with sweat and rumpled, and threw himself on it.

Try as he might, he couldn't leave it. Sometimes he couldn't leave the house for days on end. He sat on the edge of the bed with a drink in his hand. When that didn't do the trick, he drank from the bottle—scotch, bourbon, rum, vodka—anything alcoholic. He drank until he fell asleep. He saw no one. He let no one into his apartment.

"Hey. Whassup, man?" Guy called him. He was worried about Cootie.

"Nothing," Cootie said, his voice lifeless. "Just needed a little time by myself."

"Are you all right?"

"Yeah. I'm trying to put the pieces together. I need a little time to think."

"Cootie, you don't sound well. Are you sure you're okay?"

"I-I-I think I fucked up Faith's life. I fucked up Audrey's life and Alicia's too. That's why Audrey vanished. That's why Faith killed herself. Me and my bullshit. I'm not a man. I was never a good father or husband. I thought I was slick. If I just paid attention to

189

my wife and my girls, I would have known how much I was screwing up. Do you think I'm sick?"

"No. You're just under a strain with the search for your daughter. Trying to get a job so the parole officer doesn't send you back to prison. Trying to find a place to stay. Trying to get your life back on track. That's a lot of stuff to do. But you can't give up."

"Was I responsible for my wife being on drugs?"

"No, Cootie. No, you weren't."

"What about this Audrey mess? I know I dropped the ball." He put his hands between his legs and rocked back and forth on the bed. The tears wouldn't come, although he wanted them to flow on his cheeks. He needed to cry. He thought crying would relieve the tremendous pressure he felt in his chest and between his ears.

"This isn't like you, Cootie," Guy said. "I've never known you to feel sorry for yourself. You always get in a fix, but you keep on standing up. I'm worried about you, man."

"I can't shake this sadness," Cootie said. "I keep drinking and drinking, but it doesn't go away. I was just thinking about what Aunt Monie said to me two weeks before she was killed. I didn't know why my mother hated me so. I didn't know until my aunt said, 'Do you know how many black boys there are in this world who their mother treats them like shit, because the child might look like their father?' She hated my father madly."

"Did you look like your father?" Guy asked.

"You knew him," Cootie said. "Even you said I looked like him. But I have pictures of him when he was young. I really resembled him. My mother said I talked like him, walked like him, even acted like him. She despised him because he put her out on the streets to sell her ass."

"That's the past," his friend said. "You have to let it go."

"The world has no place for black men or boys," Cootie said. "It kills them or drives them mad or gets them sick, but in the end, it finishes them off. I remember reading a news article that said a man in Harlem is less likely to live to the age of sixty-five than a man in Bangladesh. And Bangladesh is one of the poorest countries in the world. What chance have we got?"

"We got a good chance, Cootie. We just have to scuffle a little harder to survive."

"The deck is stacked against us. If the virus or drugs don't get us, then heart disease, diabetes, cirrhosis, cancer, homicide, bad food, and poverty will. Being black and a man, is a death sentence in this city. Probably in this country too."

"What about the job?" Guy asked. "Why don't you ask Momo for one? Hell, he's rolling in the dough. That way the parole folks will see that you're trying to get your life straight. Call him up. I bet he says yes."

"If the white bastards want to make life hell for me, they'll send me back anyway. Did I tell you about their trip with me, while they went to some of the parolees a few days ago? They told me I had to get with the program or else."

"So you'll get with the program. Honkies are easy to fool."

"I guess. We'll see. Give me a couple of days alone."

"You're not going to pull anything funny, are you?" Guy was concerned about his pal's state of mind.

"No. I promise you that."

Satisfied that Cootie wouldn't harm himself, Guy told his friend that his kids were waiting for him to take them to McDonald's for burgers, fries, and shakes. His wife wanted to get them out of her hair. They were driving her nuts with their loud singing, video games, and running back and forth through the house, nonstop. He agreed to give his wife some time to herself, if she would let him play some pool with the boys on next Thursday.

"What's today?" Cootie asked.

"Sunday, all day long." Guy laughed at his friend's wacky habit of losing track of time and days.

"Give me a call next week, and we'll hook up over a drink," the ex-con said. "I'm going to give Momo a call about that job. That was a good idea."

After a few moments, Cootie got up, took off his clothes, put on his robe, and sat on the bed again. He had another bottle of liquor on the nightstand. In bed, he put one arm over his face to shield it from the sun that was streaming in from the windows. He heard one of his neighbors talking to someone about a drug deal that had gone awry. Finally, he fell asleep.

The fact that he didn't hear the phone ring was strange enough, but the voice on the other end was stranger yet. It was Audrey, talking very clearly, but rambling from one topic to another. He could tell she was very high, mind full of lucid thoughts and images, but its focus was faulty, and making no sense as it lost steam from where Cootie listened from his sprawl on the bed.

". . . Dad, I hear you're looking for me. Stop looking for me. I'm okay. I'm doing what you used to say, 'Go out on your own and you'll see what the world is like.' Well, I see it, and the world is a very cruel, dangerous place where women are not welcome. As Mitch always says, 'Women are just pussy, just sex, bitches whose only worth is that thing between their legs . . . that's the way men and the world think of them.'

"If you're there, don't answer; don't pick up the phone because I want to have my say. If you're there, you'll interrupt me and try to put your two cents into my conversation, and you'll confuse me. I want this talk to go one way. I remember all my family and friends used to say I was too pretty, and the men and the fast life would destroy me. Even Mama used to say it. Only you saw my worth, other than my pretty face and body. You said I was smart, tough, opinionated—had balls. You challenged me. The only other man who sees me like that is Mitch. I don't have to be anybody else with him. In my other relationships, I thought I was me, but I was really a figment of imagination of them. Mitch isn't like that. I know you don't like him. Kelly and Lotus told me.

"Working together is a strain. He can't scream at me in front of the other girls. He sometimes ignores me, so they don't feel he's playing favorites. I would love to go over and drape myself all over him, but I can't. The other girls wouldn't like it. It reminds me when I used to play you against Mom. I'd ask Mom if I could talk with her in the bedroom and then ask her if I could get a snow cone from the ice cream truck on the street. I was seven. Just minutes before, I'd ask you and you'd say, 'Hell no,' and it would spoil my dinner. I learned the advantages of playing you against Mom or vice versa. If Mom said no, I knew I could count on you to say yes. Especially if one of you wasn't around. When you were in prison, I could make Mom do whatever I wanted.

"When you were behind bars, I told you I was all right, but I wasn't. I was afraid of Mom. One morning, I found her shooting up in the kitchen, her arm tied off and the needle about to go in. I screamed at her at the top of my lungs. I told her I didn't want a junkie bitch for a mother and threw a bowl of oatmeal at her. In the bedroom, Alicia told me that Jake, one of our uncles, had got Mom high on shit and was fucking her in the hallway. And Alicia saw this. That night, Mom sat us down and pleaded with us not to tell you. She begged us. In the end, we didn't tell because she asked us not to.

"Did Alicia tell you about Mom trying to strangle me outside Macy's? Probably not. She was flipped out and trying to kick the drugs. She was on this Bible thing. Redemption and stuff. A cop on the beat outside of the store spotted her and yelled to Mom, but she ignored him. The cop ran to her as she was trying to choke the life from me, and some people were attempting to get me free. My face was pale, and I was gasping for breath. They finally wrestled her to the ground and pulled me out. I was sobbing, and they carried me in a squad car to the hospital. When they arrested her, she was stretched out on the sidewalk, shouting hymns and prayers, talking about Jesus and the evil ones. The last days on earth. She was totally wacked out. Alicia didn't tell you probably.

"Mom. Alicia, and me knew she was going to get arrested. We just knew it. We could see her getting busted and ending up at the Rose M. Singer Center, the women's jail on Rikers Island. The cops arrested her and charged her with reckless endangerment of a child. Her junkie pals tried to bail her out, so she could spend less than five days waiting for her case to come up on the court docket. At one point, she sold crack to avoid going on welfare. She quit her job as a teacher's assistant. It was hard for all of us financially. Where were you when we needed you? Where? You stupid asshole.

"Did your precious Barbara tell you about how the city tried to take us away from Mom? And she, your bitch of a sister, sided with welfare to wrestle us from Mom. Where were you when we needed you? In damn jail. Mom tried to keep us, but the city proved she was an addict. I recall Barbara standing up in court, pointing at my mother and saying: 'I love my brother's wife, but she's a drug addict and a criminal, and doesn't deserve a second chance with the kids. As a Christian, I'm for forgiving someone, and giving someone a second chance. Jesus gave us a second chance. But how many second chances do you get? How many chances do you get to ruin these young girls' lives?'

"I found out a lot that day. I found out Mom had been married before. Married to a man, Steve, in a Rikers Island chapel years before she met you. The groom was serving time for manslaughter, robbery, possession of stolen property, petty larceny, and weapons possession. Mr. Right. This was not a marriage built to last. Steve was stabbed to death as he came out of an after-hours spot on the Lower East Side. I found out Mom had been a junkie for years. I found out she had a daughter who was born addicted to heroin and died. We were afraid she was going to kill us. She was a combination of the bitch in *Mommie Dearest,* the frigid witch in *Ordinary People,* and the killer skank in *The Grifters*. But Barbara lost. Child Welfare said state law did not discriminate against parents with criminal records. Barbara cried when she heard the ruling. The welfare man said: 'Being a convicted criminal does not remove parental rights.'

"I hated you. I hated your crooked, lying ways. Other kids had parents who worked for a living, but no, you had to scam for the easy money. You have no guilt for what you did, how you treated those who loved you. All you knew was hustling. Maybe you wanted to get caught.

"Do you remember when you had me ring that apartment's doorbell, while you waited around the corner with a gun? Remember that? I was maybe eight. You kicked the door in and put the gun into the mouth of the dealer. He owed you money. You said he would pay you or you'd blast his decrepit aunt. I sat there on the couch and watched you put the gun up to the temple of his old aunt. She wet on herself. The dealer was so nervous. He really didn't want you to kill her. He paid you. What did his aunt call you? *Incorrigible.* She yelled you were a nigger bastard who used your daughter to commit crimes. *This family tree is twisted.*

"I didn't want to follow you guys' footsteps. Damn criminals. Dysfunctional home life. I've spent my entire life trying to live this shit down. I told Alicia I'm trying to get restored to wholeness. Wholeness, you know what that is? Alicia and me have been trying to outgrow a warped childhood that left us with a distorted view about ourselves and the world. I hear voices telling me: *Be a slut.* She hears voices telling her: *Be a nun.* Did you know she can only make it with her old man if she wears a nun outfit to bed? He straps her down after he gets her drunk and then forcibly fucks her. Alicia, she would never tell you that. As for me, I'm a whore.

"Even though you haven't been in my life, or our lives, I missed you so badly. A girl loves her father. A girl needs her father. But you weren't around. I kept waiting for you to come into my life and change everything around. Like Cinderella. I wanted you to be Prince Charming and rescue me. I guess I wanted every man to rescue me. I wanted you as a protector. I didn't feel pretty. I didn't feel loved. I didn't feel like a woman.

"You taught me when I was real young that I was delicate, fragile, and beautiful. That is not what the world has taught me. I know you lied. You lied just like you always do. Women do better alone than men. Women outlive men. Men are weak, just like you are. You didn't train me in the skills needed for my survival. Mom always told me to 'never swim too far.' And she was right."

Cootie eased up on the phone, turned up the volume on the message, and straddled a chair backward. He wanted to get a cigarette from the pack, but didn't dare to do that. He needed to listen, listen to his daughter's voice, listen to her cry of help. Damn, he wanted to reach out, offer his hand to her, and tell her that Daddy would be there. *Daddy would be there.*

"I'm not in awe of any man. I'm not going to play a fool just to massage some male ego. Do you know what I mean, Daddy? I'm tired of letting the boys win, and just looking pretty and keeping my mouth shut."

Cootie tried to smile. This was his girl—Audrey. Still feisty; still fighting. Now he could speak, tell her that he would be there for her.

"Darling, I know how you suffered, especially after your mother died," Cootie said quietly into the phone. "Where are you living? Tell me where. I know what drugs can do to you. Do you want that?"

He could hear her breathing—even, gentle breaths—and a light tapping on the receiver. Silence. Dead air. Nothing and nobody there. Just a humming when the line went dead. Where did she get the number from?

TWENTY

Through the window of the Lenox Lounge, Cootie saw Lotus step out of a cab onto the sidewalk, where she was immediately whistled at by a group of men. She adjusted her dark glasses, pulled her long leather coat around her, and strolled into the bar. As he walked from the bar holding a drink, she smiled and touched his shoulder.

"Hi, Mr. Cootie," she said.

"Hi yourself." He kept moving into the inner sanctum, where a jazz trio played and a fairly average-sized crowd listened to the men putting finishing touches on a Monk tune, "Straight, No Chaser."

"I called you because Mitch moved her. Audrey's not at that address anymore. I talked to Kelly, trying to see if she knew where she was. Kelly said no. In fact, Audrey's talking about moving in with Mitch. Did you say you talked to her the other day?"

"Yes, I did. She called."

"What did she say, Cootie?"

"Nothing much. Lotus, do you have any idea where she might be? She sounds like she's confused and unsure about what her next step should be. I know Mitch isn't a good influence. All he wants is to exploit her. He wants to make money off her before she wakes up and quits the game."

Lotus looked into his face, deadly serious. "She'll never leave him. Never."

"But why?"

They found a table closer to the back of the room, so they could talk while the pianist tried to copy Monk's fragmented solo, from the song to spur the bassist into playing. He was repeating a big, flowing sound to provide a rhythmic bottom for the keyboards. The patrons talked among themselves, creating a wall of sound that the musical improvisations could barely penetrate, while the drummer used the brushes over the skins. What resulted was a song barely recognizable as the only single Monk signature tune, a distorted classic. White noise.

"Mitch is safe in a way you aren't, Cootie. He appeals to her insecurity and low self-esteem. Most men don't know that the majority of women battle a love-hate relationship with their bodies. They feel uptight about them. All the media say women should have a certain type of bodies—perfect shape, perfect tits, perfect ass—and when they don't, they feel like something's wrong with them."

"What you're telling me is that Mitch lies to her. Lies to her big-time. Tells her what she wants to hear. Fills her head with all kinds of garbage. Feeds her fantasy that she's a queen."

Cootie thought about his daughter calling herself a slut. "She feels like filth. She believes she deserves to be punished; is guilty about what happened to her Mom. The woman was a junkie who neglected her girls. How Alicia turned out like she did is a real surprise."

"Mitch is a businessman—or thinks he is. He saw a weakness in Audrey, and now he's exploiting it. No doubt Audrey loves sex. Mitch only thinks of her as a dollar sign."

"Is she a whore, Lotus?" Cootie couldn't bear to think of her as a woman selling her ass. Not his daughter.

"I don't know. I know she likes to fuck."

Now the pianist started the melodic intro of a Lee Morgan number, "The Sixth Sense," joined by the bassist, who lurked around the swirls of color and rhythm, played by the man on the keys. A man, with dark glasses and an African dashiki sat in with them on trumpet, adding a searing bright tone in middle register. The drummer moved along with the same repeated intense vamp.

Cootie was suspicious. "Shit, we could have gone to Showman's or Gishen's Café or St. Nick. Why did you recommend this? What's up? Come clean."

"Have you ever thought about . . . maybe Audrey doesn't want to be found, Cootie? Maybe she just wants to keep away from you. Could you deal with that?"

"No, I couldn't. I know she's a young adult, but she's only a kid."

"This is something she told me, and you don't know where you got it from," Lotus said, motioning to the waitress. "You can keep your mouth shut, right?"

"Yes. I won't say anything."

"Sam—uh, Audrey—told me that two of the guys her mother used to date forced her to have sex with them and some of their friends," Lotus said. "She said she used to imagine she was dead. Four times she tried to kill herself. But she said she felt guilty for her sister, who she didn't want to have to go through what she was. Twice she thought about leaving, but she said she couldn't have a peaceful night knowing that she had left Alicia with those perverts. She would be driving with one of the guys, the one her mother supposedly loved and trusted, and he'd be fingering her between the legs. The shame she felt was unbelievable. She said she'd pray for them to get into a car wreck. Or he'd make her suck him off in traffic."

Cootie frowned. "I've got to make it up to her. I must."

"That's not all. The guys promised to leave her sister out of it, but she and her mother walked in on them having sex. Her mother got a knife and charged at the men, but they took it away from her and knocked her down."

"Alicia never told me anything," he said.

"You need to talk to your girls," she said. "These guys overruled their mother, taking over the house. They became jealous and told the girls not to date. They wanted the girls all to themselves. They couldn't imagine any boy putting his hands on them. Totally possessive. Once the aunt stepped forward to take the girls, then Audrey ran away."

"I was away for eight years," Cootie said sadly. "I didn't know what was going on in the world. I missed everything. I missed the kids growing up. I just fucked up everything—my life and theirs."

The reason Lotus got him there was an offer from Mitch to part with Audrey, his baby girl, for lots of cash money. She informed him that Rex, one of his male prostitutes, was coming to the club with the details of the exchange. Rex. He was one of the group who stripped at the halls and auditoriums, wiggling their booties and flashing their dicks to the ladies, but they also serviced the guys and gals on the side. Lotus warned him Rex was a bad man. He did some of Mitch's dirty work, fingering marks and ratting on those who got out of line.

"Can this Rex be trusted?" he asked. "How do I know he'll keep his word?"

"Rex is nothing—a two-bit hustler who loves to be butt-fucked and paid," she said. "No, you have to worry about Mitch. He is not to be trusted. He's the prince of liars. He'll smile and then cut your throat. You can't trust him."

"Don't worry. I won't. I'll do anything to get my girl back. Anything."

Their drinks came. He clinked his glass against hers, and they took a hearty sip. For the first time, he really noticed the curve of her full lips, how she spoke; how she smiled, how the ends of her mouth turned up.

"To freeing Audrey," Cootie said, his expression dour.

"To freeing Audrey—uh, Sam," Lotus said, and they laughed.

"Would you come over after this?"

"Why?" She knew why.

Cootie knew what he was suggesting. "I wanted to go over the details of the offer and plan strategy, if that was all right. Two heads are better than one. You know these characters and I don't."

"All right, but I've got to work tomorrow afternoon, so I can't stay out late," she said. "Is that all you have in mind? Talking and planning?"

He paused for a fraction of a second, looked down and then back at her. He was embarrassed because she knew what he was thinking.

Suddenly, Rex stood before them with his outsized bodyguard. The enormous black man looked like the Hulk without the green color. He was dressed in a black suit and had his bulging arms folded across his massive chest. As was the fashion, he was bald and scowling. Rex looked bitchy and totally effeminate.

"Answer her. The suspense's killin' me," Rex said with a lisp.

Lotus watched him take a long drink before she turned and acknowledged Rex and his muscular superhero. "Cootie, this is Rex and Mr. Clean."

"I don't think he likes being addressed as Mr. Clean," Rex said. "And what kind of name is Cootie? Is that one from the Old School of Crooks? Still, I like it. It's so dahling."

"Have a seat, gentlemen," Cootie said, waving the men to the seats at the table.

Lotus got on the wrong side of the hustler when she lit one of her cigarettes and puffed an enormous cloud of smoke into the air. She smiled at Rex and shifted in her seat.

"Please, I can't stand cigarette smoke," Rex said, groaning. "Also, I hate how it smells when it gets all in your clothes. Please, honey bunch."

The waitress came over to the table. "I'm sorry. No smoking. It's city law."

That was just what Rex needed. He loved that Lotus got her comeuppance and had to put the cigarette out. When the waitress had her back turned, he stuck out his tongue like a bratty kid would do with an older sister.

"Now, what would you gentlemen like?" the waitress asked.

"I'd like a cranberry juice with ice, and the gentleman there would like a beer, preferably Bud's or Miller's," Rex said. "Do you guys want anything else? It's on the house."

Both Lotus and Cootie shook their heads. No freebies.

"Mitch wants to help you with your search," Rex said. "In fact, he'd like to put an end to it. He knows where your daughter is, and he would like to help you get her back. All in one piece."

Lotus, only half listening to the hustler, looked about her. She numbered the Lenox Lounge as one of her favorite uptown jazz rooms, its old art-deco beauty with its mosaic-tiled floors, cut-glass doors, and leather ceiling tiles and banquettes. The place had undergone a half-million-dollar refurbishing and was worth every penny of it. The club was larger inside than it was previously. Most of the patrons were still Black, except for a smattering of young white college kids from Columbia, NYU, and Fordham.

"What's your offer?" Cootie asked.

"Like I said, Mitch wants to help you with your search," the hustler said. "He wants to make a trade. He wants to help you, but like a good businessman, he won't give you something for nothing. It's got to be an even exchange."

"Trade for what?" His question hit the hustler right between the eyes.

But then the waitress returned to the table, bringing a glass of iced cranberry juice and a bottle of cold Bud on a tray. She leaned over to set the drinks down, and the men caught a peek at her over-exposed brown breasts. They nodded approvingly except Rex, who grimaced at such a vulgar display.

"Money, but we'll talk about that in a moment," Rex said, turning his attention to the trumpeter playing the melody of Trane's "Love Supreme" with the drummer playing the brushes in the background.

Lotus had seen Mitch around with Rex and the boys, hopping to clubs and bars, drinking and carousing. "I know you, Rex. You're a true male whore. See, Cootie doesn't know what he's dealing with. If you're a client, he'll do anything if the price is right. I know the last time you said you wouldn't let anybody fist fuck you. Is that still true?"

Rex put his head up, like a dignitary about to be photographed. "Shut up."

"But he will let you pee on him for a bonus. Right?" Lotus was having too much fun. She hated Rex and his kind. Perversity for a price.

Rex was sulking, and then he swung his hand in a slap at the woman. But Cootie caught his anger in mid-flight and pressed his hand down to the table. All the while, he was looking at the beefy bodyguard to measure his response, for he really didn't want any trouble from him. The large man did nothing; he just sipped his beer.

"Who is your sugar daddy these days? Mitch?" she asked.

"Yeah. He's your sugar daddy as well," Rex said, growing. "Right, bitch?"

"He is. But I'll tell you this. When he gets tired of you, he'll throw you away just like he has so many whores and faggots in the past. He doesn't give a shit about you. Or me. I don't know what it is with you good-looking types, always stepping on people, always hurting people. He's just using you."

Rex crunched a cube of ice. "And he's just using you too. When he says jump, all you ask is how high. Don't forget he feeds you. If he turns his back on you, you'll never work again in this town."

"Play nice, ladies," Cootie said. "Talk about the offer."

"Mitch wants money—lots of it," Rex said, beaming.

"What are you saying?" Cootie asked.

"He wants money, and wants it before he releases your daughter," the hustler said. "He knows you can get it. He'll return her safe and sound. Or—"

"Or what?"

"Or he'll make her disappear," the hustler threatened.

"Fuck you," Cootie leaned forward and half-shouted at him. Some of the patrons turned in their seats, looking at them.

Rex continued chewing ice with a smirk on his handsome face. "No, fuck you. You're a damn loser. You really don't want to get Mitch mad."

"I want my daughter back," Cootie protested.

"The cash figure for her return is a hundred thousand dollars, with a penalty of a thousand dollars the first day," the hustler said. "That goes up and up, with seven thousand the second day and fourteen thousand the third day, twenty-one thousand the fourth day, and so-on and so-on. Don't make Mitch lose his patience. Don't make him hurt you."

"This is fucking extortion," Cootie said.

The hustler moved his chair, still closer to the shocked father of the captured girl, until he was almost on top of Cootie. "No, it's not. Mitch just wants what he paid for her. He has paid for all of her expenses, clothing, dental and medical care, and all her vices. You know the girl loves her rock. Her jones for rock—crack cocaine. That runs into thousands of dollars. Mitch's just trying to get his investment back."

"It's out of the question."

"Do as you please, but we must settle accounts," Rex said. "You must pay your debt. You're an honest man. You want to pay your debts, right?"

"Bullshit. I want her back. She's just a kid."

"And Mitch wants some collateral, some stocks and bonds that your sister has for that rainy day," the hustler added. "I think they total about seventy-five thousand. He wants you to arrange that release for him. Now, if you don't get the money and the collateral, he *will* sell your baby girl. She's prime. Any number of pimps and porn brokers would love to buy her, and she'd disappear from the face of the globe."

"I'll get the cops in on this," Cootie warned. "You can't do this."

"He can and he will," Lotus said. "He's a fucking monster."

"As for our deal, you have until the third of the month," the hustler said. "That's thirteen days. Thirteen days. And remember the interest that's mounting. Time is money. Just to let you know, I'm not fucking around. We'll have to put the first day cost up to three grand and then you can do the math accordingly. Don't get tricky. Don't try anything stupid. We will make her vanish."

"If you do, I'll kill you and Mitch too," Cootie said, his left eye twitching.

Rex slurped down the reminder of the juice. "And if you get the cops involved, we'll have to kill your other daughter, Alicia, and her old man as well. Then your sister, Barbara. The kids too. And then we'll come for you. Don't fuck with us."

Impulsively, Cootie said, "What's your end of this deal?"

The hustler looked at Cootie and grinned at the stripper. "A job well done."

"No, it's not." Lotus smirked. "I know all about Rex here. The end of the deal will be him sprawled on Mitch's bed with his backside well oiled, and a rendezvous with a fat black dick. You're a whore and you know it."

Rex fumed at that suggestion. "Honey bunch, you're a whore too. And a total nigger bitch to boot. I hope you don't tell him to underestimate us. You know the wrath of Mitch and how far it can reach."

"You'll have my answer the day after tomorrow," Cootie replied. "I don't like to be played for a sap. Daughter or no daughter, this smells to high heaven. I'm not a damn fool. If he wants trouble, I can give it to him. He really doesn't want that. If the girl wants to get out, Mitch should let her go. He has no right to keep her against her will."

"Oh yes, he does," the hustler joked, giggling. "She's bought and paid for. Now you must make that price, or there could be some dire consequences. Mitch is giving you that choice. A good outcome or a bad one."

The hustler and his bodyguard rose to their feet in unison, pushed back their chairs and exited. As soon as they left, the waitress came back and asked if they wanted anything else.

Lotus crossed her legs and said to the woman, "Make them doubles."

"I can't believe this," Cootie said, still in shock.

"I called my roommate and told her I'd be late," Lotus, the stripper, said. "I figured you'd be stunned by all this shit. Let's stick around and booze it up a bit. Is that okay with you?"

He shook his head. "I'll have the one drink, but I think I should turn in."

"Come on, have some fun," she said. "There will be time enough to worry later on. You deserve one night when you don't have all that trouble weighing on you. Let's have a few laughs and shit."

"Okay. Let's tie one on." He looked at the couple next to them, hugging and touching each other underneath the table.

Suddenly making up her mind, Lotus got to her feet. "I've got to make a call. I'll be right back. I've got to check on something." As she walked back to the rear of the room, she pulled out the cell phone and punched in the number of her apartment.

"I'm going to bring Cootie back to the apartment," the stripper said. "Is everything ready? He won't know that's been pre-arranged. Cool, very nice."

The drinks arrived and her male friend drunk the double whiskey. Trying to keep up with him, she tossed the drink down and pulled him to the exit after the last set was completed. She had finished her drink too fast, but she enjoyed the rush of intoxication surging through her body. He whispered into her ear, talking in a muted voice about what he was going to do to her. The waitress who had served them was sitting at the bar, drinking a ginger ale, and watching them. He noticed her tight skirt was above her knees, and the long expanse of brown legs on view.

"Come back again," the waitress said, grinning. She was talking to him, not Lotus. He was sure of that. The waitress showed her teeth again at him and let her knees part.

As they waited for a gypsy cab, Lotus reached for him in the dark night, and whispered to him, "The bitch back there had the hots for you."

He shrugged it off and flagged down the car, and opened the door for her.

TWENTY-ONE

Once inside the cab, Lotus pulled the door shut. She was silent in the dark with the richness of his male voice keeping her company. She could only see him when the cab went past the flash of the street lights. Like a strobe in a nightclub. His body was against hers, making no claim on her, but she could sense his maleness tight on her smoldering flesh. It seemed hot, searing into her smooth skin. A bony pressure.

"Why do you want to help me?" he asked her.

"Because I think you are a decent man," she purred. "You're just trying to live. And these bastards are trying to trip you up. Like this Mitch and that fag, Rex."

The cabbie watched them in the rearview mirror. He was either African or West Indian, but for some reason, the accent in his words didn't betray him. "Where to?"

Sure of herself, she gave him the address to her apartment, the quickest way to get there; the side streets, and the agreeable lights. She located the pack of cigarettes in her purse, but she asked the cabbie for permission before she took one into her lips. "Is it okay if I smoke?"

"Yes, but open the window," came the reply.

The only bright spot in the pitch black was her cigarette. She loved the feeling of intimacy, just the two of them in the inky cocoon of darkness.

"How are you connected with Mitch?" His voice was strong and sardonic. He'd asked her several times before, but he hoped that she would give him a straight answer for once.

"Why do you want to know?" She was being catty.

"I need to know before I get myself in too deep," he said, smiling in the stillness. "I need to know who my friends are."

"I'm a friend; bet on it." Her voice was soft, almost lost in the hum of the tires.

He gently pulled her down onto the seat until she was lying half on him. She did not put up a struggle or any resistance, instead, she surrendered to him, to his kisses. He kissed her lightly on the lips once, then twice.

"Why do you think I came when you called me?" Something akin to desire crept into his words.

"Maybe you were curious. About me. About me and Mitch."

"Sure, I was. I was wondering what you're doing with a no-count thug like him. He's heartless. The more I learn about him, the less I like him. He has plenty of enemies who may turn on him if the situation is right. I wouldn't want to be around him if the worm turns."

Stunned by his appraisal, she replied before she really thought about an answer. "I know he's a shit. He'd fuck me over if he thought he could make a profit."

"Exactly. Now he wants to screw up Audrey's life, and I won't let him."

She was pensive for a couple of seconds and passed her cigarette to him. "I'm sorry about the scene with Rex. I can't stand him. Fucking swish!"

"Don't worry about it. He had it coming to him."

"Cabbie, turn left here and go past the first street, then pull up at the second apartment building," she directed the driver through the maze of streets. There was hardly anyone out at that time of night.

"Okay, lady." The cabbie followed her guidance.

The cab pulled over to the curb—but not before Cootie paid the driver, tipping him handsomely—and then opened the door for the stripper. Lotus stood on the

211

sidewalk, trying to see if there was a light on in her apartment. Both of them were slightly buzzed from the booze. When they walked into the lobby, they laughed at the unstable steps on the stairs to the third-floor walk-up.

"Hello?" Lotus turned the key in the lock and opened the door.

"Hello." A feminine voice answered. "Lo?"

"Yeah. We have company." She switched on the lights, pointing Cootie to a seat on the couch where a table held an ashtray and magazines like *Ebony, Jet, People,* and *Entertainment Weekly*. After that, she walked into the bedroom and closed the door.

He slumped low on the sofa, cradling his head in his hands. He picked up the murmur of voices behind the door, arguing and debating something. Lotus wanted her to join them for a party, but the other woman didn't agree.

Finally, Lotus came back into the room heading for the kitchen. "Well, that's settled. You want a beer or something stronger."

"Something stronger." He didn't know what they had planned for the night.

"Cool, baby." She got a saucer, opened the fridge, and got two handfuls of ice.

In the doorway, Kelly stood behind her friend with a black satin robe that barely concealed her curves. He imagined she was naked underneath. She held Lotus around the waist and gave her a light peck on the neck. "If he wants some Southern Comfort, there's some Mitch left here the other day. He can have that or some rum or vodka. It doesn't matter to me."

"I don't think he wants to hear Mitch's name right now," Lotus said.

"Why?" Kelly asked. "What did Mitch do to him?"

"I'll have the vodka," he said, ignoring her. "Straight." He wanted to forget everything that had happened this night. Everything.

It was strange being there. The air conditioner was on full blast, whipping up an arctic chill. He didn't like the cold outside, but the winter winds inside were getting the best of him. The walls of the living room were some type of cinnamon with large posters of male movie stars—Travolta, Pitt, Crowe, Willis, and the like. A stack of comic books sat beside the sofa, two or three porn tapes featuring girl-girl sex, and the black-and-white TV on MTV, with rap star Fifty Cent prancing around a group of near-nude black girls showing their butts.

"Do you work out, Cootie?" Kelly asked. "You have a very tight body."

"No, I don't." He sat on the sofa and stared at the TV, watching the girls.

"I've got to pee. Be right back," Lotus said, heading to the bathroom.

Kelly suddenly kissed him on the cheek, presented him with a silver Italian jewelry box, and opened it for him. "This is where I have all of my goodies. You want to get off? I've got some great smoke. And really serious blow. Let me know what you want. You're a pal of Lo. Nothing's too good for you. I think the world of Lo. She saved my life, and that's no bullshit."

"Saved you from what?" he asked.

"I'll tell you when I know you better," she said. "You couldn't tell, but I used to be anorexic. Or maybe it was from the drugs. As you can see, I love to get fucked up."

Lotus came back into the room. "You treating him right?"

"Have you fucked him yet?" Kelly asked, words all speeded up from drugs. "I bet he's good. Oh yeah, Mitch called you while you were out. Said something about you

213

having to work on the weekend. And yeah, he said you dissed Rex, said he wouldn't stand for it. I hate that damn Rex. He's always around Mitch, always under foot. Do you think Mitch's doing him?"

"Who knows and who cares?" Lotus retorted. "Rex got out of line. I hate drama queens. The boy loves drama. He was getting all up in Cootie's face."

Kelly cooed. "And such a handsome, rugged face."

"Fuck Rex and fuck Mitch," Lotus said, pouring a half gram of the coke onto a small hand mirror. "Want some? 'Cause Kelly won't offer you none. She's greedy. Wants it all for herself. You're supposed to share with your guest."

"I did offer him some," Kelly said, sounding contrite. She lit a cigarette and put it into Lotus's mouth.

Lotus was busy cutting the pile of snow into three lines with a razor, and then she handed him a rolled five, and he leaned down and did a line. He sniffed twice and pinched his nose. Both girls watched him for a sign of approval. He nodded and gave a thumbs-up.

"Lotus said you're looking for your girl," Kelly said, doing a line and sniffing loudly.

Beyonce was on MTV, wiggling her curvy body, mouthing the words about a naughty girl. Lotus turned the volume so the music wouldn't interfere with the party in progress, but she liked to watch, especially when the camera slid around to get the singer for a rearview shot. Both of them cheered when the lens focused on her ample hips.

"Oh man, I would love to lick her fur," Kelly said, laughing. "I would rock her world. Jay Z would have to get in line."

"Damn, I've got to pee again." Lotus left the room again.

Now Prince strutted across the screen, his lithe body keeping beat with the music. He played the guitar, did some intricate dance steps, and sang without losing a breath. Kelly wondered who did his makeup and laughed.

"I forgot to get something to drink," she said. "What did you want?"

"Anything stronger than beer," he said, doing a half line.

Kelly brought back two glasses of rum and Coke—a sissy drink—but Cootie said thanks and downed it. She said the coke was community property, but she had her own stash of some glorious blow, pulling out a small vial. She took out a small spoon, dipped it into the white powder, and held it up to his nose, which she did four times. The spoon went to her nostrils six times before a line of blood dribbled from her nose onto her lips.

"Shit. An occupational hazard," she joked.

He felt a wave of dizziness surge through him, the room spinning, and maybe he should have been more relaxed, but his arms were disobeying him. He felt like he was totally drunk and had to lay down. The heat was creeping up inside him, moving up his stomach into his lungs and chest, onto his neck and head. His shirt was soaked through, even though the room was frigid.

"I wish I had some meth," she said. "Do you have any?"

"What was in that coke anyway?" he asked.

Kelly laughed and said in her finest Porky Pig voice, stutter and all. "A special blend. Do you like it?"

"I'm totally fucked up," he said.

Lotus returned with a bag of chips and pointed to his erection. "Someone woke up. Standing at attention. Want to play?"

"What was in that shit?" he asked again. His eyes were watering. He kept swallowing hard as the drug's residue eased down his throat.

"Want some more?" Kelly asked, pouring a second glass of straight rum, which he gulped down. "Want some more blow?"

He waved his hands no, sliding down off the sofa until he was sitting on the floor. He was leaning his back against the sofa. It had been a long time since he had been this high. Both girls were pointing at his stiff dick and wondering how they could get it involved with their fun.

Now everything went fuzzy after that. He was naked, except his jockey shorts. The king-size mattress was on the floor. There were candles burning, fragrant and scented with an Eastern aroma. He remembered Kelly telling him to roll over on his back and lift his legs up. She rubbed some liquid into his chest and legs with soothing, soft, circular strokes while he murmured with satisfaction. She continued to massage him, the strokes getting more heated and sensual. His dick, balls, ass cheeks. Her robe was off, and her body was open to his touch.

"Lo, she says you need this," she said. "You're way too uptight." She ordered him to switch positions on his belly, and her fingers did their magic again.

She straddled him, her crotch near his face, reaching for his thighs. His hands found her breasts, pinched their nipples gently. His head moved in position so his mouth could find her tits, his tongue could encircle them, and a sigh of pleasure came from her. She was quite aroused from his caress. He was entranced with the folds of her vagina and the small bud peeking out of them, the wetness and heat.

"His dick's so damn hard," Lotus said, moaning as she knelt and wrapped her fingers around it and put it to her mouth. "I'll save you some."

"You better," Kelly stammered while he licked her thighs before teasing her opening. He could feel her friend lean over and part her butt cheeks to let him get greater access with his tongue. With each lick, she shuddered.

"Wait, I want to get some ice," Lotus said and ran off to the kitchen.

When she returned with the ice, she pushed Kelly off, laid her down, gave her some blow, and took the ice cube between two fingers. She circled both of her friend's erect nipples with the cold sensation, sending her wiggling until she replaced the cube with her snakelike tongue, sucking, sucking. Hot desire enveloped her. He eased himself to one side of her, gently worked his fingertips into her juicy crease, while the pressure from Lotus's mouth grew urgent on Kelly's breasts.

At that point, Lotus met his eyes, saying, "Eat her. Eat her good."

The tart scent of her need, of her sex, filled his nostrils. Soon both girls were positioned where he could get to them. They said, "Take turns licking us," and he did just that. He licked their pussies, one and then the other, alternating with his lips and tongue. Lotus tasted sweet and fruity while Kelly was more of a tart lemon flavor. He reveled in their scents and flavors. He wanted to tease them a bit. He placed two fingers inside both of them, curling them into the sensitive area on top of the tunnel, wiggling them inside, his thumbs rubbing their clits. Both girls were really wet, practically gushing.

"Just a minute more," he said, slurping while his tongue did its art on both of them. Kelly put a spoon up to his nose to keep him solid and strong. He was like an animal, fueled by lust and drugs.

Then Lotus spread her legs wide as Kelly buried her face between her thighs, and the stripper bucked into her friend's mouth, moaning as if she was about to come. Her moans became frantic and intense when Kelly stopped licking and took Cootie into her mouth, while Lotus played with herself; her thumb on her clit, shuddering and coming. She pushed Cootie back on the mattress, mounted him, and bobbed up and down, crying out with pleasure. Her sex pulsed and trembled, and he drove his erection into her to the hilt. She came again and sagged off him.

"Fuck her deep, baby," she whispered as he watched Kelly's upturned ass.

Quickly, he positioned himself behind Kelly, her sex yawning and ripe, and then buried it inside, full length, while Lotus stood over her so her friend's full, bruised lips could get at her pussy. As Kelly licked her gal pal, he was compelled to ride her ass, stroke after spine-bending stroke—long, deep strokes—pulling himself out of her and then plunging to the depths of her well-lubricated hole. Lotus, tired of orgasms, got down on her knees and reached down and toyed with his dick and heavy balls, as he pushed in and out of her. With just a few more thrusts, he came, filling her with his seed as their bodies met in a moment of sheer ecstasy. He was not finished. They kept moving faster and faster until they came at almost the same time. He collapsed on top of her, with him still inside of her.

Their juices and sweat soaked the pillows and mattress beneath them. "Did you get the wet spot?" Kelly laughed.

"Hell yeah," he said, wearily rolling over. He still wondered what was in that dope. He hadn't screwed like that in years.

"Want some more blow?" Kelly asked. They turned around to see Lotus curled up, asleep and snoring like a hog caller. They laughed.

"No, baby," he answered, asking for a cigarette. "Do you treat all of your friends this way?"

Kelly led him to the bathroom, watched him pee, and washed him off then herself, with a wet towel. She got on her knees, kissed him behind the legs, and winked. Once they situated Lotus on the mattress, they went to sleep with Cootie sandwiched between them.

TWENTY-TWO

Twice in the last three nights, Cootie suddenly sat up in the bed, his mouth opened in a silent yell, his body covered in sweat. It was an unending nightmare. He kept dreaming something was going to happen to Audrey—something bad. To get rid of the jitters, he called Momo and asked about the job. The boxer said he could help his trainer prepare him for the fight, or he could file papers in the office. Take his pick. He chose the trainer, the preparation, and the ring.

As expected, the boxer was edgy, short-tempered, and abrupt. The call to accept the job should have gone easily, but it didn't. He had the second of the exhibitions to be fought in Atlantic City, a ten rounder, and the opponent had been warned to take it easy. Unlike the first one, the boxer tried to knock his block off. The Dago fought like he was trying to win a title shot.

"What the fuck do you want, Mr. Chambers?" the boxer asked. "I don't need no distractions. What do you want?"

"I didn't call to bother you," Cootie said. "I called to say I want to take the job you offered me. I'll report on the weekend if that's all right."

"Yeah, that's cool," Momo replied. "Did you find your kid yet?"

"No. I'm getting worried."

"Why don't you bring the cops in on it?"

"No cops. I'll do this myself. I know where she is. I just have to go and get her."

"Cootie, do you need any help?" the boxer asked. "I know some boys. . . ."

220

"No, I know where she is, and I'll get her when the time is right," Cootie said. "I'll handle it, but thanks for offering."

"I'm sorry that I yelled at ya. I'm as uptight as a big cat in a little room. I still have the matter with the boxing commission. And the goombahs. Did you speak with your boy on the commission?"

"No. Every time I call him, he's out of the office. I think I'm going to have to go down there. Or do something slick to get his attention. But I know he can help you. I know it."

"Are you scared . . . you know . . . about your kid?" Momo was drinking something. He slurped and rinsed his mouth out with it.

"Yeah, I am," Cootie said. "I'll do my best. Sorry to disturb you."

"No problem," the boxer said, sounding again like the young kid he was. Twenty-one and fighting for the championship. "Sorry that I snapped at you. I'm just a little tense. Take care of yourself. Hey, about the job, get there when you get there. I'll tell them to cover your butt. I hope you get your girl back safe."

"Oh damn, the tub." He hung up the phone and ran back to the bathroom. The hot water was almost overflowing. He let some of it out, and poured in Epsom salt for his aches and pains. The recovery from the other night's debauchery—lustful sex and drugs—was still taking a toll on him. He couldn't wait to soak. Thinking anxiously about the boxer and the battle that awaited in the ring, he stripped off his clothes and draped a towel around his middle.

Then the phone rang. He didn't answer it. The message was left on the answering machine, but he was curious to see who it was. It was Specs, a loyal pal of his dead father. He said he had some information for Cootie that might clear up the Audrey matter once and for all.

*   *   *

Cootie walked out of the building, pitched his cigarette away, and asked Guy to drop him at the Good Time Sightseeing Bus Line, the company that operated red British-style double-decker buses that toured various parts of the city. The message from the answering machine said that Specs, an aging hipster who knew everyone and everything in Harlem, would meet him there.

Specs, a former hard-bopper who hung out with Bird, Diz, and Monk, was still spry at his age. He never told anyone just how old he was.

"Hey, baby. What's happening?" asked Specs, the jive cat in his trademark black beret, goatee, black turtleneck, and pants.

They slapped five and took their seats on the top tier of a bus headed for Harlem. Cootie looked uncomfortable, watching the rows of tall buildings rush past as the bus started uptown. He was weary and wrung out emotionally. He wanted a cigarette in the worst way, but he was trying to stop for the umpteenth time. Almost every seat was filled with either a white person, a foreigner, or someone from another state, all armed with a camera of some type.

Specs was feeling upbeat. "Dude, you got me out of a sinfully hot blackjack game, but I had to come forward because you've done me many a good turn over the years. And your old man was tops with me. He was always cool with the cats. They don't make them like him anymore. He was a solid cat for one so young."

Finally, Cootie sat back in his seat. It was nice to hear someone speak so graciously about his father.

"Who was that thug who dropped you off?" Specs asked.

"Guy, good man," Cootie said. "He knew Dad too. I can count on him."

"Now, Mitch and his crew have been sending drugs through the U.S. Postal Service," the hipster said. "The G-men are dogging his people. These postal service inspectors are not allowed to open mail just on a whim. They must obtain a federal search warrant to open packages they suspect contain illegal drugs. And they have drug-sniffing dogs as well. They've got this Mitch character dead to rights. But they are closing in."

"On Mitch?" he asked in surprise.

"I got this from a police source—a reliable police source."

Cootie leaned forward to look at a woman walking along a sidewalk. "Do you have anything else?"

"That source also said a dozen drug dealers peddling thousands of dollars in heroin a day in city housing projects, will be caught in a surprise night-raid," the hipster said. "The officer added it's Mitch's crew. A snitch told the cops about the suppliers and now they have about seventy-five housing cops and federal agents in that raid in East Harlem and the Bronx. Hopefully, they'll catch all of these bums."

"Is that all?"

"No. The press learned of a city police lieutenant who allegedly had sex with a fourteen-year-old girl under Mitch's employ in one of his brothels," Specs added. "He was found hanged in one of the cells. He left a suicide note indicating the guilt of Mitch and how he tricked him into seducing the girl. The cop wrote that he didn't know that the girl was one of Mitch's whores."

"What were they charging him with?"

"Committing a criminal sexual act and endangering the welfare of a child," the hipster said. "The cops learned of the scandal from the teen's parents, after the girl boasted to them that she had been having an affair with someone who was a big-shot in the police department."

"Is Mitch the only one who's implicated in the crime?"

"No. There was another boy, seventeen, who was a recruiter of the young girls for Mitch's brothels, but he died from an elevator fall down seven floors in a project building," Specs said. "Either he fell or was pushed down the shaft. Nobody can tell either, but it's suspicious. There are a lot of others in this business."

"Damn. He's involved in all kinds of bullshit," Cootie said.

"But that's not all, believe me," the hipster said. "Mitch had all kinds of friends on the force. Twenty-five sex-sleaze suspects were caught in the city in a kiddie-porn sting for viewing a computer video file, showing a man raping a six-year-old girl. Now that was Tuesday before last. These are some sickos who love to see kids suffer. Mitch will be charged with second-degree possession and distribution of child pornography as well."

"If they can catch him. And it won't be easy," Cootie added. "He moves around between all of his businesses. And then there are the crooked cops involved in this shit."

"So you know these bastards who took your girl?"

"Yes, I know it's him. Mitch and the perverts."

"I knew Mitch's uncle, a thief and molester, who used to be the bouncer at The Red Top—a mean drunk," the hipster said. "He ran around with some evil characters like his nephew does. Take Rita, one rough-and-tumble fox. Used to have a bar tab at Showman's before she went up on an assault-and-robbery beef. She's Mitch's godmother. Her father, Hughes, was a trumpeter back in the bop days. Used to hang with Bud Powell before the ofays scrambled his eggs by putting all of that high voltage through his noodle."

"I know one of his women who works in a club in the Bronx," Cootie said. "All the feds have to do is to put a tap on her phone. Mitch stays in contact with her. Hell, I saw him only a few days ago."

"That's what they call hide in plain sight," Specs said. "To ofays, all coons look alike."

Meanwhile, the tour guide, a thin, white guy with long hippie hair and pimples, started his lecture about Harlem; the capital of Black America:

"This is 125th Street, the heart and soul of Harlem and home to the world-famous Apollo Theater, the premier show palace for African-American art and music. Amateur nights at the Apollo are noted for their originality and robust talent. That's the Apollo on our left."

With his instruction, the tourists turned in that direction and began filming the Apollo's famed marquee and exterior. Specs paid no attention to the tourist pitch and continued with his inside dope.

"Yeah, baby, it's somebody with juice. Maybe wise guys probably . . ." Specs continued. "Let me give you more of the lowdown on Mitch. He's a wicked cat with a blade or a gun. He'd shoot you in a wink of an eye. Don't underestimate the boy."

"I won't."

"And then there's Owl. As I said, everybody in Harlem is dangerous if you cross them. Owl's twin sis, Opal, was dating this shyster before she got married. This spade was running game on her. She showed up unexpected at this cat's pad, and put some hot lead in the vicinity of his groin. Shot him twice in the family jewels. And the chick he was balling, this real cutie—Opal rubbed red pepper in the chick's lamps, almost put her eyes out. Then she did some carving on the broad's pretty face."

Cootie said "damn" under his breath. These were definitely some bad folks.

"Harlem was full of clubs in its heyday," the tour guide was now saying. "You had the Bamville Club over at 261 West 129th Street, where the great Fletcher Henderson band played in the 1920s. Then there was Connie's Inn over on Seventh Avenue and 131st Street, where the swinging Don Redman band did their thing every week, and Bill 'Bojangles' Robinson mesmerized audiences with his footwork."

Specs listened a bit to the guide and shook his head. "I should be giving this tour, not this fool. What does he know?"

"Give me more on this Owl fella," Cootie said.

"*Ooo-pop-a-da,* my man," Specs sang. "Owl's a spade dude with some odd pals. Was in stir for a while. He has these connects to these wild, bizarre motorcycle dopeheads. He's a rock head himself. Crack. He used to have a cheap kitchenette over on Lenox on 144th Street. Moved with Madame Peach's sis, who had this croaker friend who used to set him up with phony scripts for drugs."

Cootie was lost with the lingo. "Croaker?"

"A doctor," Specs replied.

"I love your turns of phrase." Cootie laughed. "You love language."

"Anyway, this cat used to do speedballs with her. H mixed with girl. They took away my boy's license for ruining this tot's health with some bad mojo, some malpractice deal. The aunt became a lush and faded into oblivion. But Owl has many of her many bad habits, especially with that narcotics angle."

"This guy's bad news," Cootie said. "I don't even want to think about my girl in this nest of bastards' company."

"Never dug him or his ilk," Specs said. "He's not your biggest worry. Groove on this. It's Mitch, Daddy-O. The cat you should be riled about is that jive head job. He's a pervert. He's a baby raper. And a killer. He should not be on the streets. Somebody should erase this cat from the rolls. He's a damn time bomb."

"I've heard that said about the man," Cootie said. "A child molester."

Specs nodded. "Solid, jack. Everything about this cat is subterranean. Only young girls turn him on. He's been known to switch hit too. Dicks and jailbird chicks. Word is, that he flipped his wig a few years back; that he was laying up with his own mama; that they had some sort of weird sex thing going."

Cootie was full of despair. "We're fucked. A gang of perverts."

"That's nowhere, baby," Specs said. "Strictly uncool. You can't afford to throw the towel in now."

A white man asked the tour guide about the Theresa Hotel and its background. He said the guide was more interested in the jazz history of the area than anything else. The guide ignored the request.

"Someone just asked me about Harlem and its relationship to jazz," the tour guide said. "At one time, Harlem was nothing but a hotbed of jazz clubs. Over on Seventh Avenue near 134th Street was the old Club Hot-Cha, where the singer Billie Holiday—or Lady Day—was discovered. Also on the same avenue near 135th Street, was Small's Paradise, where the upper crust of Harlem congregated. Two famous jazz institutions not far from that place on Lenox Avenue were the Savoy Ballroom at 596 and the celebrated Cotton Club at 644. The Lindy hoppers and the big bands made the Savoy a household name where the swing orchestras of Cab Calloway and Duke Ellington earned the Cotton Club a reputation for fine music and good revues."

The bus turned on 135th Street near Harlem Hospital. Cootie sat slumped with his head in his hands. None of what he heard gave him any relief.

"Nothing but perverts and killers," Cootie said to Specs. "My girl's just a kid."

"Again, be careful with them," the hipster repeated. "Don't underestimate them. I'm getting off at the next stop. It's near my crib."

Cootie shook his wrinkled hand. "You need anything, Specs?"

The tour guide went on in the lecture. "Noted black photographer James Van Der Zee owned a studio at 272 Lenox, and over on Seventh Avenue near 139th Street was Harlem's most fashionable residence, Striver's Row, where many of the community's elite lived. At 267 West 136th Street, there was the Niggerati Manor, a rooming house with rent-free rooms for black artists and writers. Writers such as Wallace Thurman, Langston Hughes, and Zora Neale Hurston lived there. In fact, it was Hurston who gave the place its colorful name."

Specs stood. "I hate to hear the word *nigger* come out of the mouth of an ofay. Even if it's for business."

"How are you for cash, Specs?"

"I'm light in the pocket," Specs said. "But I didn't do this for the bread. I did this because we're cool."

Cootie slipped him two fifties. Specs inspected them briefly, nodded and smiled. He sauntered to the guide and whispered something in the white guy's ear. The guide said a word or two into his headpiece, and the bus slowed to a stop.

"See ya later, alligator," Specs said, and some of the whites laughed.

"After while, crocodile," Cootie answered, remembering the hip phrase as one that his father used often when he was growing up. The information gained from the hipster filled him with dread. His girl was in real danger—mortal danger.

TWENTY-THREE

In the following days, Lotus and Kelly kept tabs on Mitch, as did Guy, who had some brothers follow the pervert wherever he went. And who was Madame Peach? Specs told him she ran a floating fetish house from a few locations in Harlem and Brooklyn. Pretty girls did what she ordered, and exclusive clientele loved to spend cash for whatever they wanted. All-star kink.

That afternoon, Cootie was sitting in a Popeye's chicken joint on 125th Street, wolfing down some yardbird, as Specs would call it. The chicken was cool, but he loved the dirty rice. He waited until three before he called Momo. There was the third exhibition bout scheduled that night at some resort hotel in the Catskills, some stiff, some fistic work before the main bout. Momo's trainer said the boxer must get in some ring time or otherwise this white boy was going to kick his ass.

When Momo got on the phone, he said there would be a limo to take Cootie to the place of the exhibition and to take a change of clothes for the party afterward. Cootie liked that. He was trying to make up for lost time since being out of the big house. Until then, he killed time eating spicy chicken and watching the perps and suspects walk down the avenue with the groups of African women, trying to get the locals to come into their shops for braids or dreads.

Later, at the resort in the Catskills, Cootie walked around the stifling locker room under the arena. The boxers were huddled casually around their managers and trainers, as though they were going to shop at the mall for a hat. They joked and laughed, but Momo was unusually serious and focused. He was shadowboxing into the air while the others jawed about bullshit.

"Get some work, Momo," the boxer's trainer said. "Don't try to knock him out."

"Right." He punched in a series of hooks and jabs.

"Remember, it's a warm-up," the trainer added. "Toy around with him, see what he has to offer, and then do what we've been talking about. Think in the ring. Don't try to get him out of there with brute force. Use your brain."

"Right, use my brain," the boxer repeated.

"He's been handpicked, so he won't run," the trainer said. "He's going to try to test you and see what you got. He'll want to bang with you. Don't let him. Think. Plan, scheme, and then impose your program on him."

"He slaps like a bitch," Momo said. "He can't crush a grape."

"That's not true," the trainer said. "He's been in with some good boys. Took them the distance. He might be a journeyman, but he can fight and punch. Remember what I told you. Don't make this harder than it should be."

"Right." The boxer was practicing his uppercuts, right down the middle, right on the chin of his imaginary opponent. He let out a grunt with every one he threw.

The trainer noticed Cootie and smiled. "Hey, man. What's up?"

Cootie nodded. "Is the kid ready?"

"As ready as he's going to be," the trainer said. "I'm just trying to make him take this boy seriously. He thinks he's going to be a walk in the park."

Momo snorted. "I'm going to fuck him up."

"I'm sure you will." Cootie patted the boxer on the back. He recalled Momo throwing up after one or two fights, gagging because he was sweated dry and the fluids didn't switch on the kidneys soon enough but he would soon be all right when he gulped down plenty of water.

At a signal, they went down the hall and into the arena, which was packed. A full house. No doubt they came and filled the seats because of Momo and the championship fight in three weeks at one of Trump's casinos in Atlantic City. They wanted controlled violence, no slapping, but punching—but below the highly charged caliber of a title bout. The old pros gathered there to see if the boy had skills. The tourists and regular customers took photos.

Still, they wanted to see blood, even if it was just a busted lip. They got into the ring, Momo and this Mexican kid, Morales, bowing and waving to the crowd. They knew they weren't permitted to really mix it up, after all, it was just a show, an exhibition. Momo's trainer warned him that the Mex, with his hard bald head, liked to lead with his dome. He would jump in and ram into you with his head, hoping for a cut. And even though they wore headgear, a hard head could break a nose or split lips. The Mex was full of tricks, according to Momo's trainer.

It was in the third round that Momo got into trouble. They had split the first two rounds. Momo started slowly and dodged a bullet, especially when the Mex went to town on his body. Morales decided to test the black fighter with several solid punches to the belly, probing for any weakness, but Momo came on in the second round, fighting the Mex on the outside, keeping him on the end of his blows. The Mex was a bull and tried to muscle his opponent into the ropes, so he could clock him. Swing that one great punch so he could get him wobbly.

"You're a pussy." Momo was talking to him between clinches. "You're a faggot."

All that did was upset the Mex, who tried more than ever to shut his nasty mouth and put him down on the canvas. Momo won the fourth easily, shooting out combinations into his opponent's scarred face and hairy chest. The crowd loved it.

Once in the corner, Momo joked to the trainer, "Damn, that boy doesn't bathe. He smells rotten, like bad meat."

"Don't worry about that," the trainer said. "Do what I told you. Think."

Near the middle of the fifth round, the Mex got the better of Momo, pounding him over and over to the body, up under the ribs and to the kidneys. Momo crouched, trying to protect the vulnerable areas with his elbows, while dancing away from his attacker. The Mex followed him, chasing the black boxer like he was a shot fighter. He cut off the ring, giving Momo a full array of hooks and straight rights, snapping back his head.

"Don't just stand there," the trainer yelled. "Get out of there."

Momo was pinned in a corner, taking everything the Mex had, attempting to cover up the best he could. He was getting his ass whupped. He didn't listen to his trainer, who tried to caution him not to go toe-to-toe with the sturdy Mex, who had been in classic boxing wars in Mexico long before Momo had ever put on gloves. The man knew how to finish his opponent.

In the corner, Momo stood on shaky legs, disbelieving that the Mex could be that good. "I hit him with both hands, and he still wouldn't go down. I hit him with everything I had. I don't get it."

"What did I tell you?" the trainer asked. "Think, think, think. Morales is a brute, a thug. If you look for

233

his weaknesses, you can beat him. I'm glad this is happening to you. Now you finally see what I mean. You can't knock everybody out. You have to out think them. Move to your left, shoot out your jab . . . and—"

"I tried that, but he just counters," Momo said, sounding desperate.

"Let me finish, let me finish," the trainer said. "Out think him. You have power in both hands, but he doesn't let you get set, then all of your punches will be slaps. You can't pitty-patty this guy. You've got to set down on your punches and knock the hell out of him. Only then will you get some respect. Do you understand?"

Momo sat on the stool with his head down. "Yes."

"Take deep breaths. Breathe, breathe. I don't want you getting tired on me. Don't hold your breath while you punch. Don't tense up. Press him behind your jab, then everything will come." Cootie could tell the trainer was concerned.

The sixth round had Momo turning rabbit, and the crowd jeered him. They hated a coward. They wanted a man to stand and fight. They didn't mind if you mixed it up, but at least stand like a man and take your punishment. And the seventh round had the Mex using an old tactic, running in with his head, trying to ram Momo. The trainer complained to the ref, but the man just waved him off. Cootie could see Momo was scared.

But the seventh was a different story. Momo was winning and thinking. He got the Mex with his hands down and backed him into the ropes, pummeling him. The Mex tried a counter punch, a left, but Momo hit with a right hook, and then their heads clashed and somehow a cut opened. Suddenly blood poured down Momo's smooth face. His left eye was full of blood, so he held on, pulling the Mex into him. The liver shots made him cringe. The Mex grew stronger, sneaking a right-hand lead that stunned him. He didn't let go of him. He was hurt, probably for the first time in his career—really hurt. Later, Momo would swear that the Mex thumbed him in the eye or raked the laces of his gloves across his face.

The ref called time and checked the cut. Despite Momo's wanting to go on, the trainer called the bout. The crowd was shouting and booing and throwing beer cups into the ring. The trainer, Momo, the cut man, and Cootie got out of there as quickly as they could. Momo locked himself in the toilet and cried.

The trainer pushed everybody out of the dressing room, except the cut man, Cootie, and himself. He knew it was a humiliating defeat. A damn exhibition. But maybe it was better than going up against the brawler in the title bout. Momo could use the time to heal and get really ready.

"I bet they had spies at this fuckin' thing and they're reporting back to him right now," the cut man said. "They're probably laughing right now."

"Momo doesn't follow orders," the trainer said. "He's hardheaded."

"Do you want a ride back to the city?" the cut man offered.

"Yeah, that would be nice," Cootie said. "Tell Momo I'll call him tomorrow. If he needs anything from me, he knows where he can find me. Anything he wants."

"I know, I know," the trainer said, folding up some bloody towels. "You're a good friend. I'll tell him that. You'll be at his old place?"

"Yeah." Cootie left the dressing room with the cut man, who mentioned that the Mex had been a plant by his trainer to see if Momo had the right stuff to take the championship. The trainer knew his fighter and knew he wasn't ready, but he couldn't tell him that. That would have only meant some ruckus.

*   *   *

It was a cold night when Guy found him going back up into Momo's Harlem place with an armful of groceries. The eats, mainly snacks and bottles of diet soda, came from the round-the-clock bodega up the street. He had his uncle's borrowed Dodge. Cootie walked back down the stairs and leaned into the car.

"I found Madame Peach's next party," Guy yelled. "But we don't have much time. After a while, they don't let anybody in. I had much trouble getting the info from this Asian chick at this sex shop in Times Square. Can you come now?"

"Hell yeah," Cootie replied. "Let me get the groceries put away. Then I'll be right down. Do you want a beer?"

"No," Guy said, ready for action.

The Maximum Hotel, formerly an SRO, was once a respectable inn. It was slated to be torn down to be replaced by a mall, all centrally located a few blocks from the park near Manhattan Avenue. Guy explained Madame Peach's fetish parties were totally wild and frantic. Sex, drugs, and alcohol. She kept a revolving roster of black and Latin club dancers, and retired porn stars to service some of the most powerful, exclusive white clientele in her little red address book. It was invitation only.

"Kelly invited me—uh, us," Guy said to one of the security people who frisked them both as they waited in the hallway. They left their weapons in the car, for they knew they would be searched. Another squat man, possibly a Filipino, stood with his hands in his pockets, eyeing the black men suspiciously.

"I have to see if Madame Peach knows whether Kelly had you on some kind of list," the first guard said as he opened the door. "If she says it's all right, then you can get in. If not, no go. I'll have to turn you away."

The Filipino snickered. "Snug as a bug in a rug."

Cootie caught a glimpse in the parted door of a black girl wearing a black corset and some latex outfit, sitting in a chair with a riding crop. Her legs were spread lewdly as if she was open for viewing. She had plenty of cleavage, abundant bosom trying to overflow the top of the corset. There was a row of seats with white men in them, clapping and laughing.

"She says you can come in, but you have to be quiet," the first guard whispered. "A girl will show you where you can stand. All the seats are taken. Standing room only."

Walking quietly across the tiled floor, Cootie and Guy stood along the wall behind the audience and the participants in the chairs. A Japanese girl, clad in a corset and miniskirt very similar to the female in the chair, asked if they wanted a drink or a line of coke. Both men shook their heads.

"What the fuck is this?" Guy asked.

"Have you ever been to one of these parties before?" the girl quizzed. "It's a little bondage and discipline. And a session of spanking and caning. Nothing much. A few folks having fun and that's about it."

They watched as a slightly bald white man, nude with leather ankle and arm restraints, knelt down before the girl on the chair. He was blindfolded with his hands tied behind his hairy, pale back. She ordered him to lick her thigh-high boot with the spiked stiletto heel, and he squatted beneath her and took it into his mouth.

"Will you obey my every wish?" the girl asked.

"Yes, mistress," the man said, very submissive.

237

"Open wide, slave," the girl ordered, and the white man let her black fingers push a rubber ball into his open mouth. "Open, open, wider, slave."

He permitted her to let him do the task. The girl smiled and reached for a thin bit of cane, elastic and sturdy, from one of the assistants. The men in the chairs were sitting on the edge of their seats, because this was what they had been waiting for. None of that lick-and-fetch shit. In fact, they appeared to be trembling at the mounting degree of excitement and pleasure. The girl held the cane down by her side while she inspected the man's exposed ass cheeks, massaging each flat surface.

"Are you ready for a little pleasure, slave?" the girl asked, grinning.

"Yes, mistress. I am ready."

"Are you ready for the sting of the cane, slave?"

"Yes, mistress." The man positioned himself so he could take what was coming to him. He had a stupid smile on his face.

Standing over him, the girl squatted over the man and gave him a few hard smacks with her open hand on his ass. He sighed in delicious relief. She smacked him on the butt harder and harder, leaving crimson handprints. Then she went to work with the rattan; the distinctive whistle of the rattan against the warmed white skin. She knew where to strike and slash, on the precise spots on the buttocks and thighs and legs. The men in the chairs tried to predict where the cane would land because they all recognized the girl was an expert, a queen of pain and desire.

"Is it good, slave?" the girl asked.

"Yes, mistress." The man wiggled under the constant strokes of the cane.

"Is it really good, slave?" she asked, halting the cane's fall and reaching around to fondle the man's balls. He whimpered at her touch.

"Oh yes, mistress," he panted, his sex formerly at half-mast and now beginning to harden. His breathing became labored as she continued caning him, varying the aim and rhythm of the strokes.

Focused on the man's feverish desire, the girl caned him until he came, noticing the tightness of his balls primed to spurt, and hearing him gasp and cry out. His bottom was hot, red, and decorated with purple welts in a neat pattern. Some of the females in attendance leaned over, taking in the sight of the black girl imposing her will on the white pillar of society. The row of white men moaned and groaned at the intense image of the erotic torture that had just taken place and wished it was them.

Cootie shook his head at Guy. It was very surreal. It was like one of those nightmares out of a Fellini movie. The man howled in delight as the girl really let him have it with a blend of hard and light strokes, and finally his entire body shuddered while his dick erupted, his male juices dripping down his white thighs.

"Oh, shit," Guy shouted.

One of the white men put his finger to his lips. This act was holy, solemn—sacred. The room was as quiet as a cathedral at night.

"Let's go," Cootie said. He had seen enough.

One of the girls tapped Cootie on the arm and led him to Madame Peach, the old broad herself. She sported an unruly crown of scarlet dreads down her back, and a tight-fitting red leather outfit. Guy was fascinated by her crazy mole with hair on it on the bulb of her witch's nose.

"Order me some Chinese—you know what I like," she said to one of her girls. Who are these gentlemen? I don't know you."

Cootie smirked. "I don't think so. We're far too tanned to rate a seat in this place. And probably too broke. It's seems like you attract a prosperous white crowd."

"Especially with this sick shit," Guy said, laughing.

"You have to excuse my friend," Cootie said. "Kelly recommended us to you. She said you employed a woman named Audrey at a few of your parties. Mitch sent her around to you. A pretty girl, fine figure, long legs. Used to wear her hair like yours."

"In dreads?" Madame Peach asked.

"Do you know her now?" Cootie asked, showing her a photo from his wallet.

"What do you want with her?" the woman asked. "You're not the cops, are you?"

"No, we're not." Cootie said, noticing one of the girls had a line of blood from her nostril. He knew what that meant.

"Let's walk while we talk," Madame Peach said, gently shoving the men down a corridor where she explained the need for her business. She talked about slaves and dominatrixes, men dressed in women's clothing, balls and dicks trussed up, bared asses battered by paddles and lashed by whips.

"My business of S&M and bondage will continue to be popular as long as there is an AIDS epidemic, because men are scared to death of tainted pussy," Madame Peach said, walking slowly. "That's why all these guys are raping underage kids and kidnapping young girls. They figure the younger the pussy, the fresher. Nobody wants old pussy or even used pussy. See, this business has the girl clothed, and there's no risk of exchanging bodily fluids."

"But it's some sick shit," Guy said, laughing.

"Maybe, but the men love it," she answered. "Especially white men. And then you put them together with some strong black and Latin women, and it's a sexual explosion. All the men want is to please a woman. They became like little boys in that regard. They want to please mommy."

"You don't see black guys doing that shit," Guy volunteered.

"Not true. You should see these parties on Thursday nights," she said. "The place is packed with black men, strong, rich, powerful. Businessmen, judges, lawyers, politicians, sport figures, everybody male and black. They act macho but here we get them, and they are so, so submissive."

"Snap." Guy said. "The whole world's male population is sissies."

They turned around and headed back the way they came. There were shouts, jeers, and loud singing. Madame Peach walked briskly toward the main room. Two of her girl assistants helped a man up, his legs weak from the beating, his ass crisscrossed with welts. One of her guards released another blindfolded man who was hanging spread-eagle with ropes on his arms and legs from a metal cross.

"Oh, it's nothing." The old woman shrugged.

A group of the other girls in all leather stood at the end of the room, holding either canes or riding crops. A girl, almost recognizable from the rear, was sucking a guy, scooting back into the hand of another man, while he thrust his fingers in her. When she finished, she mounted yet another guy, letting him grind his knee between her crotch. The girl wore a leather mask.

Madame Peach entered the scene and slid two fingers into the girl's sex. She kissed her roughly and licked her fingers, tasting the girl.

While the girl was performing her lewd act, Madame Peach sauntered back over to the black men, whispering to Cootie. "You asked about your daughter," she said. "Well, that's her. We call her Tatiana. The girls go by many different names in this industry. She's one of the best girls I've ever had. She's dynamite."

Cootie stared at the girl who didn't appear to notice him. She was concentrating on getting the guy off. And herself as well.

"Want to taste her?" Madame Peach asked Cootie, holding up her two fingers.

TWENTY-FOUR

As Madame Peach droned on about if the house got busted, everything would be taken care within a couple of hours by a high-priced legal mouthpiece with connections to downtown, Cootie saw the man himself, Mitch, come in, slapping fives with some of the faithful. He wore all black—black turtleneck with an Armani black suit, and a long, ankle-length leather coat. A pair of shades concealed his serpentine eyes from all scrutiny. With him was the cold-blooded killer Owl, somebody who Specs warned him about.

"My brother, my brother," a white patron with sore red buns, greeted the hustler, embracing him. "You sure put on a helluva show here. Great girls, great sex."

Mitch waved him off with a regal flick of the hand. "We try to please."

Suddenly, Madame Peach strolled up to the hustler, gesturing wildly, her voice loud and shrill. Owl stepped in front of him, like a shield between the hustler and the excited sex matron. Mitch nodded, and the old woman proceeded until she stood face-to-face with the psychopath.

"These guys want to see Tatiana . . ." Madame Peach's words lowered into a non-existent low register, almost off the charts. Cootie saw she gestured at him, pointing at him accusingly, but only one or two words could be heard.

For Cootie, Mitch was a bastard of the worst kind. He had his fingers in every vice in the community, a death dealer. Scum. He was a punk disguised as a man. As Guy pegged him with his confused sexuality, Mitch

243

walked like a bitch, talked like a bitch, and dealt with others like an evil bitch. Cootie didn't understand why the women flocked to him. Money, probably. The whole world was damn nuts.

"A fucking sissy," Guy chided.

"Careful with that shit," Cootie warned. He knew not to underestimate men, regardless of what they appeared to be. Sissies could fuck you up too. But he had more to consider about this situation, whether he should go for broke, take Mitch and Owl down, or try to negotiate with the hustler for an early release for his baby girl. Still, he knew that he was not going to leave this room without her. No way. Even if it meant his life.

Mitch motioned for Tatiana—aka Audrey—to come to him. "Is she a doll?"

Madame Peach stood off to one side of the hustler, with Owl resting his hand in his jacket, probably on a gat. Smiling like a used car salesman, Mitch gestured for Cootie to join them as well. Cootie could see that it was Audrey when she removed her mask and walked briskly into the center of the group.

"Cootie . . . Cootie, isn't it?" Mitch said, shaking the man's hand. "I'm sorry that I was completely rude to you earlier. I was in a funk . . . business problems. My mind was elsewhere, but now everything is everything. You say Tatiana is your daughter, right?"

"That's right," Cootie replied.

"What was the name you went by at my clubs before you went to work for Madame Peach?" asked Mitch, leaning down to let one of his underlings light his cigarette.

"My name was Sam when I was featured at one of your Bronx clubs," Audrey said.

"What is your given name, your Christian name?"

"Audrey, sir." She said her name like a little girl.

Meanwhile, Guy walked over to the group. "I've got to go and piss. Where's the men's room around here?" He acted like he had to go bad, wiggling and prancing.

"Owl, go with him and make sure he doesn't get into trouble," Mitch said. Both men walked off to another hallway and through a set of doors.

"Can I get a chance to talk with her?" Cootie asked. "At least, grant me that. I just want to see if there is anything I can do. As her father, you should grant me that right."

Mitch turned to Cootie's daughter and shrugged. "Do you want to talk to him?"

Audrey rocked back and forth, like an addict in need of her next fix, saying, "I don't have a father. I don't see why I should talk to him. I don't have anything to say."

"That's not the way to treat your father," Mitch mocked him. "Getting all testy and shit. You're supposed to show the man respect."

"I don't want to talk to him," Audrey retorted. "He's an asshole."

"No, talk to him," Mitch said, laughing. "Never say I came between a father and a daughter. I believe in family values, Christian morality, and all that good shit. Madame Peach, take them to somewhere quiet so they can talk. I can see Audrey has issues. Isn't that what Oprah always says? Maybe Mr. Cootie can help her deal with her issues."

So Madame Peach guided Cootie and Audrey into an adjoining room where they could talk, but there was a catch: a naked white man hung from the ceiling by some kind of contraption by his arms, just dangling. He was also blindfolded. There was the frail light from two thin candles underneath him. The senior dominatrix grinned as she saw him, then she put her leather-clad arms up, indicating this was also business.

"Can you put a ball gag in his mouth, so we won't be disturbed?" Audrey asked her. "I really don't want any interruptions, please."

Madame Peach left the room, going out into the hall. Audrey signaled to her father to be quiet. When the dominatrix returned, she pulled up a stool and ordered the patron to open his mouth, then placed the gag in. As an added treat, she also put a pair of earplugs on the man, so he could not hear the chatter.

When the old woman departed the room, Audrey closed her eyes and asked if her father wanted to hit her. "I know I caused you a lot of trouble. Go ahead and hit me."

Cootie thought back to Audrey as an impish little girl, always getting in something. Talkative, restless, sassy. Faith's sister said Audrey reminded her of her mother as a kid. She pointed out her budding sexuality, even when Audrey was only eight years old. She loved her body. She loved to be naked. She loved getting attention from boys and men. Now as a young woman, she still wanted attention from men, wanted to be in the world of men, wanted to talk with men, wanted to fuck men, wanted to beat and seduce men.

Cootie also recounted how Audrey let the white man run his fingers slowly down her back and ass. He shuddered at that memory. This was his daughter, his little girl. All he could see was the supple and firm body of a young woman, no flab, no sagging flesh. He looked down at the girl who sat across from him in a chair, the small triangle of pubic hair between her thighs.

"Cover yourself," Cootie said, removing his coat.

His daughter put on the coat, wrapping herself up with its warmth. If Mitch said she must talk to this bastard, then she had to do it. It was not a request; it was an order. She wondered where they would start, since they had said so few words to each other. And her father was not known to be chatty. She knew he was locked inside himself.

She explained the situation to him. "I wanted to get back at you. I wanted to hurt you like you hurt me—like you hurt us. I know I bit off more than I could chew. Mitch is evil. They say he cut some girls' pussies out. Maybe it's just a rumor, but he doesn't give a shit about anybody or anything."

"Why do you work for him?" Cootie asked. "I asked Lotus that, and she said she didn't know. She said one man's word is as good as another. Whatever that means."

Audrey waited for him to sit down, then she spoke. "He reminds me of Granddad. He could be his son. I never thought of you as his son, but Mitch could be his son. He's evil just like the old man."

Cootie nodded, thinking back to the ailing patriarch in the hospital. Crumbling.

"I want to be like Mom," Audrey said proudly. "I want to be the whore of men—their slut, their slave. I want to be whatever they want me to be. I don't give a shit."

Her father muttered a curse under his breath.

"See, Mitch taught me to obey all men, address them as sir." She beamed. "He taught me to keep my head down. Remain submissive. I loved the power of being their slave. I would say fuck me, sir; slap me, sir; blindfold me, sir; burn me, sir; whip me, sir. I wanted to become a whore, a slave. I just wanted to be fucked."

"What has come over you, girl?" Cootie asked.

"Some women are born whores," she said, stifling a giggle. "Did you know that?"

He positioned himself on the chair so he could speak his piece. "God didn't let me choose my father or mother. In fact, he didn't let me choose my family, so I have to deal with the hand I have. But no man can stand between his child and life, between a daughter and happiness. I know I made some horrible mistakes. I hate the way I did. I failed you girls. I even failed my wife."

"Damn right you did."

He kept on trying to smile. "This should have never come to this. I need to say so many things to you. Some of it you will reject because you're so young, but most of it you'll get, because you know the life you're living ain't shit. You know that this fast life will chew you up and spit you out. Look at me."

She made her voice even, mean, and quiet. "Are you finished?"

"I did a terrible thing when you guys were young," her father said. "I was selfish. I only thought about myself. I thought I was loving you as a father, because I provided cash and a roof over your heads, but I didn't see that I was a loser as a man, as a husband, and as a father."

"Are you done yet?"

"No. I know your mother loved you girls. What happened was she couldn't adapt to the real world, so she gave up. I know that, because I almost gave up myself."

She moved her shoulders and frowned. "She was a whore, just like me."

"No, she wasn't like you. She wasn't a whore, just like you're not a whore. She was a confused, bitter woman trying to find herself. She hated her life, hated the way the drugs controlled her life, hated what she permitted to happen to you girls. In the end, she just gave up, just got tired."

"So that's why she killed herself," the girl said. "That's bullshit."

"She killed herself for what she did to you all," Cootie said. "She couldn't stand it."

"Bullshit. She was weak. She was a coward and weak. A weak bitch."

He wanted to hit her as soon as she said it, but he did not. "Hell, I can't explain everything to you. I ain't God. I'm just a man, a black man at that. Who the fuck knows why somebody does some of the shit they do?"

"So how come you're now the wise man all the sudden?" she asked sarcastically.

He knew what he looked like. Old and corrupt. And still in need of redemption. "In prison, you get plenty of time to go over your life. You pass away the time by reflecting how you spent your days. You start to care about who you are and who you should be. I can't dwell on the past. I have to look ahead."

"Did you ever think about me?" she asked.

"Yes, I did." His expression was solemn then.

"And what?"

He knew what was coming. He was afraid of it but he had to hear it. "Now I have to look at what happened. Some things don't make sense. I can't explain this to you. Your mama loved you. I love you, and I will love you forever and always."

"What difference does it make?" She was stubborn. She didn't even hear him. "I hate Mama and I hate you. I hate you for doing this to me. You did this to me. You caused me to do this shit."

"Why? Why—because I got caught and went to prison?"

"Yes. Why did you have to be a criminal?"

His head was bowed and his fingers intertwined as if in prayer. "You shouldn't blame someone else for your choices. You chose this life just like I did. I can't spend my life saying somebody else is responsible for making my life as it is. That's like niggers saying white folks are the cause of all their problems, and it ain't so. I can't say anybody is accountable for what I decide to do with my life. I fucked up, not you."

"I'm a whore. I do all kinds of rank shit," she said. "Ask Mitch. He'll tell you."

"That's not true," Cootie said. "You can change your life. You can walk away from it. You can. I'm trying to change my life. It's hard, but I know I can do it."

"Bullshit." She rolled her eyes, just like she used to do when she was a girl.

"You must forgive us—me and your mama. We're human. We made mistakes."

She stood. "I don't have to forgive you. I don't have to ever forgive you. You know what you did. You abandoned us, you neglected us. You left us to the wolves like those bastards Mama used to fuck around with to get drugs, those drunken men trying to paw me. Fuck you, man."

He could not speak. He felt bad. He felt weak and didn't want to argue anymore. He turned his chair away from her and closed his eyes. All he wanted to do was to keep her safe—his wife and the girls safe. He didn't want anybody to get hurt. He never knew the streets would do his women like this.

There was a knock on the door. Somebody said to come out, time was up. Audrey walked ahead of him. He followed her out, through the hallway to the room where Guy was leaning with his back to a closed door. He had a cigarette in his lips and a gun held loosely at his side. There was blood on his neck. His eyes possessed a hard fierceness, but it was not terror. Cootie wasn't sure what it was going on.

"Come here, baby," Mitch said, easy and gentle. His arms were up like a Nazi soldier surrendering.

"Where's Owl?" Cootie asked.

"Your friend used a blade on him. That wasn't fair," Mitch said. "He got the drop on him in the toilet.

Madame Peach said he slashed the man ear-to-ear. You should keep him on a leash."

"Good for you," Cootie said and winked. He wondered where Guy got the blade from.

"Would you take money for the girl's services?" Mitch offered. "I can make you a rich man. She's a gold mine. She's got many more years in her. Think about it. More money than you can spend."

"Fuck you," Cootie replied, his eyes narrowing. "I don't sell daughters."

"Come here, baby," Mitch demanded. "I said come here now. I don't want to repeat myself again."

Audrey was like a zombie. Her face was empty and odd, but she went to him. Remembering their talk, Cootie was going to stop her, but decided against it.

Suddenly, Mitch slapped the girl very hard with his open hand, a harsh bitch slap. She staggered with the blow. She groaned and covered her marked face with her hands. Cootie wanted to go to her as she sobbed, her body trembling. But Guy stopped him.

He was not far from Cootie, almost in reach.

"Easy, nigga," Guy barked, moving the gun up a notch. "I don't like your ass no way. All I need is an excuse to off you, bitch ass, so don't give it to me."

"I'm going to walk out of here," Mitch said boldly. "I don't think you're going to do anything foolish. You're not that big of a fool. But maybe not. You probably don't have the sense your mama gave you."

Audrey walked coldly to Guy and put out her hand, and he placed the gun in it. Cootie saw the dumb play and shook his head. He didn't want to get the girl involved in a murder rap.

"Don't do something you'll regret later," Mitch said, stepping lightly toward the door. "Give me the gun. Give

251

it to me. You don't want to do time because of somebody like me."

"He's right." Cootie could tell his baby girl meant it. She was going to hurt him, and hurt him badly if he didn't stop fucking with her head. He could tell she was messing up, high on something. Her finger was itchy on the trigger.

"Shoot the bastard. . . ." Guy was enjoying this lethal drama.

But Mitch was not. He knew the girl was serious, and as wacked out as she was, she could do any damn thing. Madame Peach had given her some ice, so she could take on the customers. Fuck their brains out.

Still, Mitch knew how to bluff. "If you're going to shoot me, shit . . . get it over with. Or else let me leave."

The gun boomed suddenly, and smiling, she put a bullet in the calf of his right leg. He went down, screaming, and crawled around on the floor. Cootie knew she was not fooling around.

"I told you, don't fuck around with me," Audrey said, and shot the sobbing Mitch in the other leg. The other guys parted around him, sticking close to the sides of the room. They were in shock. He rolled over, dragged himself to the wall, then tried to pull himself up.

"That's my girl." Guy laughed, taking a gun from one of Mitch's stunned crew. He chuckled at the hustler shrieking at his blood-soaked pants legs, his hands trying to stop the red flow.

Cootie shrugged. He didn't say anything.

"Look at what you've done," Mitch shouted, pointing at Cootie. "You did this. You turned her on me. You poisoned her against me."

"Stay put." Audrey was aiming the gun at the hustler.

"I'd kill you if you didn't have that gun," Mitch said, still pulling himself up at the wall. The blood was smearing everywhere.

There was a loud sound of another shot. The bullet spun Mitch like he was a top, and his knees folded. He pitched forward and fell on his face on the floor. He sprawled there, his eyes cold and dead. A neat bullet hole showed itself in his head above his right eye, with a bright ribbon of crimson that snaked out over his nose to the cheekbone and onto the tiles.

"So that's that," Guy said, taking the gun away from the girl and putting it into his pocket.

Cootie's heart was broken. He didn't want any of this grief for his girl. But his friends would be sure to cover up for her. Guy was a master at that shit. He looked at his friend, whose face was unreadable. Madame Peach was already talking about a deal with some of the hustler's crew, ditching his corpse away from her brothel.

The other guys were pleading for their lives, but Guy assured them that no harm would come to them. Nobody cared about this little ruckus.

His baby girl hugged him, sobbing into his neck, and he stroked her face. Stroked her head with the same tenderness that he held in his heart. He smelled her hair, her dirty hair funky with the raunch of sex and sweat. Her breath smelled as if somebody had taken a dump in it.

"Let's split," Cootie urged. Audrey followed him, tears in her eyes.

He put his arm around her waist, drew her to him. She told him that she wasn't sure how to be his daughter again. She had hated him for so long. She didn't know what to do next.

"Don't cry, baby," Cootie said. He lightly touched the dual streams of water along the young woman's cheeks. "The car's outside. We'll settle down somewhere and figure this thing out. Guy'll handle everything on this end. Don't worry. We'll be fine, just fine. Some things take a while to get accustomed to."

She had never smoked a man before. Killed a man outright. Maybe bit by bit, but never killed him outright. She was worried about her soul, but time would wipe away any grief and regret. Her father assured her the angels had drawn a black mark through Mitch's name a long time ago. Not to worry.

"I need to get fucked up." Guy laughed, walking to the elevator.

"What 'bout you, Pops?" Audrey asked, holding one of her father's calloused hands.

"Not yet," Cootie replied, holding the door open so they could get in. "I want to do one thing first. I want to visit your mother's grave."

Audrey looked solemn, and touched Cootie on the shoulder. "I could do that. But we should let Guy drive. He's the only one holding it together. I think jail made you kinda twitchy. And Guy, pull in any of those Korean stores, so we can get some flowers. Yellow roses."

Her father smiled and winked. "You remembered. Good girl." Alicia had remembered the yellow roses. Now he must remember to fit in this jungle out there to survive, scout the territory, develop his senses again, proceed slowly, work with the pack and make his girls first on his list. As a lifer back in the joint once told him, "Being a loving father and a good husband is the best part of being a man." White America would try to make him fail, but he would succeed. They were walking out to the ride as two cop cars were pulling up. Not to worry. He would work and live smarter this time, not harder. Not to worry.

IN STORES NOW

She's Robbin' the Rich
To Give to the Poor

1-893196-23-2

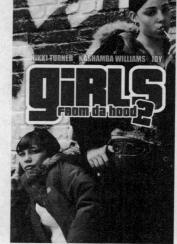

1-893196-28-3

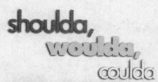

1-893196-25-9

0-9747025-9-5

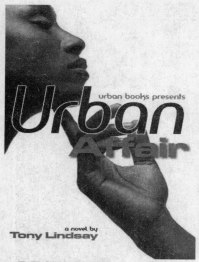

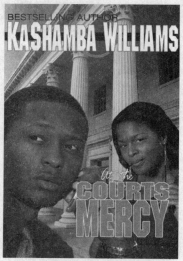

DECEMBER 2005
1-893196-27-5

JANUARY 2006
1893196-29-1

FEBRUARY 2006
1-893196-41-0

FEBRUARY 2006
1-893196-37-2

MARCH 2006
1-893196-32-1

URBAN BOOKS PRESENTS

Little
BLACK GIRL LOST
2

KEITH LEE JOHNSON

MARCH 2006
1-893196-39-9

URBAN BOOKS
PRESENTS

GIGOLO'S
get lonely too

MARCH 2006
1-893196-33-X

URBAN BOOKS
PRESENTS

Make you

LA TONYA Y. WILLIAMS

APRIL 2006
1-893196-34-8

OTHER URBAN BOOKS TITLES

Title	Author	Quantity	Cost
Drama Queen	LaJill Hunt		$14.95
No More Drama	LaJill Hunt		$14.95
Shoulda Woulda Coulda	LaJill Hunt		$14.95
Is It A Crime	Roy Glenn		$14.95
MOB	Roy Glenn		$14.95
Drug Related	Roy Glenn		$14.95
Lovin' You Is Wrong	Alisha Yvonne		$14.95
Bulletproof Soul	Michelle Buckley		$14.95
You Wrong For That	Toschia		$14.95
A Gangster's girl	Chunichi		$14.95
Married To The Game	Chunichi		$14.95
Sex In The Hood	White Chocalate		$14.95
Little Black Girl Lost	Keith Lee Johnson		$14.95
Sister Girls	Angel M. Hunter		$14.95
Driven	KaShamba Williams		$14.95
Street Life	Jihad		$14.95
Baby Girl	Jihad		$14.95
A Thug's Life	Thomas Long		$14.95
Cash Rules	Thomas Long		$14.95
The Womanizers	Dwayne S. Joseph		$14.95
Never Say Never	Dwayne S. Joseph		$14.95
She's Got Issues	Stephanie Johnson		$14.95
Rockin' Robin	Stephanie Johnson		$14.95
Sins Of The Father	Felicia Madlock		$14.95
Back On The Block	Felicia Madlock		$14.95
Chasin' It	Tony Lindsey		$14.95
Street Possession	Tony Lindsey		$14.95
Around The Way Girls	LaJill Hunt		$14.95
Around The Way Girls 2	LaJill Hunt		$14.95
Girls From Da Hood	Nikki Turner		$14.95

Girls from Da Hood 2	Nikki Turner		$14.95
Dirty Money	Ashley JaQuavis		$14.95
Mixed Messages	LaTonya Y. Williams		$14.95
Don't Hate The Player	Brandie		$14.95
Payback	Roy Glenn		$14.95
Scandalous	ReChella		$14.95
Urban Affair	Tony Lindsey		$14.95
Harlem Confidential	Cole Riley		$14.95

Urban Books
74 Andrews Ave.
Wheatley Heights, NY 11798
Subtotal: _____
Postage:_____ Calculate postage and handling as follows: Add $2.50 for the first item and $1.25 for each additional item
Total: _____
Name: _____
Address:_____
City: _____ State: _____ Zip: _____
Telephone: ( ) _____
Type of Payment (Check: ____ Money Order: ____)
All orders must be prepaid by check or money order drawn on an American bank.
Books may sometimes be out of stock. In that instance, please select your alternate choices below.

Alternate Choices:

1._____
2._____

PLEASE ALLOW 4-6 WEEKS FOR SHIPPING